By No Means a Gentleman

Ladies Who Dare
Book Two

Tanya Wilde

ARE YOU SIGNED UP FOR DRAGONBLADE'S BLOG?

You'll get the latest news and information on exclusive giveaways, exclusive excerpts, coming releases, sales, free books, cover reveals and more.

Check out our complete list of authors, too!

No spam, no junk. That's a promise!

Sign Up Here

www.dragonbladepublishing.com

Dearest Reader;

Thank you for your support of a small press. At Dragonblade Publishing, we strive to bring you the highest quality Historical Romance from some of the best authors in the business. Without your support, there is no 'us', so we sincerely hope you adore these stories and find some new favorite authors along the way.

Happy Reading!

CEO, Dragonblade Publishing

Additional Dragonblade books by
Author Tanya Wilde

Ladies Who Dare Series
Almost a Scoundrel (Book 1)
By No Means a Gentleman (Book 2)

Chapter One

"WHY MUST I marry that man?"

"Leeds is a good man," Lady Harriet Hillstow's father, the Marquess of Hatton, argued. "Wealthy in his own right. A good match."

Define "good match," Harriet thought darkly. But that was not for her to be troubled about, was it? Since she was nothing but the object of a business deal. It did, however, solidify one important fact in Harriet's mind. The Marquess of Leeds was most certainly *not* a good match.

He was the very worst.

Firstly, he did not care one whit about her. And secondly, he was a peacock who gambled, kept company with lechers, and it was anyone's guess how many skeletons could be dug up from his garden.

More to the point, why would he ever want to marry her? Somehow, Harriet found it impossible to grasp why Leeds, a *good* catch by everyone's definition and wealthy in his own right, as her father had so eloquently put it, would agree to marry an invisible wallflower. Her father must have promised a lot more than her dowry.

This entire affair stank of something rather dubious.

Harriet placed her hands on her hips, the book she'd been reading when she marched from the library resting on her hipbone. She'd completely forgotten she'd been busy reading when she'd overheard her parents discussing selling her off. Though that might be stating it a bit cruelly, she could think of no other way to put it.

"What did you have to promise him to agree to the betrothal?" she demanded from her father. "Other than my fortune, of course, since he is *so* wealthy and all?"

"I didn't offer him anything."

"And I'm expected to believe this?"

Her father sat back in his leather chair and regarded her as though debating whether to reveal the truth or not. An ominous foreboding slithered down her spine.

"Leeds approached me for your hand," her father admitted.

Harriet's jaw dropped. "I beg your pardon?"

"Is that so surprising?"

"Yes," she all but snapped. "The man has never spoken one word to me."

"Then now is the time to rectify that, don't you agree?"

"I don't have to rectify anything. You, Papa, on the other hand, must end this farce of an engagement. Today."

"Harriet, the betrothal has been agreed upon. It's done. Signed. You are wedding Leeds. He is procuring a special license as we speak."

What?

A special license?

Just when Harriet thought she'd heard it all, her father pulled the rug out from beneath her feet again. "What on earth does he need a special license for?" The dubious odor intensified.

"Enough. The engagement has been set."

"If you want me to marry, fine, I'll marry, but let me choose my husband."

Her father sighed. "Harriet, I wouldn't have engaged you to Leeds if I didn't believe him to be an honorable man. Do you doubt my judgment?"

Yes, horribly so.

"If you thought him so honorable," Harriet challenged, "why is this the first I am hearing of this engagement?"

Her father sighed. "This is not a plot hatched in advance, Harriet."

"But it is a plot," she shot back. "Why else procure a special license?"

"He wishes to marry as soon as possible."

"And that doesn't strike you as suspect, Papa?" Harriet glanced at her stepmother who hadn't said a word up till this point. "Mother agrees?"

"Leave your mother be. I investigated Leeds. There is nothing suspect about him or his circumstances."

Yet he wished to marry her by way of a special license? Surely her father must find that odd.

"The man is enamored with you, Harriet." Her father rounded up his conclusion. "I could tell."

And I am a fairy! "I assure you, he is not." How could he be? They hadn't even been introduced! Did her father truly not care about this?

"Nevertheless, the matter has been settled."

"What has prompted this sudden madness? This is only my second season." Harriet tried to persuade her father. "I ought to hold out for a"—*love match*—"duke."

Her father arched both brows.

"Is it so impossible to conceive that I could snatch a duke?"

"Not impossible," her father said slowly.

But not likely, was what he did not say. Harriet wanted to stomp her foot but refrained. "Where is Leeds?" she asked instead. "Why has he not proposed to me? Or courted me? Or, God forbid, strung a sentence together and acknowledged me? And you believe he is enamored with me? I have never heard a more laughable notion."

Her father let out a heavy sigh. "You can ask him that when he arrives."

Harriet's breath caught. "When is he arriving?"

"Should be any moment now."

"*Any* moment? What happens when he arrives?"

Her father said nothing.

Her heart sank. "I shall run away to the Americas before I marry a man without knowing *why* I'm being handed off in such a rush!"

Her father slammed his fist on the table. "Because I said so, damn it! You will marry Leeds and that is final."

Harriet turned to her stepmother. "And you will allow this travesty to take place?"

"Your father has his reasons, dear. I support him in this matter."

Harriet, however, did not.

A special license? Well, then she would have to use *special* means to get out of this underhand business. In fact, the horror she now faced—and to which she protested—gave rise to a special *determination*. As a wallflower, Harriet had never been comfortable in social settings. Her first season, she had chosen to watch from the sidelines. Everything had been fresh, sparkly, and a bit overwhelming. This season, she had planned to be more active and find her love match.

Her dream husband.

A man who would fight for her.

She had made that promise to her mother. Which was why Harriet refused to stand aside and allow this man, the dubious-smelling Marquess of Leeds to sweep aside her dreams and upturn her promise with a surprise marriage he and her father had arranged. Not to even mention the fact that the man embodied her worst nightmare come true.

No, she longed for a connection much more meaningful than a transaction between families, something her father could not understand. It didn't have to be a big, all-consuming connection, though that would be lovely, but she could build on the knowledge of a husband that fought for her. Courted her. *Spoke* to her.

But not this. By Jove, she could not just accept it without a smidgeon of resistance! Who was Leeds anyway? If the man wished to wed her, he would first have to prove himself worthy.

She glanced at the clock perched on a mantle behind her father. How long did it take to procure a special license? An hour? A day? A week?

Never mind that. Harriet did not plan on being available for Leeds to plunder her future as he pleased.

She held her chin high as her eyes flitted between her parents. She did the only thing pride allowed her to do: she turned on her heel and strode from the room with her back straight.

Sorry, Papa.

But she had made a vow she had no intention of breaking. Ever.

Harriet left the study only to be blocked by a large chest when she reached the foyer. The soft scent of leather assailed her senses before she quickly took a step back, taking in the broad expanse of shoulders and already suspecting whose face she'd find above them. Yet still her breath caught the moment her gaze collided with a pair of deep, golden eyes.

So handsome.

Not the point.

He was the last man on earth she had ever wanted to run into. But now that she had, she couldn't help but give him a thorough look. Tall, impeccably dressed, with dark hair styled to fashion, he was indeed the quintessential man about town.

Her gaze lifted back to his, annoyed that he towered a full head over her. And, in a momentary lapse of judgment, Harriet noticed the strong line of his jaw and the heavy brows that arched over deep-set eyes that were framed by a layer of thick lashes. And such a man wanted to marry her? A man who could have any woman he wanted?

She might be plain, but she was not dim.

He stood before her, the picture of a stubborn, unyielding male, crowding her space, but there was something in his expression that gave Harriet pause. A look that conveyed the impression that he was determined to get what he had come for—her.

"Lady Harriet."

Lady Harriet.

Cool. Measured. No inflection in that voice. None whatsoever. He stared at her without any noticeable expression. As if he and her father had not just sealed her fate. He could have been looking down at an ant for all the emotion in his features.

Knave.

Handsome knave, true.

"He speaks," Harriet said. "He also roams about others' halls as though he belongs in them."

That earned her a raise of a single brow.

"My lady." Only when he spoke did Harriet notice the footman, who had been invisible in the presence of Leeds. "Your father is expecting the marquess."

"So I heard."

Leeds said nothing, his gaze flicking to the book she clutched to her chest before lifting back to her face. She grasped the book tighter. She enjoyed reading romances. There was no shame in that. Granted, she was probably one of only a few who would consider Charles Griffin's new book a romance. Nevertheless, who was he to stare at her with such an odd, indistinguishable expression?

Given the current situation, where no one had even bothered to tell her about her impending nuptials—not her stepmother, not her father, and not the man before her—only she had the right to pass judgment here.

Her gaze caught on the folded document with an elaborate red seal stamped in the middle clutched between his gloved fingers. A hunch began to form. Her father had mentioned a special license. Was this it?

"You look lovely, Lady Harriet."

Harriet blinked. *This is what you have to say to me?* Annoyance and, yes, disappointment nipped at her heart. Only a fool would believe his words. "Which part of me, my lord? My lips, my eyes, or my mouth?"

"Every part of you."

She resisted a snort. Liar. "You must be here to collect the devil's contract?"

"Devil's contract?"

"Yes, the one where you rob me of my dreams and snuff out my happiness."

Two lines appeared on his forehead.

Harriet stepped up to him, taking a bold stance. "If you do not wish to be humiliated beyond repair, my lord, I suggest you bow out of the betrothal agreement you so shamelessly negotiated behind my back." Let's see what he does with *that*.

The twin line between his brows deepened. "You don't find me agreeable?"

"Agreeable? How ever did you arrive at that deduction? It's not like you and I have conversed before now. It's not like you have *courted* me." Or fought even a little for the privilege of being at my side.

His gaze bore into hers, his lips silent.

Nothing to say? "Had I not overheard my parents speaking of pawning me off, I'd probably only have found out on the wedding day." Her gaze dipped to that glaring document before they narrowed on him. "Why would you rush to marry me anyway?"

This time he didn't hesitate. "Why would I not? You are beautiful, intelligent, and unattached."

Unattached?

As in easy prey?

Harriet pursed her lips. At any moment, horns might sprout through his toffee-colored hair and his jaw could drop, revealing sharp, frightening canines while fire shot from his throat, scorching her eyebrows, and *that* would be more believable than the answer that rolled off his tongue. "Well, I have no intention of wedding *you.*" *Not without you convincing me you are able to rise to the promise I made.*

The corners of his lips drew upward—the first sign of some form of emotion. "And the gossips believe you are a timid mouse."

"I am not a mouse." She let her eyes shoot flames at him. "Nor am I timid."

"You most assuredly are not."

Harriet curled her lip, done with the conversation. She had an impending mission to test this man. And possibly a marriage to sabotage if he failed the test. "If you will excuse me, *my lord.*"

He stepped in front of her when she would have passed him. "A word, my lady."

"The time for *words* would have been before you and my father decided to parley my future without my concurrence."

"I must ask again," he paused for breath, "*my* lady." A short silence. "In what way do you not find me agreeable?"

Harriet had no intention of satisfying him by answering the question and couldn't understand his hesitating response. Could he truly not see why she should object to this arrangement? "In what way do you think that you are?"

He frowned. "I am a marquess."

Harriet's jaw threatened to drop open for the second time that day, but she recovered quickly with the lift of her chin. "So you are titled. Congratulations."

"You . . ." The corner of his eye twitched. "You will want for nothing as my wife. I'll treat you well."

"My father said as much." Harriet refused to temper the skepticism in her voice. "So many a man has said to many a woman."

His gaze never wavered. "You believe I am not a man of my word?"

"I believe you keep the company of Cromby and his cronies."

"Cromby keeps my company, not the other way around."

"Pot. Kettle. Black."

The footman gave a low cough.

Harriet ignored him.

"You will judge me," Leeds asked slowly, "by such a simple thing?"

"Is there anything simple about your companions? The company you keep? Or that keeps you?" Her arms crossed over her breast, book tucked in between. "I overheard Cromby refer to Lady Penelope North as Pudgy Penelope, and that is the *least* of his transgressions."

Leeds grimaced.

Good. At least the man had some sense of good and evil.

"I am not responsible for Cromby's tongue."

Answering for himself but accepting no charge? Harriet smiled but didn't retort, moving to step past him.

He moved with her. "Given your circumstances, Lady Harriet, I thought you would not be averse to accepting me as your husband."

"*My* circumstances? You know nothing about me, sir!"

He cocked his head to the side. "I know you've yet to favor a gentleman. I know your suitors these days are comprised of fortune hunters."

"Have you been spying on me?"

"Not spying, no. Noticing."

Honestly, what did she do with a statement such as that? Tuck it away for further examination later? Embrace it as God's truth? Disregard it as one of those things men *say* to get their way?

"Setting aside your candid revelation," Harriet said, albeit a bit too dryly, "do not expect me to favor *you* any time soon."

"I am no fortune hunter."

"Yes, yes. You are a marquess, wealthy, and honorable. I, however, remain unconvinced."

That dark gaze burned into her. "What will convince you?"

"Nothing," she said and darted past him before he could move to intercept her, and as she passed him, she snatched the document from his fingers, her mother's last words echoing through her mind. *Harriet, sweetheart, do not marry a man who would not fight for you. Promise me.*

I promise.

A loud curse was the last thing she heard before she broke into a run.

FINALLY. HE'D SPOKEN to her.

And it felt bloody breathtaking.

And thoroughly hellish.

William Fitzgerald Hamilton, the third Marquess of Leeds and better known as Will amongst close friends, had always considered himself a levelheaded man.

Until the first moment he laid eyes on Harriet Hillstow.

A day he had never forgotten.

He'd been riding in Hyde Park when he spotted her leaning against a tree in a pretty white day dress with lace trimmings with her nose deep in a book. The wind had swept up tendrils of escaped curls and she'd laughed as another gust flipped through the pages of her book causing her to lose her place.

The scene had riveted him to the spot. That had been the moment his awareness of Harriet Hillstow had awakened. After that, he noticed her at balls and events and found himself surprised that she kept company with the wallflowers of the *ton*.

He'd never believed that she belonged in a row along the wall with all those timid creatures. She belonged at the center of all the stars. The more he studied this beguiling wallflower, the more his awareness of her soared.

He only had one problem.

Will had always been terrible at conversing with women. As a boy, he'd stutter in times of utmost pressure. This agitation seemed to present worse in the presence of girls. With time, his stammer had cleared to some extent, but his sentences had dried up into uncomfortable, short, and stunted responses. So much so that he eventually stopped interacting altogether in fraught circumstances—with women in particular. It was much easier to avoid painfully awkward conversations than to be in the midst of them.

Until this woman.

Lady Harriet.

He wanted to interact with her. So, he had tried on multiple occasions, but she flabbergasted him every time with her beauty, her grace, and he ended up losing his voice even before he approached her. The times he did manage to drag his feet within talking distance, his mind drew a complete blank and he continued straight past her without so much as a glance. An unprepared mind equaled a slew of stutters.

Heartrendingly agonizing, that.

Observing her at present, defiance flashing in her blue eyes— right before she snatched the special license from his hand—he knew he had been right. Harriet Hillstow did not belong in the shadows of a ballroom.

She was no timid mouse, even though her heart-shaped face and perfectly arched brows gave her a delicate appearance.

The woman possessed pluck.

And she had just stolen the most important document of his life.

Will cursed, breaking into a run after her.

He spotted the hem of her skirts disappear up the stairwell that led up to the second floor and picked up his pace.

Sensing his pursuit, or perhaps hearing his footfalls, she glanced over her shoulder. Will noticed her eyes widening with grim satisfaction—she hadn't expected he'd chase her down. He was not about to let her destroy those papers. Not after he'd pulled strings to get a meeting with the archbishop on such short notice. If he had to turn up on the archbishop's doorstep again, what would he say? His future wife stole the papers because she refused to marry him?

No.

Absolutely not.

A man had his pride.

He reached her bedchamber just in time for the door to slam against his boot. Will pushed his way into her room, shutting the door behind him, his gaze fixing on her like a hawk. This woman always had the power to send his heart chasing after its own rhythm. The difference between today and any other day in the past was that there was so much more at stake.

"Are you mad?" she asked astonished. "You cannot enter my bedchamber!"

"We are to be—"

"No, we are not! And even if you manage to force me into wedlock, my chamber will be barred to you!"

"Force? Is this not too strong a word?"

"What would you call it?"

"An arranged marriage?"

"Isn't that just another word for forced?"

Will stilled and swallowed the retort perched on his tongue. He could feel the blood rush to his ears, sweat forming on the palms of his hands, two tell-tale signs that his words were about to twist over his tongue.

A curse exploded in his mind. *Please not now.*

He considered the woman before him. A little tigress.

His logic didn't seem to work with her. He sensed that confessing the truth—that he had been enthralled with her since the moment he'd laid eyes on her—wouldn't work either. Even if he did confess, Will wasn't confident that he could say it in a way that would sound romantic and not increase her suspicions.

Truth be told, Lady Harriet was right to be skeptical of him. She was quite right in saying that he had never conversed with her, never asked for a dance, nor had he ever called on her as a suitor ought.

He could hardly tell her he became tongue-tied whenever he attempted to approach her. Would she even believe that? Perhaps if the circumstances had been different, she might have. But certainly not today. He could only hope that with time she would glimpse his sincerity through his actions.

Will inhaled a deep breath, collecting his words. "We are betrothed." Weren't arranged marriages still an acceptable method of finding partners?

"So I've been repeatedly told," she retorted.

"That's not what I meant."

"Oh? Pray tell, what did you mean? Sir."

"I mean, that we are betrothed is a fact. But the wagers circling about you are becoming more troubling, Lady Harriet," Will said calmly, and slowly the tension left his shoulders. "Neither I nor your father is scheming behind your back. We are trying to protect you."

"My father's protection I understand, but yours?" She paused, then drew back in shock. "Wait, wagers? What wagers? Why have I not heard of this?"

Damn it.

Her father must not have told her yet.

Will preferred the anger over the hurt that crossed her features. He couldn't stand it. But he was a selfish man. When he had got wind of a list of heiresses attached to the betting book of White's—and discovered Lady Harriet's name was on it—he had been livid, yet strangely calm.

The list noted the good and bad attributes of each heiress, and by that content alone, he suspected the man—whoever he was, as no one had claimed ownership—hadn't meant for it to be circulated. Only, it fell into the hands of Cromby.

Another point against the man.

Will hoped whoever was responsible for that list was ashamed. As they bloody should be.

It didn't matter whether the attributes they'd assigned each woman had been ridiculously silly, the women listed would still suffer from it. *Did* suffer, as Leeds had presently negotiated to marry one of them.

"Wagers about your ruination."

Her brow furrowed. "What do you mean?"

He didn't hold back. "Your name made a list of heiresses, and it landed in the betting book of White's."

"That explains my father's actions. I suppose." She tossed her book on the bed. "But not why I should wed *you*."

Will froze. What did a man say to that? He chose the safest answer, one not even his tongue could stutter over. "I'm in want of a wife. You are in need of a husband."

"Who says I'm in need of anything? Just because of the wagers?"

Will nodded.

"Have *you* placed a bet?"

"Of course not," Will said, stiffening. "I have my honor."

"Then why choose *me* if you are in want of a wife?" she asked. "There are many eligible young ladies who will fall at your feet if you show them even the slightest interest."

"But not you, I gather."

Her silence echoed her sentiment.

"You would also make an excellent marchioness."

"You don't know that."

"I may have many faults, but I am not blind." Will couldn't help testing the waters. "I have noticed you at balls."

Her eyes brimmed with doubt and disbelief. As expected. Still, Will felt a pinch of disappointment. He couldn't say the words he wanted to say. Not before he had a chance to show her his sincerity.

But with the wagers, time had run out. Her father had eagerly accepted his proposal, and the betrothal agreement had been signed.

Will had believed she'd been informed.

Truthfully, it hadn't occurred to him to ease her mind when he'd approached her father for her hand as he had thought she would be eager to marry. Were not all ladies? Plus, he met the standards of a catch according to the gossip rags. Titled. Wealthy.

Good teeth.

Today was full of surprises.

And curse Cromby.

She may have considered the two men friends, but Cromby had always inserted himself in Will's space without invitation. Will had just thought it too tiring to expel him. Not worth the breath. But the moment Will had learned Cromby had put the list in the betting book, he'd been dead in Will's mind.

And maybe he should have endured his awkwardness and approached Lady Harriet in a different fashion, like courtship, but he hadn't wanted to take the chance of her being ruined by a wily fortune-hunter or risk her father marrying her off to someone else.

He'd seen his chance. He'd recognized an opportunity to marry the woman he'd been obsessing over day and night and hadn't given thought to anything else.

But he couldn't tell her any of that.

To the *ton*, she had the reputation of being a demure chatterbox, which was utter nonsense. There was nothing meek about Lady Harriet. Chatterbox? He had yet to glimpse such a thing.

"So you think I'll be a useful addition to your estate, and these so-called wagers make me easy pickings, is that it?"

Will flinched. "That's not what I meant, either."

"You say a lot of things you don't mean, don't you?"

"We are a good match, Lady Harriet. Can't that be enough?"

"Nothing about this marriage feels right."

Will racked his brain for a solution. "How about we go for a ride in Hyde Park? There is nary a cloud in sight today." He could watch the sun dance off the hue of her hair *and* set her mind at ease.

Something, emphasis on *thing*, caught the corner of his eye.

Will's head swiveled to the crawling creature and cursed, putting himself between Lady Harriet and the *thing*, backing her into the wall.

"What are you doing?" She pushed at his back.

"There is a creature approaching us. Do not be alarmed, I shall protect you." Will looked around for an object he could use as a weapon.

Lady Harriet snorted. "That is not a thing. That is Chester."

Will glanced at her in shock. "*Chester?*"

His gaze whipped back in horror at the thing-creature-Chester crawling slowly toward them.

"What the bloody hell is that thing—um, Chester?" Will asked, unable to keep the disgruntlement from his voice. The thing had nails as long as pikes and a short, flat head.

Lady Harriet slipped from behind him and strode over to the animal and picked it up. Its long arms circled her neck.

Christ above.

"It's a sloth," she said.

"A what?" He had never heard of such a thing.

"A sloth," she repeated.

"Lord no, that must be the ugliest animal I've ever set eyes upon."

"Oh pish, he is adorable." She patted its head. "A friend rescued him from a merchant who collects exotic animals. I'm caring for Chester until my friend returns."

Will stared suspiciously at the sloth in her embrace. It truly was the ugliest thing he had ever seen. But somehow, the look she bestowed upon the animal made him want to yank the thing from her embrace.

Will sighed.

Jealous of an animal. He really had sunk too low. Before he could reply, a knock at the door interrupted them.

Her eyes widened. "Yes?" she called out.

"My lady, the priest has arrived."

If looks could scorch, Will was pretty sure he'd be in a grave right about then.

Chapter Two

"A DRIVE THROUGH Hyde Park?" Harriet used the most sarcastic tone she could muster. "The priest is here!"

"My lady?"

"Thank you, Beth. Please give me a moment," Harriet directed at the door.

"As you wish."

She turned back to the rotten man before her.

"Harriet," the traitorous beast began, having the good sense to look sheepish. Had he maintained his stoic manner, she would have clubbed him over the head. "You weren't supposed to find out like this. Your father said he'd inform you. I believed you already knew."

"As you have very well discovered, I did not. And I did not give you leave to call me by my name."

He let out a heavy sigh and dragged a hand through his hair while regarding her as though he didn't quite know how to manage her.

Good. She'd rattled his pristine composure.

Did he believe she would just accept this? Believe that merely noticing her at balls was enough for him to know he wanted to marry her? It was just more proof he did not know her at all. Because if he did, he wouldn't have used this backhanded approach to secure her hand in marriage. She felt like a cornered animal with no way out.

Harriet pushed that suffocating discomfort aside. She might have been born helpless, but she did not grow into a helpless woman.

"And this," she held up the envelope. "Is this the special license my father told me about?"

He didn't deny it. "Yes."

"What happens if I tear it up?"

"I shall have another within an hour." He paused. "Or so."

"Your contacts are so lofty?"

"I am that determined."

Her grip on the document tightened. "I truly have no choice then."

"Lady Harriet," he said softly, advancing a cautious step before lowering onto one knee so that he did not tower above her anymore. It still did not diminish his presence. "I know this is not what you want, and God knows you deserve to be lavished with gifts and poetry. But I will do my utmost do make you happy."

Leather. Rosewood. A hint of something unfathomably male. Lord, if supreme manliness had an *eau de cologne*, this man would be the king of fragrance.

Smoky. Earthy.

And to go along with his all-consuming arrogance, a touch of deceit. Another reminder of the man's character.

Her perfect man would never act like the man before her. At the very least, her perfect love match would *care* for her feelings. Because he would *love* her.

Leeds . . . She didn't know what Leeds wanted from her, nor did he betray any of his thoughts. The man could have been a statue for all the emotion he painted on his face.

Tears threatened to burn her eyes, and she clenched her jaw while she willed them away. Anger, disappointment, the threat of not being able to keep her promise to her mother, she didn't know what she was feeling as she stared into that unfathomable, dark gaze that held no sentiments whatsoever.

By Jove.

She would not stand for this!

Her gaze dropped to the broad expanse of his chest. If she kicked him right in the center, would he even budge? If he hadn't resembled a crouching tiger who looked ready to pounce, she might have tested her leg strength.

She did not trust this sudden kneel either. Did he hope to appear less intimidating? Hah! It had the opposite effect. Truly. The man appeared even more formidable.

It made Harriet uneasy. It was as though she—the prey, a little deer in the forest—had caught sight of a predator. She could either remain frozen in the hope that he would move on or run for her life.

The former was not an option. He had already caught her scent. Locked his sights on her. And she suspected, once this man put his mind to something, he wouldn't stop until he got what he wanted.

"Compelling me into marriage this way is the last thing that will make me happy."

He paused, shooting a glance at Chester before finding her gaze again. "I admit, I've made some blunders, but I will give you everything you want."

She waved the special license in his face. "I want my name crossed out of this document."

"Anything but that."

"And you expect me to believe your intention is to make me happy? To protect me? You've done a wonderful job so far, sir. Do keep it up."

"I realize we've had a poor start—"

"*Poor* start?" Harried interrupted. "I daresay there was no start to speak of!"

"Harriet—"

"Did I not say not to call me by my name?"

"Love—"

"Do *not* call me *love*." Was the man trying to provoke her into an early grave? "Why would you call me that?"

No pause. "A blunder, my apologies."

"You are quite the blunderer, sir." Harriet bit down on her teeth. "We are not familiar enough with each other for you to address me so intimately."

"Which is why I am trying to close the distance between us. You can call me Will."

Harriet started. Close the distance? A rushed "arranged" marriage was not enough? This man truly was in a class by himself.

"Well, I don't want you to call me by my name or any endearment. Nor do I wish to close the distance between us." There was no intimacy between them and there could never be until he proved himself worthy—the same standard she had for any man. Best he understood that from the start.

"Lady Harriet, then."

Harriet gave the man a suspicious glare. She might have won the battle—*no*, he surrendered this battle—but he did it to win the war.

The man was trouble.

She should have just gritted her teeth and let him call her "love" no matter how annoying the tingle of gooseflesh. If he wanted to fool himself that a name would close the distance between them, let him. *She* was no fool.

"Fine," she bit out. "Call me Harriet, if you must."

He raised one dark brow, surprise lighting his gaze. "Harriet."

A rush of butterfly wings skittered over her skin. How could her name sound like that? So . . . so sultry? He did that on purpose, didn't he?

Scoundrel.

"What have I done to deserve this?" Harriet questioned. She set Chester down. "Surely, you do not find me that pleasing to the eye?"

A glimmer of determination marked his countenance. Too late, she realized she probably shouldn't bait a wolf when they were alone in her bedchamber with the very means to wed her immediately clasped in her hand.

He was on her in a second.

Harriet had no time to react before his lips seized hers. His tongue swept into her mouth at once, claiming her small gasp of surprise. Instinctively, she understood that unless she put an end to it, this man wouldn't stop until he had claimed every single part of her, stolen every single one of her breaths.

Mother Mary.

A romantic at heart, Harriet could appreciate all the elements—such as kissing—that went with romance. And this kiss . . . she could almost believe in things that did not exist and surrender everything without any caution.

Almost.

A small spark ignited deep within her and took flame. A fire lit in her heart to teach this man a lesson.

I can play this game of yours as well, Lord Marquess.

She crumbled the special license in one hand as the other shoved into the locks of his hair. She returned his kiss with the fervor of a lover reunited with her long-lost love.

"You taste like a dream," he breathed against her lips before deepening their kiss again.

So did he. There was no denying that. He tasted of something dark, something so intoxicating that it brought chills to her skin.

No!

She could not forget what he was doing—thrusting an unwanted marriage of convenience upon her!

She twisted out of his embrace, retreating a few steps to gather her wits. Game or not, it was a dangerous one to play. She couldn't believe she kissed a man! *This* man.

"Harriet."

There he went again—pronouncing her name as though it tasted like a sweet piece of candy. "You've proved the point that, unsurprisingly, your arrogance knows no bounds, sir. How dare you accost me in my bedchamber? We are not wed yet."

And the fact remained that no one had thought to ask her about her feelings about the marriage. Not her father and certainly not the Marquess of Leeds. She might as well have been invisible for all the care they had shown. She was not about to make it easy for them. They didn't take her feelings into account, so she would not consider theirs.

"I'm proving to you just how pleasing I find you, Harriet. And you enjoyed my kiss. I may be wrong in many things, but I'm not mistaken in that."

So what if she did? She would never admit it. And a kiss didn't prove anything.

"And what about the priest? Is that not a bit presumptuous on your part?"

"Whether we wed today or wait until the banns are read, we will wed—we must for your own sake. I see no reason to delay the inevitable."

"What about me? Did it ever occur to you that I might want a big, lavish wedding?"

His brows knit together. "Is that what you want?"

"Is it not a bit too late to be asking me this?" Did he expect her to suddenly reveal her dreams to him? Just like that? She lifted the document to his face. "*This* is what I want." A forceful yank ripped the special license in half.

There. This is what I think of your methods.

He clenched his jaw, but other than that, he remained calm. Too calm. "This won't change anything."

No.

But it would give her time to give him a tough tussle. Test this mettle of his. Harriet had not been jesting when she'd threatened to run off to the Americas. In fact, mayhap this was the best way to put his determination, his commitment, to the challenge. He'd have to either fight for her or give up.

"I know," she said, ripping the paper in two more halves for good measure before tossing it to the floor. "But it shall be a pain having to explain to the archbishop why you need another license."

And give me the opening to escape you.

TWO HOURS LATER, Will entered the Hillstow residence again with another special license. This time, he didn't make the mistake of keeping the document in his hand but instead secured it in the pocket of his jacket, nestled safely against his chest.

He, a worldly man of eight and twenty, still couldn't quite believe the turn of events. He had conversed with Harriet without breaking into a slew of stutters. He had kissed her. And he had been shocked to his core when she'd kissed him back. He had wanted to prove that he found her captivating, yet she had turned the tables on him and proved in turn that she would not be taken lightly.

Not that he'd been taking her lightly before, however his social reticence might have appeared to her. And it troubled him that Hatton hadn't informed his daughter of the betrothal or the wagers—that was bad—but Will still hadn't expected such a vehement reaction against their union.

It stung his pride.

And she hadn't been wrong. It had been a pain to secure another license. Damn embarrassing. Luckily, not as impossible as he had feared.

Will pinched the bridge of his nose.

Most would consider him a catch. Yet Lady Harriet considered him the worst of rogues. To say he'd been caught off guard was a deep understatement.

And all this because of his perceived connection to Cromby?

It seemed highly unlikely. Her mistrust of him must run deeper. But for the life of him, he couldn't decipher why. He must be missing something. That or it boiled down to not being able to fathom the inner workings of the female mind, which no man had any hope to unlock.

Damn it.

He should not have lost his grip on his restraint in her chamber earlier. If anything, it had strengthened her defenses against him. Never mind. No matter what, Lady Harriet would be his wife after today. He had the rest of their lives to woo himself into her good graces.

However, the moment he entered the hall of the Hillstow residence, he knew something was wrong. He certainly had not expected the scene before him—the priest he'd procured cradling his distraught future mother-in-law. He could hear doors slamming in the distance, and two maids dashed up the stairs to the living quarters while two footmen whispered to each other in low, panic-stricken tones.

Alarm spread through him.

What the hell was going on? He would give his right leg that this current mayhem had something to do with the little spitfire who had raised hell with him today.

"Where is Lady Harriet?" Will asked the marchioness without beating around the bush. Given Lady Harriet's lack of enthusiasm earlier, there was no telling what she might have done after he'd left.

"Oh, this is terrible!"

An icy shiver ran down his spine at the woman's cry. "What happened?"

"Harriet has run away!"

God's blood. Of course, she had. And why not? Nothing else had gone as planned today.

"Where is Hatton?"

"George is out searching for her," the marchioness wailed while the priest dutifully patted her back.

Will swallowed a breath of frustration; the dramatics of his future mother-in-law brought an ache to his temples.

Did she leave a note? Will started to ask, but his tongue couldn't roll past the *D*. He inhaled deeply, forcing air into his lungs, mentally repeating the question in his head five times before he finally asked, "Did she leave a note? Any indication of where she might have gone?"

She waved about a small piece of paper.

He strode toward the pair and snatched the note from her fingertips. The neat scrawl was short and to the point.

Tell Leeds he can rot in perdition.

Will shut his eyes to draw strength from within. He should have considered there was more to her motive for ripping up the license than simply causing him inconvenience or embarrassment. He should have . . . should have locked her in her chamber.

No. He could never do that.

Put guards on her? Have her shipped to his residence and held the wedding there?

It's a moot point now.

In truth, as much as he blamed Hatton for not being forthright with his daughter, this was just as much his fault as it was Hatton's. He should have made more of an effort with her. Should have danced with her at balls. Conversed with her. Perhaps then his offer for her hand would not have come as such an unwelcome shock. His desire to marry her would be clear and not be so suspect to her. At the very least he could have dealt with her opinion of him, showed her he was not the blackguard she claimed him to be.

But his awkwardness had always been a hindrance. When it came to her, it was downright painful. But to flee from him? Was that not a bit extreme? While he admired her gumption, his patience was wearing thin.

And *that* had never happened before.

For all his flaws, Will had always prided himself on his patience. But Lady Harriet had exceeded all his expectations, and it seemed, much to his dismay, that she did so to the detriment of his virtues. He'd always known her to be more than the mousy creature most of the *ton* believed her to be. To him, she was a little swanling yet to spread her wings and claim the center of everyone's attention. Now, he discovered, this swan had already developed a bite.

"Would she leave London?" Will asked the marchioness. He wouldn't bother with her friends or family. If Hatton was out searching for his daughter, they would be the first doors he'd knock on.

"Leave London? Oh, dear! Would she do that? She is all alone!"

Bloody hell. "Madam, I know you are distraught, but please think. Would Harriet leave London? Would she go to the country? Anywhere else?"

She sniffed. "I do not think so."

Will wasn't so sure. Although to be fair, he wouldn't discount that she would hide in plain sight either.

"The Duke of Calstone has arrived," the butler announced.

Calstone appeared in the doorway with a bright smile. "Am I late for the wedding?"

Will had never been so relieved to see his friend. "Yes. However, you are lucky in your lack of punctuality as my bride has run off."

Calstone's jaw went slack. "You were left at the altar?"

"Not exactly an altar, but yes."

"The lady has some big b—" he cut off when he spotted the priest and the distraught marchioness, ". . . grievances."

"She has every right to be upset," Will said, dragging a hand through his hair. "She only found out we are to be married a few hours ago."

Calstone's eyes widened. "Give a bride some warning, man."

"She was supposed to have ample time." He shot a look at his future mother-in-law. "No one saw fit to inform her."

"Even so," Calstone said, "you must have done something for her to run off."

"She believes I'm robbing her of her dreams and snuffing out her happiness."

"Aren't you being a touch overdramatic?"

"Her words, not mine."

Calstone whistled. "Brutal."

Yes, brutal. "She said her parents pawned her off on me."

"She actually used the word pawned?"

Will nodded.

"Savage." Calstone whistled, then clapped his hands together. "We're going bride hunting?"

"Yes."

They strode from the room without a word of comfort to the priest and weeping marchioness. All of Will's focus had shifted to a little beauty who, it was becoming apparent, was as slippery as an eel.

"So, where will we look first?"

Will racked his brain but could come to no good conclusion. The post? The underbelly of London? Bow Street? Bow Street would be best. He also had some acquaintances who owed him a favor. The more people he had searching in all directions, the faster they would find her.

"Wait!" the marchioness called just as they reached the door.

Will and Calstone both turned at her call.

"Harriet . . . she . . . might have mentioned a place earlier when she argued with George."

"What place?" Will demanded.

The woman's tears started anew.

"Madam, I will ask again," Will paused, feeling a disruption of his words coming on. His temple twitched. *Damn it.* Not now.

Calstone patted him on the shoulder and sent him a reassuring look. "Where did Lady Harriet go?" his friend asked in his stead. Some of the tension left his jaw. "Do speak up, madam."

"The Americas!" she cried in a loud wail, throwing herself onto the priest's shoulder.

The Americas? What bloody madness was this? Surely, Harriet wouldn't go that far.

Will suddenly recalled the book she had clutched in her hands when he had run into her earlier. He hadn't thought much of it then, but now Will's blood froze in his veins at the memory. It had been Charles Griffin's accounts of his travels around the colonies. Hadn't the newspapers gushed about how the author found his true love in a foreign land?

Will clenched his jaw.

Calstone gave an uncomfortable laugh. "A lady wouldn't travel to that godforsaken place alone."

Not an ordinary lady, no. But his friend had never met Harriet Hillstow.

Will strode through the door and descended the steps in a hurry.

"Leeds?" Calstone called, keeping pace. "Where are we going?"

"To the docks."

Chapter Three

"I NEED TO board this ship!" Harriet waved a hand at the captain of *The Royal Oak*, the only ship bound for the Americas on the dock. In the last three hours she had prepared several money pouches, packed a valise, written a note, snuck out of the house, hailed a hack, and been driven to the West India Docks.

Ninety minutes of which were spent peeking through the hackney's window to assure herself she hadn't been caught.

By now, her father would not only have learned of her absence but be scouring London for her whereabouts. Hell, even Leeds might already have returned with another special license. The only advantage she had was that they had no clue as to where she was heading. They would be searching in all the wrong places.

Served them right.

Harriet didn't give herself any time to think because then she would start to dwell on all the reasons boarding a ship as a woman alone was an extremely bad idea. The only thought she allowed herself was that she must get as far away from this arranged marriage as possible.

Plus, she would only be alone for the duration of her journey on the ship. Once she arrived at her destination, she would join her friend, Rohan Graves.

"We're about to pull the gangway, miss. We cannot board you."

What nonsense! The only way she couldn't board was if they had already pulled it!

"Why not? The gangway is still there. Let me quickly cross it!"

"Those are my orders. No more passengers board once we decide to lift the gangway, miss."

"Please," she waved a fat purse in her hand. "I will pay triple the fees."

The captain's gaze flicked to the bulging black leather pouch in her hand. Harriet wanted to jump for joy. If a woman could not appeal to a man's instinct to save a damsel, she could always count on her purse.

"Please," Harriet implored. "This is a matter of life and death." It was no exaggeration as far as she was concerned. Marrying Leeds now meant a certain death to the promise she had made to her mother. Desperate circumstances called for desperate measures.

"Hold!" the captain shouted to a sailor. "One last passenger to board."

Harriet heaved out a breath of relief.

She hurried onto the ship before the captain could change his mind again and handed him the pouch.

"How long until we arrive at our destination?" Harriet asked the captain, a short, stocky man with a thick beard.

"A month, miss, permitting the weather favors the voyage."

Speaking of destinations. "Where exactly is the ship docking?"

"Charleston, miss."

Ah good. Rohan had business in Charleston.

When she arrived, she could secure a room in the local inn until she found him. He might be at sea, but no matter, she could wait. Then he could help her with this wretched situation. She would need it if Leeds did not show any inclination to fight for her hand. And maybe even if he did.

This was by far the boldest thing she'd ever done. However, she had to take a stand. For her promise, yes, and to show her father that they couldn't treat her as nothing more than a bit of business to be transacted. Of course, she understood arranged marriages, but being informed on the day of your wedding that you're about to be wedded? This was not to be borne!

There were lines. Lines not even a parent should cross.

And honestly, she probably would not have gone this far if not for Leeds. While he did not appear to be a man easily deterred, showing up out of the blue with a special license and a priest? What was that if not suspicious? Why was the man so dead set on marrying her and doing it today?

Speaking purely practically, she supposed she could do worse than marry the Marquess of Leeds even though he was nothing she wanted in a man. As a matter of fact, he was the exact opposite of what she wanted—he was bossy, intimidating, and had questionable morals.

She preferred a man whose essence spoke of love, caring, and good character.

What had her father been thinking?

The captain motioned to a sailor overseeing the gangway being lifted, drawing her from her inward rant. "Brett will show you to your cabin once he's done."

She nodded her thanks, turning to lean against the railing and watch the bustle of the docks below. Only once they'd cleared away that plank, that last connection between land and ship, did the reality of her actions set in.

I'm leaving England.

She was on a ship bound for the Americas.

She firmed her shoulders along with her resolve. She would write to her parents as soon as she arrived in Charleston. Then she would wait to see if Leeds followed or not. If he crossed the ocean to collect her himself, she would reconsider the man. If he ordered her home, she would do so, but only once her parents called off the betrothal. Perhaps she might even return with an

American husband.

Harriet smiled at the thought.

Who was to say that this might not be the start of the most magical romantic adventure of her life?

In the distance, a black carriage led by two proud black horses rolled onto the docks. Harriet tensed for a moment before relaxing again. The crest on the door did not belong to her family. But for some reason, she could not tear her gaze away from the scene.

A scary premonition filled her.

No, it couldn't be.

Who could predict that she would ever board a ship bound for another country? Not Leeds. The man knew nothing about her. Unless . . . had someone spotted her on her way to the docks? She had told no one of her plan. Not even her lady's maid.

Harriet held her breath as the horses came to a halt and the carriage door was flung open. A man emerged. Tall, broad, and most certainly the very rogue she was running from.

Harriet dropped to her haunches in an attempt to be less visible, her heart pounding in her ears.

How had he guessed?

Inhaling a deep breath, she cautiously peeked over the taffrail with two wide eyes. He was there, speaking to a man in shabby clothing who suddenly pointed at her ship.

Harriet dropped to her knees again.

Impossible.

This could not be happening to her. How had he found her? Well, it didn't matter, did it? He had. Luckily, the gangway had already been removed. There was no way the captain would allow him to board the ship. She had barely made it by the skin of her teeth!

"Hold the ship!"

Harriet's eyes widened. She would never mistake that deep, gruff voice for anyone else's.

The captain stepped up to the edge. "Can't do that, sir. We

are about to depart."

Harriet clutched her valise to her chest.

Thank Heaven.

"You have a passenger on board your ship who does not belong there."

The captain cast her a curious look where she hunkered at his feet. "All my passengers have paid for their passage. We've already searched for stowaways. There are none."

"I did not say they were a stowaway," Leeds called. "The passenger is my betrothed. She would be this high, with blue eyes and brown hair."

Harriet held her breath as the captain arched a white, bushy brow.

"There are many women with your description," the captain said. "And none of them is my problem."

"She is my betrothed," Leeds repeated, this time steel coated every word.

Harriet flinched.

"Then why did she plead to board my ship as a matter of life and death?"

"So, you have met her?"

"Maybe."

"It's an arranged marriage," an unfamiliar voice filled the air. "The lady is a bit skittish."

Harriet resisted the urge to jump up and curse the man.

"You'll have to meet up with your betrothed in Charleston. We are weighing anchor as I speak."

"I will meet with her now," Leeds insisted.

The captain just stared. Harriet wanted to kiss the old man.

"Allow me to introduce myself," the other man called out to the captain. She still did not recognize the voice. "I am the *Duke* of Calstone, and I'd advise you to let the *Marquess* of Leeds retrieve his lady, who happens to be the daughter of the honorable *Marquess* of Hatton. They are to be married today."

The captain scowled. "A pleasure to make your lordships'

acquaintance. Allow me to introduce *myself*. I am the *captain* of *The Royal Oak*. Here, *I* have the highest rank. I make the rules. I am the law. As I said, you can meet up with your betrothed in Charleston."

Harriet sagged in relief.

"Name your price." Leeds, that scoundrel, refused to relent. "I'll pay it."

Harriet started, and before she could stop herself, she shot upright, pointing a finger at him. "Captain! Do not believe this wretched rogue's tongue. He is penniless!"

Leeds's gaze locked onto her. Narrowed.

Drat it! Why had she gone and done that? Not that it truly mattered, she supposed. The old man had already let the cat out of the bag.

His gaze turned back to the captain, not even bothering to counter her accusation. "Everyone has a price."

The captain nodded. "Aye, everyone does. My price is that you adhere to my schedule. My ship waits for no man."

Harriet watched as Leeds's face darkened into thunderous clouds. She quickly retreated several steps, so that she could no longer see him.

Yes, everyone had a price. And so did every action. She suspected the price she would pay for today would be very steep. No.

Harriet firmed her shoulders.

No. No. *No.*

She took a step forward again, lifting her chin as she gazed down at Leeds. *I am the one in charge here.*

Your move, sir.

IN ALL HIS life, Will could not recall ever being so furious and so terrified at the same time. He had spotted that little minx on the ship the second he leaped from his carriage, right before she had vanished from his view. The sight had hit him like a solid punch in the gut.

She truly had boarded a ship to the Americas. She wanted to escape him that much. If he didn't get her off this ship, she would disappear from his life.

He couldn't lose her.

Wouldn't lose her.

Not bloody happening.

But the captain refused to let him board the ship. Not as surprising as it was frustrating. Will hadn't held out much hope in the first place. Once the gangway was pulled—as the captain said, he was the law. Even Calstone dropping their titles like they were hot as blazing iron hadn't worked. Neither could money change his mind. The captain had all but told them to bugger off.

Will shut his eyes and inhaled deeply. *Relax.* To him that possessed the will, ways were not wanting.

Beside him, Calstone chuckled.

"I've got to meet this woman of yours. She appears quite spirited."

Will ignored him.

He'd be damned if he let Harriet set sail across the ocean all by herself. But he needed to get on *The Royal Oak* first. He could always chase the ship down with another, but by the time he got another captain to pursue this bloody captain, who knew how long it would take to catch up with them.

"I suppose this is fate," Calstone went on.

Will grit his teeth. "Fate will not dictate the outcome of my future. I will."

"I believe it already has, old chap." Calstone's claim did hold substance, as the anchor lifted right before his eyes, and too soon, the ship was pulling away from the docks.

"This can't be happening."

"Oh, but it is."

Will sent a menacing look at his friend. "You are not help-ing."

"No," Calstone agreed. "All I can do now is lighten the mood."

"You are not lightening anything." Will swept his gaze over the dock. "There must be something I can do. Today does *not* end like this. I can't . . . c—" Will stopped.

"No need for words." Calstone threw an arm over his shoulder and grinned at him. "I shall buy us a ship so that we can give chase."

"No," Will said slowly. "If I don't act now, I'll only meet her in Charleston. That can't happen." The moment she stepped foot onto American soil, she might be lost to him.

"You have a plan then?"

No. He didn't have a plan. He only had an option—one—left.

If the captain of *The Royal Oak* wouldn't accept their titles or their blunt, he had no choice but to force the captain to take them.

Very well.

Let the ship leave but, by Christ, it was not leaving without him.

Will shrugged out of his coat and tossed it to Calstone before removing his boots.

"What the devil are you doing?" Calstone exclaimed, which he followed with an oath. "You cannot mean to do what I think you mean to do."

"I do."

Will didn't take the time to explain any further and dove off the pier and into the black water, Calstone's curses fading as the Thames engulfed him. Needle pricks stung his skin, the chill seeping into his bones. He steeled his focus against the cold, inhaling a deep breath when he resurfaced.

Shouts came from the docks.

Will paid them no mind. He started to swim in pursuit of the ship. He didn't stop. Didn't look back.

He'd always been a strong swimmer, but at this moment he couldn't tell whether this madness would work. One thing he knew with certainty: he would get on that ship, or he would perish in his attempt. Fortunately, the vessel had pulled from the dock only moments before, and the distance wasn't yet very great.

He could reach her.

Would reach her.

Each stroke brought him closer.

Will had never swum with so much might, and he didn't pause or hesitate, not even when another call reached his ears.

"Captain! That fellow jumped off the docks! Look! Bleeding 'ell, has he lost his mind?"

Will didn't hear anything else. He just swam. Stroke after stroke. *Harriet.* He pushed everything else from his mind, the swell of the water, the taste of salt in his mouth, the bite of iciness nipping at him. Everything except her.

He had one purpose.

One goal.

Harriet.

And the Heavens answered. For once, every element fell into alignment.

"Toss a rope!" The captain roared. "Toss a rope!"

It seemed his title did mean something after all.

Will caught a glimpse of the thick rope that flew over the side of the deck and directed his strokes straight toward it. He snatched onto the line and gripped it tight.

"There's another one!"

Will glanced over his shoulder. Calstone, that devil. Why the hell had he jumped in after him?

They were both hauled out of the water, not allowed to catch a breath before being confronted by a furious captain.

"What the bloody 'ell are you thinking?" the captain roared.

Christ above. He plugged a finger in his ear to dampen the force of the captain's voice—it could have sunk the damn ship had the man's bellow been an octave deeper.

"You refused to let us board," Will said, opting for a calmer approach, removing his socks and cravat as he slid down heavily onto the deck. Calstone dropped next to him.

"Crazy bastards," the captain muttered.

Will took a moment to regain his composure. His muscles ached and his bones were chilled, but none of that mattered. He tilted his head up to the captain. "Where is she?"

The captain snorted. "So eager to find your little bird. You're not going anywhere before we have a talk." He motioned to a rough-looking, red-haired sailor. "Find them dry clothes."

The man nodded and disappeared from the deck.

"Shouldn't you order him to put down anchor?" Calstone asked between heaves.

The captain laughed. Dry. Without any humor. "I've never turned a ship back in my life. I won't start today. Welcome aboard *The Royal Oak*," his mustache quirked upward, "my *lords*. Destination: Charleston."

Damn it.

Not an ideal circumstance. But not one Will would complain over. Not while they were both on the same ship.

Calstone, however, didn't give up. "We're not that far from the docks yet. Lower us on a boat and send us back."

"You mean that I should spare my resources to escort you back?" The captain crossed his arms. "You're on my ship now. Where I travel, you travel."

Will glanced at his friend. "Why did you follow me?"

Calstone tossed a sock aside. "And miss the fireworks? You are jesting, are you not? Besides, I have nothing better to do anyway."

The sailor returned and hurled them each a bundle of clothes.

The captain shot them a scowl. "Get dressed and meet me up in my cabin."

"There are no socks," Calstone said while ruffling through the items.

Will gripped his friend's shoulder and nodded at the captain. "Just get dressed," he hissed from the corner of his mouth, "before I toss you back into the sea."

Calstone grunted, and they hurriedly changed clothes. Seven minutes later, they were all seated in the captain's cabin, the man stroking his beard while regarding them with a thoughtful, yet distrustful scrutiny.

"I expect triple the fare for your antics."

Will inclined his head.

Calstone snorted. "You expect triple the fare, but you didn't even hand us a pair of socks. Shoes, I understand. You don't know our size—"

"*Blake.*" Leeds shot a warning look at his friend.

"Fine. I shall wiggle my toes for warmth."

The captain ignored him. "I won't have you disturbing my passengers."

"That shouldn't be a problem," Will said. He only wanted to disturb one.

"That includes the woman you are here for."

Will scowled. "She is my betrothed."

"But she is my passenger." The captain leaned forward in his chair. "I'll tell you straight so that there are no misunderstandings while you are aboard my ship. Do not bother my passengers if they don't wish to be bothered. Bothering one guest bothers the rest. I won't have my ship's reputation tarnished because of a lovers' tiff, titled or not."

Will could practically feel the disdain dripping from the man's voice. "We don't plan on making trouble."

"We are your passengers, too," Calstone spoke up.

The captain leaned back in his chair, a shrewd look on his face. "No. You are two fools I dragged from the sea. Although, for a fee, I would be willing to hail another ship to get rid of you."

"I've never been called a fool in my life," Calstone growled.

Neither had Will, but he still inclined his head. "Duly noted. However, when that time comes, I will be taking the lady with me."

The captain stroked his beard. "So long as you don't bother

my passengers, and so long as I don't see that it's against her will, I won't come in between you and your lady. I also have only one cabin left, so you two will be bunking together."

Will didn't miss the captain's emphasis on *I don't see*. "That won't be a problem. I will handle the lady."

"Problem." Calstone slapped his hand on the desk. "Leeds might be a gentleman. I, however, am not. I won't promise not to bother your passengers."

Will arched a brow.

"If you don't let us off this ship now, I will make it my mission to bother every single one of your passengers as well as your sailors, your chef, and whoever else you have on this ship."

The captain leaned back in his chair. "Then I'll toss you in the brig."

"Do you think your men can take me?" Calstone tilted his head thoughtfully. "They probably can. But I promise you this, captain: I will take down enough of them with me for you to feel the loss. How will *that* look for your reputation?"

The captain let out a foul curse. "You little bastard."

"Big bastard," Calstone corrected.

"Send us back," Will said, leaning into his friend's play. On the one hand, he'd mostly resigned himself to the journey and the chance to calm Lady Harriet and give her time to adjust to the thought of marrying him. On the other hand, he wanted to get back as soon as possible to make her his in every legal sense of the word. "It would be best for all involved."

"I'm not sparing any of my men to chaperone you back to the docks."

"We don't need you to spare us a man, only a boat," Will said. "We will row back to shore."

The captain laughed. "The two of you?"

Calstone scowled. "We swam here, didn't we?"

"Expending most of your energy, I imagine."

"We will be fine," Will insisted.

"I'll be one boat short."

"We will make it worth your while," Calstone said.

The captain pursed his lips before finally giving a curt nod. "But I still expect your fare, and we will clear Hole Haven first. It shouldn't be too much of a task rowing to shore from there."

Will gave a curt nod. It was more than he expected, given their circumstances. "Agreed. Now can you please show me to the lady's cabin?"

The captain nodded at the sailor from earlier who'd been stationed at the door. The man motioned for Will to follow him.

Will couldn't wait to see that little minx.

Chapter Four

HARRIET LEANED AGAINST the wall and stared out of the small window of her cabin in deep thought. She still couldn't believe she'd boarded a ship all on her own with an uncertain journey ahead of her.

Before her mother had passed away, she had always encouraged Harriet to follow her dreams. Truth be told, she couldn't recall much of those days, but she did remember one day announcing to her mother that she wanted to wed a prince—and to do so in a beautiful gown fit for any princess.

As she grew older, Harriet lost all misguided notions about marrying a real prince. The prince, after all, had only been a metaphor for the perfect man—a man she loved. A man who loved her. A man who would give her a fairytale life.

Her father had ruined that dream for her.

Instead of a prince, he'd peddled her off to a pauper, perhaps not in terms of actual wealth but certainly in terms of character and feeling, falling short in all ways that mattered to Harriet.

And what of her dream dress? They hadn't even given her that.

She sighed.

The only thing she could hold onto now was the promise she had made to her mother, that she would marry a man who would at the very least valued her enough to fight to be with her. Her current predicament was, however, rather alarming. Leeds would surely chase her down to Charleston—there could be no doubt about it. But . . .

Was that enough?

His insistence on the docks, his determination, and his chasing her down. Could this be considered fighting for her? Or did it just demonstrate a sense of entitlement and desire to win?

Already, her mind spun with all the ways she could provoke Leeds into showing his true motivations once he caught up with her. Luckily, she had more than enough time to come up with all sorts of ways to test the man.

A gentle rap prompted Harriet to divert her gaze from the window. It must be the tea she'd requested. However, the moment she opened the door, Harriet was pushed back by a large man who didn't hesitate to step into her cabin.

"What are you . . ." The words died on her lips as she stared into the depth of two glowing embers. Her eyes widened.

Leeds.

Harriet shook her head, certain she was hallucinating the man before her. She looked at him again and blinked. He didn't disappear.

A resounding thud signaled her only exit had been sealed.

"Harriet."

For a moment, all words lodged in the back of her throat, refusing to pass. "How . . . how are you here?"

"There is one thing about me you should know, love: I will always find you. Do you know how dangerous it is for a woman to travel the seas alone? Be thankful I got onto the ship before you were irrevocably out of my reach."

Thankful my derriere. How had he even got onto the ship? Harriet gave the man a thorough look. He wore simple clothes. Brown breeches with a white shirt. No shoes. Strands of wet hair fell over his forehead. Had he swum here?

"Do not tell me—did you jump into the Thames?"

"Dive would be the more correct term." His gaze bore into

her. "You left me no other choice."

"Are you mad?" She goggled at him. "I won't even mention the filthy water, but what if the captain hadn't pulled you out? Or are you telling me you scaled the side of the ship?"

The corner of his lips itched upward. "Why? Are you worried about me?"

She snorted. "I'd rather not have your death on my conscience."

A glint of humor entered his gaze. "How heartwarming of you, love," he murmured the final word in that deep voice that made her body tingle all over.

She could not deny that him leaping into the River Thames after her did cause a thrill to skitter down her spine, but she needed to stay focused. She folded her arms across her breasts and regarded the beast with all the contempt she could muster. It mattered not that he was here. It would make her task harder, true, but as long as she could get word to Rohan once they reached Charleston, all would be well.

"What do you hope to accomplish?" Harriet asked. "Do you wish to marry me so badly that you would risk your life for my hand?"

"You wouldn't believe me even if I told you."

"Go on, let's see," Harriet challenged.

"I find you captivating."

"Captivating? Me?" She blinked before she threw her head back and laughed. Unbelievable. "You are right, I rather think I don't believe you."

He might as well have confessed his love for all the hogwash in those four words! How could he find her captivating when they had only met today? The man didn't know her at all. If he did, he would *know* she was the least captivating person on this planet! At least, in comparison to all the diamonds of the first water gracing the *ton*.

Leeds stared at her for a long moment before rubbing his temples with the fingers and thumb of one hand. He nodded to her travel bag. "Is that all you brought?"

Harriet scrunched her brows. "I fail to see how that is any of your business."

"Oh, love, it's all my business. The second we leave the Thames, the captain will lower a boat for us, and we'll return to shore."

No.

How could her rebellion end so soon? A flutter of unease danced in Harriet's belly. The type that warned peril was nigh, that she was about to step onto a road there might be no way back from. She needed more time.

"Who exactly is *us*?" Surely even if the captain did agree to such a thing, he would not spare one of his men or wait for that man to return. Then again, enough blunt could make anything possible.

"Me, you, and Calstone."

Calstone? That must be the duke who had bellowed their titles as though the world revolved around them alone. Harriet scratched the tip of her nose. This was all too much.

"And what if I refuse? I can refuse, you know."

"You can refuse," he said slowly, seemingly trying to find the right words. "However, that means we shall become travel companions. Are you sure this is what you want?"

"Better traveling companions than marriage partners."

"Well, I suppose a ship is smaller than London. We shall have more time to become acquainted with each other."

This man . . . time for a change of tactics.

"You have a nasty habit of entering a lady's quarters without her permission."

"I shall break it if you return to London with me."

Harriet almost laughed. He might speak slowly, but he had an answer for everything. "And who will row us to shore? We'll be on open sea once we exit the Thames."

"Calstone and I can manage. It's a clear day and the waters are favorable."

She glanced at his arms for good measure. "You seem confident in gambling with our lives."

"Is that not what you've done since you boarded this ship?"

"Perhaps you ought rather to ask why I took such extreme measures."

A muscle in his jaw flexed. "Oh, you've made your reasons abundantly clear, love. As clear as I have made my determination, wouldn't you say?"

Actually, she would. Perhaps returning to London would be better suited for her than living together on a ship for a month. There were bound to be more opportunities to test this man off ship than on it.

He motioned to her travel bag. "Get your things. We must be on deck soon."

And that was it? Did he expect her to just pick up her bag and leave with him? Her eyes narrowed on the man. "What if I don't leave with you?"

He stared at her. "Then . . . we stay."

"After the trouble you've gone to securing us a boat?"

"I'd rather return to London, but if you insist on staying, I won't fight you." He studied her a moment. "You seem surprised by this."

"Not surprised no, but I had thought you would forcibly remove me from the ship. Is that not the male way?"

"I would never do such a thing."

"In any case, I still cannot believe the captain would do this for you."

"He was made to see the light, love."

You mean you paid him off.

"Don't call me *love*. I'm not your love," Harriet hissed. "I am the exact opposite!"

A hint of impatience entered his gaze. Hah! The man wasn't an emotionless statue after all. Well, to be fair, he had already shown that with his kiss. A kiss she'd been trying not to think about at all. No matter, Harriet still felt a measure of satisfaction at having ruffled at least one of his perfectly arranged feathers.

"I am not your enemy, Harriet." His voice had lowered, almost to a whisper but not quite, yet the blow to her midsection wasn't any less impactful. He was so close that a shiver ran from the back of her neck to the tips of her toes.

"Not my enemy?" Harriet shot him an astonished look. "Everything you have done since I met you has been in direct opposition to my wants. How are you not the enemy?"

"An arranged marriage is hardly the stuff of horrors."

"So you say. In truth, you only think about yourself. Neither you nor my father ever considered me, how I feel, or what my wishes are. I was not even given the courtesy of being informed. Again I ask, how are you not the enemy?"

"I agree that your father and I are at fault. Forgive me for my presumption that you would embrace the arrangement of our betrothal."

"Will my forgiveness change anything?"

His lips parted, then closed.

What did she expect? She wanted nothing more than to poke the man in his heart. "And what if I have affection for another?"

He visibly stiffened. "If you did, you would be running toward him and not another country."

"Who is to say I am not running toward him? Why else would I travel to a lawless country when I have no friends or family there?"

"Why would I not know of such a person?"

She shrugged. "If you had taken the time to court me, you would not be as in the dark as you are now. All I wish to know is whether you would let me go if I were in love with another man."

Harriet almost lost her nerve at the intensity of the gaze that bore into her. As if that weren't enough, his nearness made her a touch dizzy and breathless.

"No."

Hot color flooded Harriet's cheeks. She couldn't say if it was because of anger, exasperation, or something else entirely.

"So it doesn't matter if I love another?"

"It matters."

"But you won't change your mind?"

"No."

The glare she shot him would have cut him to bits were it a set of knives.

"Do you love another?" Leeds asked.

"Since it matters a little bit but not a whole lot, why should I tell you?"

"Harriet . . ."

She lifted her chin.

He cleared his throat. "I don't believe you are the sort of woman to sit idly by when you are in love. That is why I don't believe you have affections for anyone—you would have been with him already."

"How would you know when you know nothing about me?"

"I am hoping we can change that." His gaze swept over the cabin. "Are we returning to London or traveling to the Americas?"

Lawd, she wanted to ruffle more of his feathers. She wanted to obliterate his patience. "I don't rightly care about my destination," she goaded, "but you shall have to carry me off the ship yourself if you mean to return to London."

"If that is what it takes—"

"Tut, tut," an amused voice interrupted. "It's too beautiful a day to bicker and quarrel over trifles, old chap."

Harriet's gaze moved beyond Leeds to a big silhouette that appeared behind him. A look of delight plastered on the new-comer's face.

This must be the Duke of Calstone.

Harriet had never met the man, and had he not appeared today with Leeds, she'd never have known they were acquainted. The duke rarely made appearances at balls and events. Because of this, he had got the reputation of being the most elusive duke in

London. Harriet had almost believed the man to be a myth. This sly, foxlike grin certainly did not fit the man of her imagination.

He looked like a ruffian fit for the streets. In fact, in their current state, both men did. And Leeds was already difficult to deal with. With this duke added to the mix—

No matter.

Harriet steeled herself for what was to come.

She would not go down without a fight.

WILL GROUND HIS teeth as he glowered at his friend. The relief he felt upon laying eyes on Harriet was almost crippling, though out of habit, he had schooled his features not to give away any of his inner turmoil. Or more aptly, the wreck that was his heart. He had come through their conversation stammer-free, but beads of sweat rolled down his cheek and his neck felt flushed with heat.

All his life, he had struggled with the burden of his speech. He didn't want to blunder in front of the woman he was about to marry, nor did he wish to scare her with all the emotion churning inside. He could see clearly where he had gone wrong. He had allowed his handicap—or perhaps even his pride—to hold him back from approaching her so that when the wagers meant that time had run out, he had to trust in the process of arranged marriages rather than that of courtship.

He had been too optimistic.

From the first moment he had met Lady Harriet, he had been drawn to her. She embodied so much more than the labels she was assigned: a bookworm, a wallflower, a "demure chatterbox" as the list in the betting book claimed.

Should he just confess that they had met before today? That she'd forgotten that first encounter in her family's library?

No.

He couldn't do that. With her low opinion of him, she might think it a ploy or a diabolical scheme to win her over. He couldn't take the risk.

One step at a time.

The wagers about her made by fortune-hunters were more pressing than anything else. Once she was safely secured as his marchioness, and the world could no longer harm her, then he could turn all his attention to nurturing her heart and confessing his own. He clung to that single thought like he'd clung to the rope that had hoisted him onto the ship.

However, he never imagined she would jab him with a question about having another love. Did he believe her claim? Not for a damn second. Though her attempt to provoke him had been admirable.

"Are you not going to introduce me to your fiancée?" Calstone attempted to nudge past him but Will blocked him.

"Shouldn't you be on the deck?" Will retorted.

"What would I be doing there when you are here? With your lack of social skills, I thought you might need help convincing the lady, so of course I followed."

"Damn it, you—"

Calstone elbowed Will out of the way and bowed. "Lady Harriet, I have heard so much about you. It's a pleasure to finally meet you."

She eyed him warily. "I cannot say the same about you, sir."

Calstone laughed. "I see you have reservations about wedding my dear friend, Leeds. You should tell me all about them."

"You wish to hear *my* impression?"

"What's so shocking about that?" Calstone asked with interest.

Will almost groaned.

"A man who wishes to hear a woman's opinion. I'm dumbstruck."

"Certainly," Calstone went on. "You don't think so little of the male of the species, do you?"

"I do." Her chin went up. "I think a lot more than that, but I'm not about to waste my breath on reciting my thoughts."

Will yanked Calstone from her view. His friend was not helping. At all. "Enough, Calstone. We are leaving."

"Ah, so you have decided we should return to London," Harriet murmured. "Sadly, my legs are *so* tired and sore. I need to rest them."

Will no longer hesitated. She seemed determined to test his resolve for some reason. Well, she hadn't said she wouldn't go, after all—just that he'd have to carry her off the ship. And he could certainly rise to the occasion on that score. He stepped up to her, dipped, and scooped her over his shoulder. Her gasp echoed down his spine in a small shiver.

She tried to wiggle from his embrace. "You, you rogue! What are you doing?"

"Aren't your legs sore?" The question rolled off Will's tongue with ease, carrying with it a fleck of amusement. "I shall carry you."

He snatched up her travel bag and tossed it to Calstone, striding from the room. He would rather not test the captain's patience lest they find themselves actually traveling to Charleston. Unless Harriet insisted on staying on board, they would return to London.

One step at a time.

By now, it ought to be clear that he was not after her dowry, if that had ever been a concern for her. He had spent a hell of a sum for those two special licenses and a small fortune for the captain to let them off this ship. Unfortunately, with the way she seemed to think of him, she'd likely find a way to accuse him of involvement in some dirty plot anyway.

From their conversation at the house, it appeared that a good deal of her cheap opinion of him had developed because of that fool Cromby. Will had never liked the man, only endured his presence, as most people did. But if Harriet didn't like him, Will would no longer even bother being polite in the future.

Regardless, he would wipe out her reservations about his character one at a time.

"Ah, here we are," Calstone said as they emerged on deck.

A group of sailors already waited by the boat. At their appearance, the men began to lower it. The captain was nowhere in sight.

"Put me down!" Harriet hissed in his ear. Will could practically feel the rage she was emitting soak into his body. He lowered her to her feet, and she promptly punched him on the arm twice. "That's for acting like a barbarian!"

Will rubbed the spot she'd clubbed, amused that such thin arms could punch so effectively. "My apologies."

She puffed out a breath. "As if you mean it. I cannot believe you hoisted me over your shoulder like that."

He arched a brow. "As a gentleman, how can I not help a weary lady in distress?"

"Distress, my arse," she muttered. Her gaze moved beyond him. "You expect me to climb down that rope ladder? What if I am afraid of heights?"

"Then I shall carry you down." In fact, he wouldn't even mind if it meant he could hold her some more.

"How? On your back?"

"No, not the back. The front."

Her eyes widened. "Am I a child?"

Will tilted his head to the side. The more he conversed with her, the easier it seemed to become. "Are you afraid of heights?"

"Of course not." She straightened her back. "I'm not afraid of anything."

Will's lips twitched.

"I'll go last," Calstone said, and Will nodded. Nestled between the two of them, she'd be safe in her descent. He glanced at her. "I'll go first. Follow close behind." *I'll be there if anything happens.*

Will grabbed hold of the ladder, carefully climbing over the edge of the ship, motioning for her to follow. "Don't be scared."

"I am *not* scared!"

He bit back a smile and began descending to their boat.

Above him, her head appeared over the rail and she swept a glance over the situation. Adorable.

"I still can't believe I'm doing this," her mutter floated to him. "Luckily, I am wearing breeches beneath my skirts."

His brows furrowed. "Why are you wearing breeches?"

She scoffed. "Why, in case I had to quickly disguise myself as a boy. I even have a cap and everything."

Will's brain immediately spiraled into images of Harriet's breeches hugging her thighs and . . .

Dear Christ.

That would be a bloody dangerous sight. He inhaled steadily. Everything so far had gone wrong. He would require all his wits going forward, not distractions like the idea of Harriet in breeches. However, no number of steady breaths could slow the wild beat of his pulse.

"Come."

Will slowly made his way down the ladder. His eyes never strayed far from Harriet's progress. The moment his feet landed on the boat, he shifted his weight to keep it steady and fix himself into a position to help her step into the boat.

When she reached the last rung, which stopped a bit shy of their boat, she glanced over her shoulder. She attempted to lower herself but promptly pulled herself back up. "I'm too short."

"I have you." Will gently clasped her waist in a firm grip. "Let go."

Her eyes met his. "What if you let me fall?"

"I will never let you fall."

She gave a curt nod, and the air stuck in Will's lungs. Would she trust him? For one brief, disappointing moment, he thought she would resist his help. But to his swift surprise and utmost relief she let go.

Will swiftly lowered her onto the boat, holding her steady against him until Calstone joined them.

"Ye ready, sirs?" A sailor called from above.

"We are good and ready," Calstone called back.

"Godspeed, then."

Will nodded at the man before pointing to a seat in the center. "Sit over there, love. Calstone and I will do the rest."

She settled in without meeting his gaze. He hadn't done himself any favors today. But he was determined that the future could remain bright, and he hoped in time she would come to understand him and his motivation.

There was nothing else but that small hope to hold onto.

Chapter Five

HARRIET HAD LIED.

She was afraid. Very, very afraid. And not just of heights but many other things as well. A stiff, hopeless marriage for one. Also spiders—she hated spiders. And moths. In fact, any insect at all should be added to the list. Even the splashing ocean water surrounding them terrified her. And then there were the marquess and the duke and their small boat.

Well, the boat wasn't *that* small. But it wasn't that big either. It was just the right size for two men to row it. The water, however, was vast. And deep.

Very deep.

Most importantly, Harriet couldn't swim, which made it even more terrifying to her. But, and this was a big but, she would not show any fear before these two men. For then she would provide an opening. A crack in her composure. A breach that could be exploited to the benefit of others.

And she remained determined to be the one who benefited.

So, she did what she imagined any war general would do in a time of battle. She drew on all the long years she spent mastering her fear of spiders, moths, and insects to school her features and manage her heartbeat, while directing her mind away from the salty water lapping at the perfectly normal-sized boat.

She darted a glance toward the horizon where *The Royal Oak* was already the size of a child's toy. Perhaps it was for the best that this particular plan had failed. The last thing Rohan could afford was a feud with a marquess *and* a duke. As a friend, she would hate to bring him trouble. Anyway, getting to Charleston and finding Rohan had not been her only chance to escape this marriage should Leeds fail to convince her.

He jumped into the Thames after you, a voice in her head reminded her. Did that make him worthy? It made him a lunatic, more like.

In any event, now that she had caught up to her *before* Charleston, Harriet didn't think Leeds would let her out of his sight again.

If she were him, she wouldn't.

Never mind that. There were more ways than one to achieve a goal. Of course, she couldn't say she would not attempt to run away given half a chance. If nothing else, it would vex the man giving chase after her. How many times would she get away with setting him on a merry chase before that cool composure of his snapped and he showed his true thoughts?

Leeds's motives still confused her. No sane man would go to the lengths he had to secure her hand in marriage without being downright mad, would he? Jumping into the Thames proved that. That was purely ludicrous. And what about Calstone? Diving in after his friend? They both belonged in Bedlam.

This had to be about her dowry. In her experience, besides love, no greater motivation than money existed. She could come up with no other reason. He must have lost his fortune and somehow kept it secret. Harriet wasn't stupid. She knew she was no diamond. She was just a wallflower who longed for love—a sentiment that rarely belonged to powerful people like Leeds and his friend Calstone.

And what about these wagers he had spoken of? Whatever the wagers, they couldn't warrant this sort of pursuit, could they? Unless he had a stake in the business.

Harriet sent the man a suspicious look.

"The shore is in sight," Calstone said with a heaving breath. The first words that had been spoken in the past hour. It almost felt out of place in their unusual setting.

"The shore has always been in sight," Leeds pointed out.

"But now it is *more* in sight. I can practically feel land beneath my feet."

Leeds nodded. "We should reach land in about thirty minutes."

Harriet let out a relieved breath. They'd already been rowing for an hour, and the skies were darkening with gloomy clouds. The last thirty minutes would surely pass in agony.

She snuck another glance at the insufferable marquess, her gaze dropping to the muscles in his arms bulging with each stroke. Did he have to look so handsome while rowing them to shore? Even shoeless and half-bedraggled the man still cut an imposing figure. Even more so with this rugged look.

Striking.

She tried to recall how he'd looked earlier when he went on one knee and promised her happiness. She'd always thought her future husband would ask for her hand in a heartfelt manner. Nothing too grand but endearingly soul-stirring. And she would leap into his arms and enjoy a happily ever after future.

Leeds had robbed her of that.

Now, the idea of him lowering down on one knee and proposing properly was laughable, and her response would be an immensely satisfying, albeit rude, *"No, I will not."*

The mental picture calmed the tempest brewing in her heart a bit.

Telling Leeds to go to hell, even just in her head, was indeed gratifying. Would he lose some of his composure if he knew she'd whacked him over the skull countless times with her suitcase in her mind? Or would he just arch one of his brows in that infuriating way?

And why should she care if he was handsome, rich—maybe— and titled? Harriet had never weighed her options in such an old-fashioned way. Her father had been wrong. She could do better than Leeds. All that was required of her was to find happiness.

If she were to have him chase after her again, how and when could she do it so that she would *not* be caught so soon? No matter how she looked at it, she would not be able to board another ship. Her family would offer no shelter to her, and she did not wish to drag her friends into her personal matters.

Her only option was to hide in a burrow that Leeds could only find after he had overturned every single rock that led there.

Unfortunately, she knew of no such burrow.

Her gaze returned to the shore. She couldn't tell which beach they were approaching, but they had headed in the direction of Canvey when they first set out to shore. They would either find lodgings, since the hour had already turned rather late, or they would head back home without delay.

"You are awfully quiet, Lady Harriet."

Harriet ignored the duke. The wind was sweeping through her hair, and she tilted her head back to soak up the soft beams of the last rays of sun filtering through the dark, approaching clouds. Just for a moment, with her eyes closed, she could imagine herself free and content. It was the only small glint of happiness she found in the otherwise miserable journey to shore.

Do not marry a man who would not fight for you.

Her gaze lifted to Leeds, and their eyes locked.

A shiver trickled down her spine.

"The next part might get a little tumultuous," Leeds said. "Hold on tightly, love."

Harriet's shoulders snapped back as that *love* reached her. Why did he insist on calling her by that wretched word? Every time he did, she had to remind herself the meaning was as shallow as their proposed union. *He* was shallow. Merely a ruffian taking advantage of her and using words he didn't mean in an offhand attempt to placate her.

Harriet looked beyond him to the waves rolling onto the shore. Sure enough, their journey was about to come to an end.

She reached out to grip onto the edge of the boat.

"Where exactly are we?" Harriet asked to no one in particular as she studied the houses in the distance.

"Hell if I know," Calstone muttered. "But anything is better than a ship bound for the Americas."

Harriet snorted.

"It doesn't matter," Leeds remarked. "We're almost home."

Home.

How laughable was that?

Calstone glanced down at his shirt. "I can't wait to get out of these clothes. Ruined a good jacket jumping into the Thames after you."

Harriet scanned their clothing and paused. That's right, they'd changed clothes, and she hadn't seen them bring their ruined garments along.

Which might mean . . .

Was the newly-acquired special silence ruined?

A spark of hope lit her breast.

If the document was ruined or lost, that would give her more time. In any case, even if it was still back in London, at least he couldn't try to compel her to marry as soon as they reached the nearest town—there would be more preparations to be made than that. But instinct told her that Leeds would not have let that special license leave his possession.

Chances were, he had placed it in his coat pocket. And he would probably not have jumped into the water with a coat that would weigh him down. If that coat had been left on the dock, unless a footman or driver smartly snapped it up, it would surely have been nicked by a passerby.

Interesting.

As if sensing her gaze, Leeds suddenly lifted his head, and their eyes met once more. Her pulse leaped. Could he tell what she was thinking? A lifetime of meaning seemed to be packed into the one second he held her gaze.

Harriet's grip tightened on the edge of her bench as they rode the waves to shore.

Lord, please don't let the boat overturn.

Water sprayed onto her face and soaked through her clothes. She didn't care. As long as she remained safe inside, a bit of wetness would not hurt. Remarkably, Leeds kept her fear at bay. Not the man himself, of course, but the stark concentration as they navigated to shore. His complete focus brought a measure of comfort to her heart.

She reluctantly admitted that the men were quite impressive. They had taken rowing to safety extremely seriously. As if at any moment the sea might turn on them.

The moment they reached shallow waters, both men leaped from the boat to pull it onto the sand. Harriet could finally relax.

Leeds held out his hand.

Harriet paid him no mind and rose, moving to the opposite side of the boat and disembarking there. She might be impressed, but she wasn't about to forgive him.

This was all *his* fault.

The moment Harriet's boots sank into the beach, the stiffening in her joints sank along with it. The worry she had been holding back melted away, and her knees hit the sand with a small plop.

How utterly mortifying.

"HARRIET!" WILL RUSHED to where she slumped and fell down beside her. He studied her face. "What's wrong? Are you all right? Are you hurt anywhere?"

"I'm fine."

"If you are fine, why the hell did you collapse?"

Her cheeks were growing pink. "It's nothing."

Will glanced at her legs. "You said your legs were sore."

She gave an awkward laugh. "Oh, that? That was a jest, I assure you."

Will had assumed so himself, but now . . .

Calstone joined them. "A fever, perhaps?"

"I do not have a fever."

"Then why are your cheeks red?" Leeds asked. He placed a palm on her forehead. "You're not hot."

She swatted his hand away. "That's because I don't have a fever. It's just . . ."

"Ah," Calstone said. "I believe I know what ails the lady."

"What?" Leeds asked. Christ, the beat of his heart had turned damn near painful.

"Embarrassment."

Will frowned, his gaze once more attracted to the pink that colored her cheeks. "Are you sure you are all right?" he asked again.

Harriet glared at them.

There's the Harriet I know. Will let out a sigh of relief.

"Let me up," she said.

He rose and held out his hand. This time she didn't reject his help. She placed her palm in his and allowed him to pull her to her feet.

"And now all's well that ends well," Calstone said, dusting off his knees.

Will shook his head at his friend, though he couldn't disagree. They had done several dangerous, reckless things today that were utterly out of character for him, but he hadn't felt he had much choice. And if Calstone hadn't been present, they would both be on their way to Charleston now.

Will retrieved Harriet's valise from the boat with a measure of relief.

"I shall carry what's mine," Harriet said, reaching out to take the bag from him.

Will evaded her hand. "No need."

"I insist."

"Your legs just gave out. It's better for me to carry your bag."

"That's just because . . ."

Will raised a brow in query when her voice trailed off.

"Never mind, carry it if you must."

He wanted to take her into his arms. Comfort her. Reassure her. But for the moment he would have to settle for carrying her valise.

Calstone strode over. "The sun will be gone in a few hours. Are we finding lodgings or transport to start home?"

"Lodgings," Will said. He had a lot of nerve. This much he had discovered about himself today. But when faced now with Harriet's fall, he lost a bit. At least the part that pressed him to return posthaste.

He would give Harriet this night. They might even be able to have a decent talk before they wed. Perhaps they could understand each other better. Will didn't hold out much hope, but he ought to at least try.

Tomorrow they could set out again at a leisurely pace. More time for them to form an understanding.

"Good," Calstone said. "It's best to get a pair bloody shoes and a good night's rest. Tomorrow, you wed."

At Harriet's dirty look, Will shot his friend a glare.

His words only provoked her to put her shield up higher. Lest he wanted her to do something even more reckless than boarding a ship to another continent, like executing them both in their sleep, it was best not to mention their wedding until they were back in London.

Should he abandon a hasty marriage and instead have the banns read after all? That would surely allow her time to warm to him. He never wanted a reluctant bride. Never imagined their betrothal would come to this. But boarding a ship to the Americas moved her well beyond putting up a degree of resistance. Every grimace and glare on her part equated to rubbing coarse salt in an open wound.

No. He just couldn't take the chance to delay this marriage. Far more worrying than the chance that she might run off again, she could also be snatched away by one of the men who had a fortune to win on a wager. Men without good intentions at all.

When he thought about all the wagers going around London, the greediness reflected in them, the discomfort in Will's heart outweighed anything else.

The risk was too great.

His little bride had inspired the most wagers of all the women on that list. He simply couldn't wait. If anything happened to her because of his hesitation, Will would never forgive himself. If only his good intentions did not make him a villain in her eyes.

He would start remedying that from this moment onward.

Will patted his chest where the license . . .

Christ.

He had stuffed the license in his jacket which he had carelessly disregarded at the docks before diving into the water. That coat would already have been carried off by a quick-witted thief.

Will cursed.

Why the devil had he been so careless? But he knew why. He lost every bit of his common sense when it came to Harriet Hillstow. Not only did she rob him of his breath, but she also robbed him of every sensible faculty, leaving only a chaotic mess behind. He'd never bumbled about like this in his life.

"What's the matter?" The vixen smiled at him, her gaze flicking to his chest and back.

She knew. Or at least she had already deduced the possibility.

Will arched a brow, willing his heart to remain calm. And utterly, unequivocally failed. "I'll get another one."

The corner of her lips quirked. "You have quite the contacts."

Calstone looked over. "What's the matter?"

"The special license," Will muttered. "Jacket pocket. Docks."

Calstone froze before he burst out laughing. "What is it with your luck, old chap?"

"Perhaps fate is hinting at something." Harriet's smile turned crooked.

"Fate is certainly testing my resolve."

"You are clearly resolved," she agreed. "Uncomfortably so."

Calstone slapped him on the shoulder. "Thought you didn't believe in fate."

Will shrugged him off. "I make you uncomfortable?" he asked Harriet.

She shrugged. "Your resolve makes me uncomfortable."

"You do not find determination a good trait?"

"Normally I do. I just don't understand yours."

"I believe that with time, you will."

Calstone chuckled. "It took me a while to warm up to our Leeds here as well." Another clap on the shoulder. "Don't worry, even if you used up all your capital and called in all your favors, I still have some clout."

Will nodded. He hadn't called in *all* his favors yet, and he might become the laughingstock of England, but it did not matter. Let him go down in history as a lovelorn fool. He would walk into the bowels of hell to protect this woman and spend the rest of his life attempting to win her heart.

"But first," Calstone went on. "I won't be happy until I have shoes, a hot meal, and a soft bed. I can barely feel my arms."

Harriet scoffed. "Your requirements for happiness are quite simple."

Calstone laughed. "Yours aren't?"

Will glanced over to Harriet.

She lifted her shoulders. "I had once thought my requirements to be indeed uncomplicated, but the world has shown me they are actually impossibilities."

Will frowned. Impossibilities? Did she mean her happiness?

"Oh?" Calstone murmured. "I'm intrigued. What are your requirements?"

Her gaze flicked to Will before averting. "Love."

Will stiffened.

Who could ever want a boy like you? You can't even speak properly. The teases of his childhood echoed in his mind before he could shut them out.

Will ruthlessly pushed the memory from his mind.

He was no longer the boy who stuttered to such an extent that he could barely form a coherent sentence. But he could feel his mouth, tongue, and throat tense even as the thought formed in his mind.

His palms broke out in sweat.

He couldn't speak. The moment he opened his mouth he knew what would happen. He'd humiliate himself.

Snap out of it, man.

Will dragged a hand through his hair. He'd keep on sinking farther into what seemed to be a bottomless pit if this continued.

"Love?" Calstone questioned. He sent a glance at Will "Are there not more important things than love?"

"Such as?" Harriet returned mockingly. "Clothes, a hot meal, and a bed?"

"Why yes, those are basic needs."

Love is also not an impossibility. I will show you . . .

He had faith in himself. In her.

"Don't," Will stopped to clear his throat, and repeated his sentence in his head before he went on. "Don't listen to him. He is a simple man with simple needs."

Calstone shot him an astonished look. "I'll have you know, I'm an exceptionally complicated man! One with extremely complicated needs!"

"Yes, we have certainly experienced your extraordinarily complicated needs." Harriet's chin rose. "In fact, you remind me of Chester, an animal I'm looking after. He, too, has a labyrinth of complicated needs."

The corner of Will's lips inched upward. He recalled that horrid creature. He couldn't say he did not agree. His friend was rather straightforward in his requirements for happiness. Rather like a sloth, as Harriet called the thing, he was sure. It had been this way since their school days.

Calstone's face blotched red. "Are you comparing me to an animal?"

"Don't be too shocked, Duke. Aren't all men animals?"

Will sighed.

This woman and her mouth—she possessed a truly exceptional weapon. Each jab hit the heart of its target. He wouldn't compare himself to a sloth, but she did make him feel like a beast.

"Leeds, are you hearing this? Your woman is mocking me."

"I'm not his woman yet, Duke."

Yet . . .?

"And you!" She suddenly pointed a finger at Will. "Why are you grinning like a fool?"

Will's lips lost their shape.

But she'd said *yet*.

They inched upward again.

Her eyes narrowed to slits. "Are you even a gentleman, sir?" she challenged.

Gentleman? He certainly carried the title of one. However, she obviously believed otherwise. Apparently when it came to marrying Harriet Hillstow, a gentleman he was not.

Will couldn't hold out any longer.

His lips transformed into a brilliant smile.

Chapter Six

HARRIET STARED AT the bed so hard that the bedding, mattress, and frame might catch fire at any moment, such was the intensity of her gaze.

That smile . . .

They had secured a room at the first inn they had come across. It was also the only inn in this little town whose name she could not recall. How she wished she could be in her own room with her own bed!

A small sigh escaped her lips.

Smiles notwithstanding, this day had been horrible. What person had to face several of their deepest fears in the span of a few hours? *Lord Almighty.*

She rubbed her shoulders as a prickle of irritation poked her heart. She itched to pace back and forth, as she'd usually do when vexed, but she was all too aware of the men occupying the chamber with her.

The truth of the matter was—a truth she reluctantly admitted—she was more vexed that she *noticed* Leeds than anything else. Even now, her body thrummed with awareness of his presence, the back of her neck tingling with his vigilance.

Since she couldn't pace, she directed a glare at the two men hovering in her shadow. "Why are you both crowding *my* room?"

Calstone looked to Leeds. "You tell her. I'd rather not lose any of my limbs.

Harriet's eyes narrowed. She hadn't been there when they negotiated with the innkeeper. She'd been swept to a nearby settee with a warm cup of tea. She had welcomed the reprieve then. That probably hadn't been the wisest choice.

"They only had one available chamber." No emotion inflected Leeds's voice, and his face resembled a marble statue.

"You mean to tell me we are sharing?" Her gaze darted from Leeds to Calstone and back to Leeds. "*All* of us?"

Leeds nodded.

"That is preposterous! Sharing a chamber with one man is already crossing the line. But two? I cannot share a chamber with two men!"

"One man," Leeds said flatly.

She pointed to Calstone. "Then what is he?"

"I'd like to know that, too," Calstone grumbled.

"The chaperone."

Harriet sent them both a piercing look. She couldn't believe her ears. "Surely you are jesting."

"I am not."

"When has a strange man ever been a chaperone to a woman?"

"I'm not strange," Calstone said, affronted. "But I am a man."

God's blood. It was like talking to a child. "You are both strangers to me."

"I am family," Leeds said.

"Not yet," Harriet pointed out. "Perhaps not at all."

He didn't take her bait, but merely stared at her. Either this man was an emotionless brick, or he had an impressive amount of patience.

No, no. *Nothing* about him was impressive. If she kept telling herself so, one day she might believe it to be true. However, she now knew him to *not* be emotionless either. Lord, his grin on the beach had near blinded her. Just thinking about the pure delight that lit his features brought on another set of heart palpitations.

Beneath that sculpted marble *feelings* churned.

"Chaperone or not, there is only one bed," Calstone lamented. "Where are we all going to sleep?"

Leeds tapped his foot on the ground pointedly.

The duke cursed. "The stables would be more comfortable than the floor."

"Then go sleep in the stables."

At any other time, Harriet would have laughed at the aggrieved look that crossed the duke's face.

Calstone turned his attention to the fireplace and grimaced. "There isn't even a fire lit. I'll go arrange for wood, shoes, and food."

Leeds nodded. "And a carriage. We start for London at daybreak."

"Wait," Harriet called when Calstone strode to the door. "You can't leave—you're my chaperone!"

The duke paused. "I won't be gone long," he said and hurried off, but not before Harriet caught the look on his face. There was still something they were not telling her.

She shot a meaningful look to Leeds. "What are you hiding?"

"Who says I'm hiding anything?"

"If not the look on your friend's face, then the way he scurried off."

Leeds sighed.

So, she was right!

"Either you tell me, or I will hunt down the owner and ask him myself."

"No need." His gaze met hers. "I told them you are my wife."

Her jaw slackened. "That is awfully presumptuous of you."

"You say presumptuous, I say optimistic." He plopped down into a chair. "It couldn't be helped."

Harriet wanted to club the man over the head with a fire poker. Where did the man get his confidence from?

So infuriating.

She turned her back to him. She didn't want to stare at his

unnecessarily handsome face.

What to do next? Would screaming into the bed pillow help? Pummeling it with her fists? She opted for falling back onto the bed and staring at the ceiling.

"Harriet?"

She turned her head to the man. "If I ask you to leave, will you?"

He sat back and threw an arm over his eyes. "I can't do that," he whispered.

"I meant the room, not me."

He peered at her from beneath his arm. She caught a flash of amusement in his eyes. "Will you climb through the window once I leave?"

"We are on the third floor." She grinned. "Perhaps."

She caught the quick quirk of his lips.

"Shall I give you a moment then?"

His voice was tired, and he looked as weary as she felt. She was not completely unfeeling—let them both have a reprieve for the night. The knowledge that he would give her a bit of space enough for now.

"No need." She returned her gaze to the wood beam that crossed the ceiling. "I do have a question though. Is jumping into a river to swim after a ship not a tad too much? What if the captain hadn't helped you?"

"What did you expect me to do?"

"Board another ship to give chase. Hire people to retrieve me."

"I'd never do that." A small pause. "I'd never hire someone else to do a job that belongs to me."

Harriet went hot all over.

Words such as that could rob a woman of her breath!

She cleared her throat. "Just so that we are clear, you are sharing the floor with Calstone."

"As you wish."

The man's soul hadn't fully turned to black coal yet. A drop of decency remained. And some peace did return to her heart at his answer.

Her eyes drifted shut.

Why was it that the more she conversed with him, the more *gentlemanly* he seemed to become? So unlike the man that hadn't even thought to speak to her before he waved a special license in her face.

"Are you all right, love?"

"Yes."

"You're not just saying that, are you?"

The concern in his voice was almost touching. "Spending hours on a raft has a way of tiring a lady out."

A light chuckle. "Food will arrive shortly. You should eat."

"I'm not hungry. You eat."

"Food means energy."

"Eating also takes energy." *Speaking too.* But somehow Harriet didn't mind it so much. With her eyes shut, she could blot out today's difficulties just for a moment and imagine they were a normal man and woman in a normal conversation, everything else melting into the distance.

"Harriet, this misunderstanding you have of me—"

Her snort interrupted him—so much for normal conversation. "There's no misunderstanding."

A soft sigh. "You've yet to tell me why you find me so disagreeable."

"Do I? I thought I'd made it abundantly clear."

"You mentioned Cromby, but he is not a reason."

"Neither is being beautiful, intelligent, and unattached."

A lengthy silence stretched between them before his voice once again filled the room. "What will convince you that I'm an honorable man?"

"A courtship might have convinced me."

"If it's any consolation, if I had the power, I would go back in time and do things differently."

Don't get sucked in by words or that whispered tone, Harriet.

"It's no consolation at all."

"I seem to have offended you in some way," he said softly, almost cautiously. "Can you tell me exactly what I did?"

Her eyes snapped open. Quite frankly, she should answer that question. Should confront the biggest thorn in her flesh. She rose to her elbows and met his gaze head on. "Are you not friends with Cromby?"

"So, it *is* Cromby who offended you? I said before that I am not friends with him."

She let a question fill her eyes. *And you expect me to believe that?*

"What exactly did he do to offend you?"

How to answer? She hadn't ever told anyone what had happened. That Cromby had cornered her one evening, pushed her up against a wall, and tried to steal a kiss from her that she was not willing to give.

On the surface, it was not unlike what Leeds had done back in her chamber. Only nothing about that situation, or the kiss Leeds had snatched, had felt so slimy. Plus, she'd met his challenge by returning the kiss. She'd had plans of her own for that moment.

With Cromby . . . the entire affair had been different. She could still feel the slobber of his mouth on her cheek after she'd evaded a full-on assault.

Harriet had barely gotten away that night. Gah! She didn't want to remember it.

She'd been so distressed but was too afraid to breathe a word of his harassment, scared she'd be forced into a marriage with that odious man. She'd also clearly seen Cromby later that night, almost right after that incident, laughing with Leeds.

"What if I said he *forcibly* kissed me?" Harriet asked, studying his face for his reaction.

Leeds shot upright. A dangerous, almost lethal, glint entered his eyes. Even his voice lowered to a menacing whisper. "He did *what?*"

A shiver shot down her spine. Harriet couldn't look away. "You heard me. The experience was vulgar enough; please don't make me repeat it."

"When was this?" he breathed, and Harriet's gaze dropped to the sudden rise and fall of his chest, as though he was holding back something, something fierce.

"What does it matter?" She sat back down onto the bed. "Anyway, I won't suffer anyone associated with that man." She angled her head to him. "What do you say about that? To me, there is no difference between him and anyone who mingles with him."

"But there is a difference." His voice lowered even more. "The difference is that I asked your father for your hand."

True.

Still . . .

"The difference is that he was dead to me the moment you said you didn't like him."

Lawd. *He did it again.* Said words that set her pulse racing.

"Harriet . . . I'm sorry that happened to you."

Harriet couldn't miss the sincerity in his gaze, his voice, the look of anger that still darkened his face. She averted her gaze and shut her eyes once more. "I saw you laugh with him right after."

"It was fake. It's always fake."

Harriet smiled at his quick reply. Somehow, she believed him.

"In any event, I don't want to talk about that odious man anymore." Drowsiness was beginning to set in. And with it, the prickle of that particular thorn slowly melted away.

If she was being entirely honest with herself, while she did hold a bit of a grudge against Leeds over his behavior and his cronies—all right, a bit of a big one—the true culprit in *this* situation was still her father. He could have spoken to her about Leeds's offer. He could have declined.

And if at the end of all this she chose not to fulfill the betrothal agreement, she would still have to return home. To her father. Suddenly Harriet didn't want to return home anymore to people who only wanted to be rid of her. But then just where did she belong?

It wasn't until the pull of sleep had dragged her to its depth that a resonating thought fluttered against the walls of her mind.

Leeds smelled nice.

WILL COVERED HARRIET with a blanket. He reached out to draw his fingers through a wayward strand of her silky hair but stopped before his fingers made contact.

His strong desire for the woman in the bed almost brought him to his knees. He wanted to claim her in every way imaginable. He wanted there to be no doubt in anyone's mind that she belonged with him. And no man would ever dare touch her again. No man would dare hurt her.

He retracted his hand before he made another blunder. What he needed to do was come up with a plan. A plan to woo his bride-to-be.

He couldn't change what had already happened, but he could try to make her feel secure and safe from this moment on. At the very least, try to prove that he was not of the same deplorable character as Cromby.

Turning on his heel, he returned to his seat, taking up the position of her protector. He stared at the outline of her slight form while trying his best to control his breathing, not certain if he was succeeding or not.

Fury swirled in his gut. Deep, all-consuming fury.

What the devil had Cromby done? How dare he force a kiss on an innocent lady? *His* lady. No wonder she resisted this match so much. She'd gone through a horrific event, and she'd gone through it alone. Suffered what Cromby had done in silence.

Damn it.

Cromby had never been a man of character—that was not a secret—and they certainly were not friends. But clearly even his tolerance of the man had been a mistake. One he paid for now.

Regardless, Cromby's actions were unforgivable. He *would* deal with the man. Now, at least, he had a clearer idea about why Harriet was so bent on running away from him. She truly did associate him with Cromby's ilk and had good reason to fear such men.

His chest hurt.

He could not even imagine what she must have gone through in those moments. Yet, being the woman she was, she not only bore it alone, but also did not cower and hide. She'd shown to ball after ball, event after event. Hopeful and chin high.

He admired the hell out of her.

But allowing Cromby's name to be in any way connected to his own wasn't his only mistake. Why the hell hadn't he courted her? Why had he allowed his own fear to hold him back? Making an utter fool of himself wouldn't have been the end of the world. He would have survived the embarrassment.

He'd known from her first reaction that he had approached the entire situation wrongly. But he couldn't go back in time no matter how much he wished to. *It's no use dwelling on regret.* All he could do was try to make up for his failures from now on.

She was the bravest woman he had ever met. Much braver than him.

I don't deserve her.

The door suddenly creaked open and Calstone appeared, a brow rising when he saw Harriet curled up in the bed.

"Is everything all right?"

Will nodded. "Is everything arranged?"

Calstone nodded and traipsed into the room, setting down a pair of shoes at his feet. "They are preparing food as well."

"You eat. I've no appetite."

"What of Lady Harriet?"

Will shook his head. "Let her rest. She will eat when she wakes. You've sent word to her father?"

"Yes, and the priest." A short pause. "I've also sent a note to the archbishop. However, I can't promise word won't get out that you lost not one, but *two* special licenses. Your rigid reputation will be ruined, I'm afraid."

"That might not be a bad thing," Will muttered.

"And they'll send someone to light the hearth soon. There's a sofa in the drawing room downstairs with a lit hearth already. I'll make myself comfortable there."

Will looked over at his friend. "Are you sure? Harriet might take offense that her chaperone did not do his duty."

"Do a *husband* and *wife* even need a chaperone? What century is this?"

Will's mouth curved into a half-smile.

"I see you can still smile. So you survived her wrath after confessing your sins—some of them at least."

Will ignored him, his gaze returning to Harriet.

"Well, all is not lost. She must trust you on some level."

"How can you tell?"

"She's *sleeping*, you cretin. I'll have you know, sleep is the human's most vulnerable state." Calstone chuckled. "You chose a very spirited lady."

"I had no choice in the matter. You know this."

There was a fire in Harriet Hillstow. A light so strong he could not resist its beckoning. It wasn't an obvious fire, but neither was it too deeply hidden. One only had to look past the surface to encounter its embers. There was no other woman for him.

"It would be remiss of me not to point out that your bride-to-be, trusting or not, is terribly resistant to this match."

"I know."

"Did I mention the *terribly* before resistant? Her resistance goes beyond any acceptable level."

"I am aware."

Calstone nudged him with a boot. "And you're still going through with it?"

"Like I said," Will looked at his friend, "I have no choice."

"But she has. You know this, too."

Will dragged a hand over his eyes. "Which is why I didn't rush us to London through the night."

"So long as you know nothing is set in stone until you are registered as man and wife. Not the betrothal agreement, not your heart."

Will scoffed. "One day I'll see you swallow those words."

"Very well, very well. I will wait for that day, though I'm quite certain it will never come. As you are well aware, I'm a simple man."

"What happened to being a complicated man?"

"I tried it on for size, but one look at all your complications, and I realized simplicity trumps complexity. As you embark on this journey to seduce your bride-to-be, you should consider doing the same."

"A simple seduction, you mean?"

"Right. Flowers, sweet things, poetry, waltzes. Kisses in the dark, secluded corners of gardens. That sort of thing."

"Poetry?"

"Or little love notes. It's better than saying romantic drivel out loud."

"You are hopeless."

"Between the two of us, I'm not any more hopeless than you are, old chap."

No denial on his part.

"I'll be off then. Tomorrow we have quite the day ahead of us. Try to get some rest."

Will nodded and waited until Calstone left the room before pulling the chair up to the bed and settling in again. He had said he'd sleep on the floor with Calstone, but since Calstone would be sleeping elsewhere, the chair would do.

Harriet wouldn't run off tonight, but for his own piece of mind, he wanted—needed—to stay close. Her warmth beckoned him, calmed him even while exhaustion pulled at him. Every muscle in his body ached. Also, every little muscle of his heart . . . but it was better not to think about the discomfort there.

Chapter Seven

HARRIET'S LIDS WERE heavy as she entered Leeds's residence the next morning at the unholy hour of ten o'clock half-asleep, half-awake. Having been coaxed, *tricked*, out of her warm cocoon at an even more ungodly hour—Harriet didn't care to ask—and ushered into a carriage. At least the men had the foresight to pack the carriage with hot bricks. So, she'd merely been transferred from one toasty spot to another and had slept all the way to London.

I have no choice.

She'd awakened to hushed voices and only heard Leeds's reply to the duke before sleep claimed her once more, those four words accompanying her back to her dreams.

He had no choice?

Why not? What exactly did he mean?

And she wouldn't even mention the fact that the next time she had awoken, she had felt her hand clasped in his. A gentle touch, but one she couldn't miss or mistake. She was sagely deciding to ignore that little matter. He must have been worried she would run off again. In one way, she could somewhat understand his concerns. And, as an avid opportunist, she had been intending to see if she *could* find a moment to escape. Well, at least before they'd arrived at the inn.

I have no choice.

Again, the suspicion in her heart solidified. He needed some-thing, and that was compelling him forward. And Harriet was the most convenient way to get it. The *only* way, judging from the conversation last night.

Dratted man, confusing her with his words and actions.

I shall get to the bottom of you, Leeds.

Leeds led them to the drawing room. They hadn't spoken much to each other since last night. Even now, silence stretched between them. In fact, up to the moment the carriage drew to a halt before his house, Harriet half expected pitch black drapes and gargoyle statues to announce his lair. However, everything appeared right and proper. Warm even—and not in the hellish kind of way. She couldn't even claim the silence had been uncomfortable. It was just . . . silence. The kind that didn't need to be filled with words.

She'd told him her guarded secret—what Cromby had done—but so far he didn't seem to be taking advantage of the knowledge. Truth be told, she didn't really believe Leeds to be like that vile man. Cromby did sly things in the shadows. She couldn't imagine Leeds forcing himself on an unsuspecting lady like that. No, Leeds operated in broad daylight. He might have hidden truths, but he didn't have hateful intentions.

She glanced at Calstone, who followed them into the room. Then there was *this* man—the duke. Without experiencing their friendship firsthand, she wouldn't have been able to believe his claims about his friend as easily as she was beginning to.

Next to the two of them, Cromby resembled a cockroach more than anything else.

"I'll have the servants send sandwiches and tea," Leeds said as she lowered onto the chaise that looked the most cozy.

"Don't bother."

"You didn't eat last night and refused the bread prepared earlier. You need to eat."

Harriet almost smiled at his stern tone. "I'm still asleep. This is a dream."

"Dream or not, I'll have them send a tray anyway. Calstone will stay with you. I'll be back in a few hours."

The duke plopped down on the sofa. "I won't decline food."

"Don't worry," Harriet said. "I shall be a dutiful prisoner."

"Thank God," Calstone said. "I didn't sleep a wink last night, and the carriage was too cramped to rest comfortably."

"See you soon," Leeds said, sending her one last look before striding from the room.

Today is the day, then.

A decision needed to be made. Leeds would get his special license, collect the priest, and she would have to stand beside him and either devote herself to a yes, or execute a no. Either follow her father's betrothal agreement, or fight for the promise she had made her mother.

Fight . . .

It all came down to whether she believed Leeds had fought enough to be worthy of her hand or not. But then, her mother had never given her any qualifying measurements to define what it meant to fight. She would have to determine that herself.

"William isn't a bad man," Calstone suddenly said in a lazy voice. "I gather you must have some misunderstanding about him, but he is a good man."

Harriet dropped her head back against the sofa. Perhaps he was telling her true. Since meeting the duke, and throughout their encounters, she hadn't sensed any malice or ill-intentions in him. But then again, men could hide their true nature very deep—just take Leeds as an example. Trusting the word of a man, even this one, would be the same as trusting a wolf not to bite you when you turned your back.

"I know, but forgive me if I don't take your word for it, Duke."

"What a tangled answer."

She peeked at him from the corner of her eye. "I suppose such a labyrinthine answer is too much for you."

"Christ, yes. It hurts my brain." He glanced at her. "Time will tell, I suppose."

Time might tell, but what exactly would the hour reveal?

"How long have you known Leeds?" Harriet asked. She had been curious about their acquaintance since she'd met him.

"All my life."

As I expected. Two peas in a pod.

"You seem to care for him a great deal."

"He is a brother to me," the duke admitted. "Do you wish for me to recite our adventures as children? The days at Eton are especially vivid."

"I'd rather you didn't."

He slanted her a glance. "Not curious at all?"

"My curiosity has nothing to do with your childhood or your days at Eton."

"I suppose you want to know why Leeds wants to marry you."

Straight to the point. Then she would be as well. "Yes."

"Do you possess so little belief in your charm?"

Harriet almost laughed out loud. "What I want to know, Duke, is why he is so determined to marry me so hastily. Charm has little to do with his motives, I'm sure."

"He has told you about the wagers?"

She scoffed. "That is not a reason."

That earned her a brow lift. "Do you know what the wagers entail?"

"I don't care about wagers or lists or the people behind them. They have little to do with me. I only care why I am being chased down by a crazy marquess."

"Ah well, I can't answer to that," the duke said.

"But you know, don't you?"

"Perhaps."

Harriet wanted to punch the man. "But you're not going to tell me?"

He shrugged. "It's not for me to do so."

"Not even when the man himself won't tell me? Not even if it will help dispel my reservations?" He opened his mouth to reply, but Harriet cut him off. "No, *time* will tell, isn't that right?"

"I have all the faith in the world that Leeds will banish your worries. You should give him a chance. You might be pleasantly surprised."

"We shall see."

They fell into a lengthy silence, but again, not the uncomfortable sort. Harriet didn't mind. Her brain had still to wake from its slumber. Her gaze swept over the room, taking in more detail. This would be her home after today. *Could* be. Would be?

Harriet couldn't quite describe her feelings on the matter. The desire to test and challenge Leeds hadn't disappeared. In fact, it had burrowed deeper, and yet a shift seemed to have taken place in her mind. But another element had risen to take its place next to her goal to test Leeds. The desire to hack away at all his layers until she got to his hidden truth.

She didn't know what the marquess might want besides her dowry, but one thing she did know . . . he was not getting anything else until she reached the very core of him. Not her body. Not her heart. Not her soul.

Had he fought for her?

Chasing her down. Jumping into the Thames. Swimming after a ship. That certainly counted, even if just a fraction.

However, his willingness to weather the storms to Charleston, the concern in his voice when her legs gave out on the beach, his outrage at what Cromby had done to her, and yes, even the clasp of his hand during the night, these were what made Harriet realize . . .

He is fighting.

In his own way, Leeds fought for what he wanted. And for whatever reason, he wanted her.

Is it enough?

Before she could answer that heavy-laden question, Harriet first required a bath. One did not venture into a life-altering decision without a fresh mind, fresh spirit, and a fresh set of clothes.

Her gaze slid to the door.

She *could* ring for a footman to prepare a bath for her. She glanced from her crumpled attire to the travel bag at the door. Had she not been so stubborn, she could have enjoyed a bath at the inn. But would Leeds have left her side?

Yes, he would have. Don't blame the man for your laziness, Harriet.

Fine. She'd been too lazy.

A light snore reached her ears.

She whipped her head toward Calstone in surprise. Had he fallen asleep? Truly?

She measured the distance between the duke and the door. This . . . well, even Harriet had to admit this turn of events couldn't be considered anything but quite astonishing.

Dare she take the chance? *Is this a test?* From the simple-minded duke?

Nooo, surely not. Yet there was only one way to find out.

As a clock struck in the distance, she slowly rose to her feet, careful not to disturb the sleeping man across from her.

The light snoring never stopped.

She smiled, shaking her head at the duke.

She had no plans to send Leeds and his trusting follower on a merry chase. But a little trouble wouldn't hurt either. Would he think she'd return home? There was no place the marquess couldn't ferret her out. He had proven that much. But he wouldn't expect her to *not* want to flee again.

She smiled at the thought. And it would be nice to take a bath in the comfort and familiarity of her own rooms onc last timc.

Small pleasures.

A plank beneath her foot creaked as she reached the door, and her breath caught at the slight sound that may as well have echoed off the walls of the drawing room.

She slipped from Leeds's home, heart pounding in her chest.

The crisp morning air embraced her like a long-lost friend. It could not be considered the break of dawn by any means, but most of Mayfair's elite were likely just waking or still enjoying the pleasure of their cocoons. The city streets were practically deserted, save for a lone carriage rattling by in the distance, some servants leaving for their daily tasks, and a few country-risers.

Her steps slowed.

Did she burst into her home, slip through the side gate, or rap on the door knocker?

Scratch the first.

Annihilate the last.

Side gate it is.

No.

No.

Why not just turn the knob and enter and breeze past the butler, Lee?

Yes, why not?

What did it matter that she didn't feel as though she belonged? Or, perhaps more truly the case, that she did not want to face her father.

She, Harriet Hillstow, was no coward. *Her* determination had also ever been unfaltering. She would return home as if she still lived there—which she did—take a bath, and regain her wits.

"Lady Harriet?"

Harriet nearly leaped out of her skin.

She whirled around. "Lord Rochester?"

His brow wrinkled in concern. "Are you unwell?"

Why did everyone keep asking her that?

"I am healthy as a horse. Why? Do I look unwell?"

"No, no," he hurried to say, even though his gaze still traveled over her quizzically. "At least allow me to walk you to your door."

Harriet flushed. She must be having something of a singular moment. "Of course." She smiled up at him. "I would appreciate the company."

STILL WARM.

Will stared at the wax stamp that held all his hope and all his heartache in one imprint. *Was this it?* The last one he would have to procure? He settled back against the leather seat of his carriage, finding comfort in the softness while his heart beat with a mixture of anticipation and trepidation.

This should be the last. The final one.

He shut his eyes, blocking out everything except the clatter of wheels as they rolled over cobblestones, adding a comforting murmur to his mood, mimicking the sound of heavy rain.

Calm.

His finger traced over the seal.

This piece of paper would not leave his sight. Certainly, he claimed a measure of pride as a man, but acquiring a third license had stripped him clean of any he might have had left.

He didn't care.

However, Calstone's words, that bastard, still had him on edge. He had the betrothal agreement, and he had the license, but that meant nothing without her agreement.

Ah, Christ.

I should have done better sooner.

He hoped Harriet had eaten something. Should he rather have sent her home?

Damn Hatton.

He did not trust the man's competence or judgment any longer. What irresponsible father did not inform his daughter of a proposal? He could have prevented so much turmoil if he had just communicated with his daughter. They could have addressed her concerns together. More than that, Harriet had run away on Hatton's watch. Will didn't expect parents to know the whereabouts of their children every moment, but surely it shouldn't be that easy to slip out of the house in broad daylight with baggage, hail a cab, and set off for the docks?

Anything might have happened to her.

His gaze fixed on the streets and the people bustling about. The rush seemed to have a harmony about it today. A simplicity . . .

Dear God, he'd spent too much time in Calstone's presence.

The carriage slowed to a halt. Sweat broke out across his palms, his temple. His thumb traced across the seal for a final time.

"One step, Will. One step. Everything will be all right."

Will stepped from the carriage only to come up short when the door of his home yanked open and a man leaped over the three small steps and onto his yard. Calstone's frantic gaze met his, and he came to an abrupt halt.

Will's heart sank. Right down to the heels of his boots.

"You're back?" Calstone strode over.

"What happened?" He demanded without preamble. "Where is Harriet?"

"I fell asleep," Calstone said with a scowl, dragging a hand through his hair. "When I woke up, she was gone."

Will cursed.

His head swung to the street.

"Perhaps she's still in the house?"

He turned to Calstone. "You didn't ask the servants?"

"Forgive me for receiving the shock of my life."

Stay calm and think.

She would be on foot unless she'd been able to hail a hack again. She probably had coin on her, and she wouldn't go home. Hide at a friend's house, then? Set out for Scotland? Perhaps Wales?

Fear squeezed his heart.

He'd gotten lucky the first time. Remarkably lucky. Will wasn't so sure he'd be that fortunate again.

"I asked but one thing of you," he growled at Calstone. "One bloody thing."

Calstone swore. "I know. The deuced fire went out and my feet were cold all night, keeping me awake. Never thought I'd fall asleep though. Where do you think she could have gone? Back to the docks?"

Will clenched his fists. "No."

"You must admit, it is rather comic, this entire ordeal."

Will glared at his friend. "This is not an ordeal; this is my life. And there is nothing comic about it."

Calstone scratched his head. "When you have the woman, you don't have the license. When you have the license, you don't have the woman. I'd call that rather comic."

"This is not funny," Will growled. One day, he might have a good chuckle at his misfortune, but not today. Come to think about it . . . no, he wouldn't no matter how many years passed. Which was entirely beside the point.

"If you want to laugh, go home," Will bit out through clenched teeth. "And forget about our friendship."

Calstone lifted his hands in surrender. "Wait a minute, old chap, I'm not laughing. I'm merely making observations."

"Then keep your observations to yourself."

"Are you sure?"

"Yes," Will growled. "Do you want a beating?"

"No, no. Just confirming." His lips quirked. "Then suppose I shouldn't say anything about the woman that looks awfully like your runaway bride off yonder."

Will's gaze whipped back to the street, his probing eyes settling on the couple Calstone pointed at not far in the distance. He instantly recognized the petite woman speaking to a tall man.

Thank God. So long as he had her in his sights, he would not lose her.

His legs were already carrying him in her direction, his eyes never leaving her silhouette. He spoke only when he was within a few feet of her.

"Harriet."

She blinked at him. "Oh, you are back."

"Yes, I'm back."

Lord Rochester turned at his arrival. "Leeds? Are you also taking a stroll?"

Will nodded. "I saw Lady Harriet pass my house and thought to catch her to discuss our—"

"We've discussed all that needs to be discussed," she hurriedly interrupted with a wide smile.

Will quirked a brow, half stunned by her sudden brightness. "Is that so?"

She nodded.

"We are speaking of the same thing—our mutual beneficial agreement?"

"Mutual beneficial agreement, you say." Her entire body lit with challenge. "What is so *mutually* beneficial about it? I've found it to be quite one-sided, which is why I'm enjoying a stroll so early in the morning—I'm quite suffocated and annoyed by this mutually beneficial agreement."

"I see the two of you have some things to discuss," Rochester suddenly put in. "I'll take my leave."

Will nodded to the man before turning his attention back to Harriet. He half expected her to cry for help, but to his surprise, she merely sent the earl a reassuring smile.

I want that smile to be mine.

"He's not wrong," Will said. "We have things to discuss."

Those big, clear eyes lifted to him. "You want to discuss things now?"

"Don't you?"

"I want to go home first."

Will hesitated didn't trust anyone in that house to keep an eye on her. "Haven't we been down that path before?"

"I want to bathe."

"You can bathe at my house. I'll have someone send for your maid."

"I need to pack my wedding trousseau. It's a thing, you know."

Will's breath stalled. Did she mean . . . Will was too afraid to ask. He cleared his throat. "I'll have a footman collect it."

She gave a curt nod. "Then shall I bathe at your residence?"

He nearly groaned at the image that question provoked. Was this another scheme after being caught once again? Had she even run away this time? "Of course. It's to be your home now, too."

She started to walk back toward his house, but Will stopped her by grabbing her wrist. He had to know. "Wait. Why are you suddenly so amenable? Just yesterday you were set on fleeing to another country."

"Would you believe me if I said I've come to see the light?"

"No."

Her laughter wrapped around him like a spell.

She'd changed her mind. Dear God, she'd changed her mind.

A force unlike any he had ever felt overcame him in that moment, and he lowered to one knee, unable to stop himself. "I know this is not how you wanted to marry. You deserved a proper courtship. I can't change the past, but I ask nonetheless, Lady Harriet Hillstow, would you please do me the honor of becoming my wife?"

Her eyes turned to saucers. She glanced left and right before she hissed, "What are you doing?"

"Asking for you hand."

"Get up!"

"Not until you give me an answer," Will said. "You might not believe me, love, but I *am* trying here. I want nothing more than your favor."

"*Fine*, I shall marry you. Are you happy?" Her cheeks flushed red. "Now get up, people are staring at us."

Will straightened to his feet. "You said yes."

She snatched his hand and dragged him in the direction of the house. "Do you believe me to be plotting a diabolical scheme?"

Will stared at her. "No." He just didn't think he'd ever hear those words from her mouth.

"I do, however, have one condition."

"What is it?" He would give her anything.

"We marry tomorrow."

Anything but that.

"No, we must marry today."

She stopped and whirled on him, demanding, "Why the rush?"

"Why the delay?" Will returned. He hated pushing her this way, but he needed a reason—a real reason—to delay. A reason to believe she would keep her word.

"I want a win."

His brow furrowed. "You want . . . a win?"

She nodded, her chin lifting in a defiant manner. "A win."

Will admired her bluntness, and he understood. He could give her a win. "Very well, you have your wish. Tomorrow."

Her smile started small but grew to beaming. It fairly blew him away.

They stood in the street and looked at each other a moment, neither speaking. They'd been through a great deal since yesterday. How could one woman drive all rational thoughts from his head and leave him with the intellect of a tree stump? However she managed it, Will didn't mind. He sensed the truth in her words, saw it in the depth of her gaze.

She wasn't lying to him.

She'd said she'd marry him, so she would.

"Do you still wish for me to return to your house now that I've answered you?"

"Are you willing to?" Will didn't want to part with her. And he couldn't say he'd be at ease with sending her home.

"Yes, I'm willing."

"Very well then." Will offered his arm, both of them making their way back to his townhouse.

Her *yes* meant more to him than anything else in the world, but deep in the corners of his mind, he couldn't help but wonder what mischief Harriet Hillstow might have up her sleeve now.

Chapter Eight

"I CAN'T BELIEVE you're staying at the Marquess of Leeds's house the night before your marriage!"

"We are wedding."

"I cannot believe you are *wedding* the Marquess of Leeds!"

Harriet stared at her friend, Lady Leonora Heart with a sense of amusement. Yes, she had agreed to marry Leeds. She also decided to stay at his house instead of going home. Her reason was rather simple. She hadn't truly wanted to return home. She could face her father if she had no other choice, but she couldn't quite forgive him yet.

Oh, she understood their world, understood what he'd done. But to give her not even the tiniest consideration as to inform her of the betrothal? And then to have her betrothed appear moments after her confrontation with him?

Harriet doubted she could explain it convincingly to her friend, but she'd rather remain with Leeds than return home.

Marry a man that would fight for you.

She'd already made up her mind before he found her with Rochester, yet it occurred to her, as the man was kneeling in the middle of the street, not caring who witnessed such a shockingly embarrassing scene, that her mother would have approved of him.

She would have approved their betrothal, their marriage.

And his proposal . . .

While certainly not romantic and a little bit too late, her heart had still burst into a thousand fluttering butterflies. Even though it had only been a courtesy proposal, she had still felt a spark of excitement.

Leeds might not love her, and she certainly didn't hold all that much affection for him, but he would make a worthy husband.

In any event, she had given him an official yes. She would never go back on her word. *And* she even managed to get a startled look from him. Anything that ruffled that man's composure could be considered a treat.

He had almost looked as stunned as she had felt at the time. But as her words settled between them, Harriet had known in her bones that she'd made the right decision. She would marry Leeds and peel back every layer of him until he was stripped utterly bare before her. Her victory in that would have the sweet tang of honey.

"If fact," Leonora went on, "I cannot believe I am sitting in a bedchamber with you in that man's house. He is *so* . . . dreamlike."

"He is just a man."

"What are you talking about? He is not *just* a man." Lenora smiled, her eyes sparkling like diamonds. "Besides the fact that he is big, tall, and has the face of a god, he is an *unmarried* man. We are unmarried ladies. You must admit, there's a certain thrill in it all."

Well, putting it that way, Harriet supposed she could agree, but she hadn't thought about that part of it as much as that from tomorrow onward this would be her new home. Her forever home.

However, she still didn't plan on staying alone in the house of her betrothed on the night before their wedding. Leonora was right—it wouldn't be seemly. And a part of her still didn't entirely trust the man. It would be foolish to do so that quickly, especially after he'd kissed her in her own bedchamber and clasped her hand last night! The other part of her . . . well, the other part needed a friend.

"Do not get too excited. This is not a romantic union."

Leonora's wide eyes shot her a searching look. "What do you mean?"

"I mean this is an *arranged* marriage."

"Well, it's certainly not your average arranged marriage if you are living with your husband-to-be *before* you marry."

"It's complicated." She had thought of all the ways a marriage could be positioned. Just because they were married, didn't mean they had to *be* together. Perhaps she ought to rephrase it. "Think of it rather as a marriage of convenience."

"Does *he* know that?"

"He'll find out soon enough. Being wed does not mean we shall be together in the sense of man and wife. As I'm still not sure of his motives, I shall give him nothing except my name next to his in a register."

"You can still run away. I shall help you any way I can."

"I already tried that avenue." Harriet smoothed out the pillow on her lap. "Besides, I've already given my word. I won't break it."

"Then you have made up your mind?"

Harriet nodded. "I shall gradually uncover each one of the secrets he is keeping from me."

Leonora arched a brow. "Won't that just make you miserable? You've always held out hope for a love match."

Harriet smiled. "On the contrary, I believe it shall bring me great delight. As for love . . . I can read books for love."

Leonora shook her head. "Always the true optimist. Have you thought about how to make him reveal his secrets to you?" Leonora asked thoughtfully.

"I suppose I shall have to first discover his motive for marrying me, though I have no idea how. It's not like he'll admit to his intentions."

A mischievous glint entered Leonora's eye. "Then you shall have to lure it from his lips."

Harriet gave her friend a thoughtful glance. "You have some advice to impart?"

Her friend shrugged. "How have women across the ages lured men to the brink of ruin?"

"How?"

A loud bubble of laughter escaped Leonora. "Temptation. Seduction. Jealousy."

The first two she could understand but . . . "Jealousy?" Surely that could not be right. Besides, how would jealousy—if Leeds was even capable of such a thing—help her discern his motives? "I don't think that one will work."

"Why not?"

"Leeds? Jealous? Over me? That would imply he cares for me, which I assure you, he cannot."

"Even if he doesn't care for you, he cares about his *name*. All men do. Besides, no man wants to be cuckolded."

Harriet's eyes widened. "What are you talking about? I'm not going to embark on an affair."

"Who said anything about an affair?" Leonora grinned. "There are many ways to ignite jealousy in a man."

"Lord," Harriet muttered. "Do I even want to know?"

Leonora clapped her hands together. "I have a fabulous idea! You should dance with Lord Dare, the most handsome and blackened rake in London."

"I do not even know Lord Dare." She slanted a glance at her friend. "And why do you pronounce his name with so much intrigue?"

"Because I find him intriguing."

"You shouldn't find a rake intriguing, Leonora. That's how ladies are ruined."

Leonora sighed. "I know, but there is something about the thrill of dancing on the edge of danger, don't you agree?"

"I don't," Harriet said. "I've never wanted to reform a rake."

But imagining ruining the calm of her soon-to-be-husband, it did hold immense appeal, so she could hardly judge her friend for her quirks.

"Oh, I don't mean to reform him. I'm just enjoying myself."

"Well, be careful. The last thing you want is to end up like me."

"Oh, cheer up, Harriet. Tomorrow you become a marchioness."

Harriet bared her teeth. "I'm cheerful. See?"

Leonora laughed. "No one needs to be *that* cheerful."

Harriet wrinkled her nose. "I cannot believe my life has come to this. At least I kept my promise to my mother. As much as I could."

"That is all that counts," Leonora agreed with a smile. She fell back against the pillows stacked against the wall. "If I don't find a match soon, my father will probably arrange one for me as well."

"You have no one in mind?"

Leonora shook her head. "All I want to do is have fun. All my parents want is to suck the fun out of everything."

Harriet chuckled. "That's a bit harsh."

"Well, I shall steal a bit of fun from every moment I can as long as I can." Leonora poked Harriet's waist. "You can still find love, you know. Or a spot of *fun* here and there."

"*That* would mean I'd have to embark on an affair."

"Maybe not. Perhaps you will find love with Leeds."

Find love with Leeds? "Impossible."

"Why?" Leonora asked.

Why indeed.

"I admit, it's rather unfashionable for wives to fall in love with their husbands."

Harriet hit her friend with a pillow.

Leonora laughed and hit her back with hers. "Well, if Leeds does not come up to snuff as a husband you can always demand a divorce from the House of Lords after you marry."

What absurd nonsense was this now? "They would never

grant it," Harriet said with confidence. Given how much that man had done to secure her hand, he would never let her go. Not without a fight. Yes, Leeds was a fighter.

But rather than be terrified by the thought, it thrilled her.

Harriet remembered something. "Leeds mentioned wagers about women. Do you know anything about that?" She hadn't believed him at the time, but his motive could be tied to the wagers as he'd told her.

Leonora pursed her lips in thought. "I can't say that I do."

Was it a lie then?

Had these wagers just been an excuse—a way to try to placate her and to make her believe his reasons were pure? The more she thought about it, the more Harriet began to question their existence. Wouldn't she or Leonora have heard about this list and these wagers had they existed? Such secrets could not be kept in the *ton*.

Gah! What a conundrum!

One thing she did know for a fact. If Leeds expected a biddable wife, he was in for the biggest surprise of his lifetime.

THE EARLY MORNING light bathed the drawing room in soft, golden hues, casting long shadows across the carpet and walls. The scene would have been quite romantic, if the mood hadn't been so serious and solemn.

Will adjusted his waistcoat and straightened his cravat, his fingers trembling with nerves. He stood near the grand fireplace, his heart pounding heavily in his chest.

The day had finally come.

The thought brought equal parts joy and trepidation to his heart. He'd gotten what he wanted most, but the journey to this moment still left a bittersweet taste in his mouth.

He hadn't slept a bloody wink, doomed to pace his chamber, alert to the slightest of noises. He trusted that Harriet wouldn't back out after giving her word, but he still wasn't entirely at ease. After all, the events after he met her had left a deep impression in his heart. He had already experienced firsthand how easily she could slip through his fingers.

I do.

I take you, Harriet Hillstow, as my wife.

You look lovely, Harriet.

To have and to hold. Until death do us part.

He had practiced the lines he would recite today—as well as some additional ones—over and over in his mind to avoid a stuttering episode.

He knew she wasn't at ease in her heart, either. He'd wanted to have a conversation over dinner, but upon returning to the house she had slipped away to bathe after which she had sent for her friend. Will had let her be. They had their entire lives to talk, and she probably needed a friend more.

He glanced at Calstone.

If only he could get rid of his. The duke had been clinging to him like a shadow. What man in his right mind smiled *that* much? Did his face not hurt? However, his appreciation outweighed his spurts of annoyance. His friend was the only person who knew how much he struggled in times that might cause his weakness to flare.

And upon hearing the woman's chatter approaching, his heart sped up. Will tugged at his cravat.

It was their wedding day.

She would be arriving soon.

Will shifted on his feet, and beside him, Calstone offered a reassuring nod. "Don't fret, your bride won't abandon you here."

"That's not what I'm worried about."

"Do you have the case of nerves?"

Yes, but they were under control. "Her parents aren't here."

"Did you invite them?"

"No." Will had thought Harriet would inform them, but it seemed he had been mistaken.

"Ah," Calstone murmured.

"Ah, what?" Leeds asked. "Do you know something?"

"No, no," Calstone said. "But her outrage must be stronger toward her father than toward you."

Will winced a little. She didn't appear to be angry at him at all. Not anymore, at least. However, he also didn't want her relationship with her father to suffer because of him.

"Should I send word to them?" Calstone asked.

"No. If Harriet is not willing to face her father yet, I won't interfere."

"Look," Calstone said.

Will's gaze returned to the door. A vision appeared in his line of sight and his breath hitched. Harriet entered, accompanied by her friend, and everything else flew from his mind.

She wore an elegant gown of pale blue silk that draped gracefully over her slender form. Her chestnut curls cascaded down her back, caught in a delicate pearl hair comb that shimmered in the morning light. Her eyes, that captivating shade of blue, held a mixture of confidence and determination. He could also glimpse the vulnerability there, but despite that, they burned as brightly as the sun.

His eyes caught on the soft bow of her lips, the pink in her cheeks, until it reached the silky expanse of her throat.

Christ.

The woman still stole his breath whenever he set eyes on her. Even at her angriest, at her weariest, she always managed to light up a room with her presence.

Will stepped forward, offering his hand. She accepted without hesitation. Their fingers touched, and even gloved, a jolt of electricity shot through Will, reaffirming his conviction.

She is the one.

It hadn't been easy for him to get to this moment, and despite his excitement, that tinge of apprehension still lingered in his mind. He still had her heart to win, and the battle wasn't over.

In fact, he suspected her battle had just begun. He could tell from just that one look. His wife might not be spitting flames at him anymore, but the challenge in her gaze was as strong as ever. Did she know she wasn't very good at hiding her emotions? Everything she felt was clear to see on her face.

The corner of his lips lifted. Was it wrong of him to look forward to every challenge she tossed his way, whatever her reasons for doing so? Although he did hope that one day in the future, no matter how long it took, she would look at him with a different expression—one of affection.

"Are my eyes deceiving me?" Calstone murmured low. "Both the bride and the groom are smiling. Why am I getting shivers?"

The ceremony commenced without hindrance, and Will could not escape the awareness of her that crawled over his skin as they stood before the priest and recited their vows. For his part, every word he said was filled with sincerity, each syllable carrying the weight of his commitment to the woman beside him. Clear. Unfaltering.

Harriet, on the other hand, claimed every word with a hint of defiance. Ah, yes, his little spitfire was going to give him one hell of a battle, he was sure.

It the end, only five words spun in his head.

I shall protect you forever.

Calstone clapped him on the shoulders. "Congratulations, old chap."

Harriet gave a small snort, but she still sent him a wide smile. "Yes, congratulations, husband."

A shiver shot up his spine.

"Where is your family?" Leonora murmured as her gaze swept the drawing room.

"As my father didn't see fit to inform me of my betrothal, I didn't see fit to inform them that I was wedding today," Harriet admitted.

Will kept his features cool. "We can invite them for lunch, if you like."

Harriet shook her head. "They are aware I've returned, are

they not? You must have sent word, and my trousseau was gathered and removed from the house."

"Calstone did send word," Will admitted.

"Well, then, there is nothing to be concerned about since my father is clearly not concerned."

The priest coughed behind his hand.

Will didn't bother to glance at him as he pulled Harriet to the side. "They are still your parents. I don't want you to one day regret not including them."

She held her ground. "I have never been a priority to my father since he remarried."

"That's not true. Your father loves you very much."

"My father loves my stepmother and half-brother. I lost all importance the day my mother died. While I might have thought otherwise for a while, the very betrothal agreement you signed without my knowledge reaffirmed that as a fact. I won't regret my decision not to invite them. For all we know, he may have believed we were already married since I never returned home."

Will's heart clenched.

"Harriet . . ."

She shook her head. "I do not need your pity, Leeds. I have long accepted my position in my family."

"I will do my best to make you happy."

She didn't reply, but Will could almost hear her heart retorting: *If you wanted to do that, then you should not have married me.* But if it hadn't been him, it would have been someone else. Someone even *less* worthy. With the wagers luring all sorts of ruffians out of the shadows, he was the best possible choice for Harriet.

He believed that with all his heart.

He cared for her. He would not do anything to hurt her. He would give her anything in his power to provide her the best life possible. Even if it took his entire lifetime to accomplish.

"I do not expect you to believe me. All I ask is for a chance."

"We shall see," she murmured. "Now, if you will excuse me, I can't keep my guest waiting."

Will arched a brow, but he let her go.

Patience, Will. Just take one step and then another.

That thought seemed to have become his lifeline.

He hadn't given his wife a proper courtship. They both were keenly aware of that. But now that they had the biggest obstacle out of the way, Will could pay more attention to wooing his wife. To winning her heart.

Once the conviction settled in his own heart, the corners of his lips lifted. Despite everything, today was a marvelous day. If he were still a child, he would be doing a merry little dance right about now. As a grown man, however, he refrained—it was better not to provoke his wife's ire, after all.

"Why are you smiling like that?" Calstone asked. "And this is two smiles in one day? Wedded bliss must be real."

Will flattened his lips. "Who is smiling?"

"You are," Calstone said. "However, you should practice your lip movements in the mirror. You are smiling like you just smelled something foul."

"Would I smile if I smelled something foul?"

"I don't know. I couldn't really tell whether it was a smile or not, but it was more of a smile than it was anything else."

Will punched his friend in the arm.

"Damn it! What was that for?"

"Talking nonsense."

Did his smile look that odd? Would he have to practice smiling if he wanted to court his wife in the future?

Chapter Nine

Harriet stared at the tumbler of gin—very strong gin— that seemed to have gained a companion. She narrowed her eyes on the *two* tumblers before her.

"What are you looking at?" she mumbled. "None of this is my fault. My father—that's who to blame. And that man. I did test him, though. He passed, as you know." She hiccupped. "Now I am married to that man."

She paused. "What's his name again? Ah, *Leeds*. I'm married to Leeds."

Her gaze flicked over her new bedchamber, but she couldn't make sense of the room.

Harriet blinked. Everything appeared hazy.

She shook her head. "See his daughter wed? Father didn't deserve to get a notice. I don't feel bad about it. *I don't*."

The flickering candlelight seemed to dance before her eyes, casting eerie shadows on the walls. She poked one of those shadows.

"What's tonight?" It seemed to be an important night, but she couldn't quite recall. She had wedded that man so . . . tonight . . .

Her head fell back.

That's right!

Tonight was her *wedding* night—a night that was meant to be filled with love and tenderness.

Not for me.

No, she was rebelling against any wifely duties. She glanced at the bottle in her hand. But not against gin. She'd drunk a lot of this stuff. Illicit stuff, apparently—nice and strong.

Harriet chuckled.

It might be her wedding night, but there would be no night of the wedding. That man, her husband, *Leeds*, he could sleep in the stables for all she cared. He might be just acceptable to marry, but she still had standards. Her bed was off limits to him. This night and every night that followed.

She laughed, the almost evil giggle bouncing of the walls surrounding her. The crystal glass in her hand caught her eye, its translucent contents beckoning to her once more.

Harriet reached for the bottle, filling her glass. This gin had been given to her by Rohan, and she'd secretly stashed it in a hatbox. If she could not celebrate her wedding night, she would commiserate and lay to rest her past expectations, and the fiery liquid promised temporary solace.

She raised the glass to toast. "To the end of the single life of a lady and the beginning of an unknown plot."

The room seemed to tilt, and she grasped onto the edge of the dressing table, her knuckles turning white, droplets of gin spilling to the floor.

"Ah, drat." Her chamber would smell like liquor now.

Harriet caught a glimpse of herself in the mirror she'd placed against the wall—a disheveled bride, her hair undone, cheeks flushed with both the remnants of the day and the lush pull of alcohol. She traced the delicate lace on her gown, the texture beneath her fingertips a reminder of the promises she had made, the commitment she had willingly entered into.

No matter.

Just because she hadn't married a man she loved, didn't mean she had to be unhappy.

She hiccupped.

"That's right, one can find happiness anywhere." She nodded

at her reflection in the small mirror "A man is not the source of happiness. Why, a sloth can make me happy. I shall have a dozen. Then I will be dozens happy. Sloths make for good old-age companions. Ah, I should retrieve Chester from my old house tomorrow. How could I have forgotten about that sweet thing? How cute would a sloth be for our own home?"

Home.

She brought the glass to her lips and swallowed another gulp. "Ah yes. My new home. *His* home too. But if that jackanapes thinks we will consummate this marriage, he should think again." She stared at the crystal glass in her hand. "What do you think? Shall we box his ears if he tries?"

She hiccupped. "He is handsome, though. It's just his character that's a bit stiff. Why are there only a few men in this world with pristine characters? Most of them are rude, overbearing, and pompous. It's better to get a sloth—a *dozen* sloths."

She snorted. "Leeds probably won't agree to a sloth. Maybe it will be best to get a dog."

Hah! Wasn't he a dog himself?

No, no. Dogs were sweet, cuddly, and loyal. Leeds wasn't a dog.

He was a wolf. Just look at how he'd hunted her down.

"A big, snarling wolf. Wolves don't make good companions. They bite." Harriet groaned. "I don't want to be married to a wolf. I want to be married to a sweet dog. Is that so much to ask for?"

You can always tame the wolf.

She gave another snort. "That man cannot be tamed. But I can still provoke him, find out his secrets, and bring him to heel. Hah, Leonora said to divorce him, but since this is a marriage of convenience, would an annulment not be more fitting?"

Not that she truly planned to break her vow or even annul it.

She grinned. But she could rile him up! Ah well, he couldn't blame her. A woman had to find her delights wherever she could, and she suspected she could ruffle his feathers with that.

Harriet laughed. "I wonder what my husband will do if I toss out the word *annulment*."

She lifted the glass to her face. "That's a splendid idea, isn't it? These little enjoyments are the next best thing, since I didn't marry a man that I love. That's not too bad of me, is it?" She poked a finger of her free hand at the tumbler. "I know, I know, it's hard having a dream. Dreams are the hardest."

Someone knocked on the door.

"Harriet? Are you all right? Who are you talking to?"

Ah. That man had arrived.

Harriet angled her head in the direction of the masculine voice that had interrupted her conversation. "I'm discussing an important matter," she called to the door. "Go away."

A short pause. "What matter are you discussing?"

Harriet chuckled. "About how I shall not annul this marriage."

"That's good to know."

She blinked. That couldn't be right—he wasn't supposed to like it. Something must be off with her words. "I mean, I am not *consummating* this marriage." She balled her free hand in a fist and announced with conviction, "I shall not submit!"

The doorknob jiggled. "Did you lock the door?"

"Of course I did."

"Even though it is our wedding night?"

"Especially because it's our wedding night." Harriet scowled at the door. "I said I will not consummate the marriage, ergo there is no reason for you to seek me out." Hiccup.

A pause stretched between them before he slowly said, "Love, you are in *my* bedchamber. The marchioness's chamber is the adjoining one."

"Well, you can sleep there. This chamber is bigger. I need a lot of space."

"I'd rather sleep next to you."

"Hah! Don't you mean consummate the marriage?"

"I won't force you to do anything you don't want, love. We

have all the time in the world to get to know each other."

"Well, you have to *earn* that spot."

"Then I shall do my best."

Harriet frowned. She'd thought he'd be more rattled by her little act of rebellion. "I thought you would be angry."

"Why would I be angry?"

"You are a man."

"I am a man. Your man."

Her cheeks heated. My man? Yes, yes, he was *her* man. Why did that sound so thrilling?

"Have you been drinking?" He suddenly asked.

"What if I have?"

Another pause. This one longer than the last.

Harriet strained her ears. Had he left?

She smirked.

She had won again. Things were looking brighter by the moment! She giggled. A giggle that was interrupted by the opening of the door that connected the neighboring chamber.

A large figure filled the doorway, eyes blazing as they settled on her, fleetingly dropping to the glass in her hand.

Drat.

She'd forgotten to lock that door! She pointed a finger at him. "Don't you dare step into this chamber."

He lifted his hands in surrender. "Am I allowed to stand in the threshold?"

"That much is allowed."

He leaned against the door, causally crossing his arms over his chest. "What are you drinking?"

She shrugged. "Nothing much. A spot of gin."

"I see. And just where did you get the liquor?"

She pointed at the box containing her collection of hats and bonnets.

"Not where you hid your liquor. Who sold it to you?"

"Oh, no one sold it to me. I got it as a gift from a friend."

"What friend gives gin as a gift?"

She grinned at him. "A *good* friend."

"You do know that stuff is likely contraband? Just how much *did* you have to drink?"

She shot him a reproachful look, lowering herself to the floor before the bed, leaning back against the frame. "What does it matter? All that matters is that this gin is keeping me company on my wedding night."

He hunched down as well. "May I have some?"

She arched a brow. "You wish to drink with me?"

"Why not?" He sat and leaned against one side of the door-frame. "It seems like you are having fun."

Harriet nodded. He looked carefree as he joined her on the floor. Had he always cut such a dashing figure?

She reached for the bottle and rolled it towards him. He caught it and removed the cork, taking a swig. His gaze once again burned into hers. "Strong."

She waved her hand. "You will get used to it."

"I did not take you for a gin drinking wench."

"Wench?" Harriet laughed. "I suppose I am."

"Did you worry about tonight?"

Harriet shrugged. "Well, a woman can never be too cautious."

"Against your husband?"

"Well, you have a history of barging into chambers and cabins and kissing unsuspecting ladies."

He took another swallow of the gin, his lips inching upward. "I seemed to recall that a specific wench kissed me back."

"She must have been overcome by madness."

"He must have been as well."

Harriet stared at him as his gaze took in the chaos that had become this chamber. Dresses flung all over the bed. Bits and baubles scattered everywhere. So far, he'd been exceedingly considerate. Yet, beneath his good humor something else lingered. He almost looked . . . hurt.

Come to think of it, he had the same look when she told him

the reason why she hadn't invited her father. Then another image popped into her head—a flash of expression after she accused him of all sorts of things the first day they met in the hallway.

She cleared her throat, taking a sip of her drink. "It's true that we both have done some outlandish things. It seems to be a theme."

His gaze returned to her. "Will there be more outlandish things coming my way?"

She lifted her glass at him in a salute. "You shall have to watch and see."

"Was mentioning the word annulment part of this watch and see?" He put the bottle aside. "I might as well tell you now, that is not happening. I don't plan on ever separating."

"I know."

"I suppose I should be grateful you didn't drink directly from the bottle."

"Speaking of which," she lifted her almost empty glass. "Give it back. It's mine."

"Let's not talk about what's yours and what's mine." He took another swig from the bottle.

Harriet angled her head. "Why? Because what's yours in mine and what's mine is yours?"

He grinned at her. "Exactly."

Gosh, she couldn't get used to that smile. Lawd, what was happening to her? She was hot all over. She patted her cheeks. "Is that why you had my belongings brought to your chamber?"

"The chamber was mine before we wed. Now it's ours."

"You do know that husbands and wives don't share rooms. It's highly unfashionable. Just look at my parents. The perfect example of an arranged marriage."

"How about we make our own example?"

Their own example? That didn't sound half bad. "I quite like that idea. We are even off to a good start. A wife stealing her husband's chamber and ushering him into the adjoining one."

"Tell me, love, is this what you wanted when you accepted

our marriage yesterday? To bar me from my own chamber?"

"I believe the term is actually 'marriage of convenience'."

"What if I don't want," his voice lowered, causing all sorts of tingles to rush over her skin, "a marriage of convenience?"

"What marriage do you want then?"

"A real one."

Harriet glanced at him, blinking as his visage blurred a bit. Still, she understood his words, and she laughed. "There cannot be a real marriage."

"Why not?"

She sent him a smug smile. "You haven't earned the right to a real marriage."

⟫⟫⟫✳⟪⟪⟪

WILL STARED AT his wife, half amused and half at a loss for words. A truly intriguing woman. Moonlight spilled through the half-drawn drapes, casting long shadows across the carpeted floor and over her. She grinned at him, and he swore, as he always had, the sun had set on her lips, such was the effect of her smile.

He had seen a similar scene before, only it was in her home, the evening they first met in person. Only, she didn't remember that night, that moment.

She didn't remember him.

A few months before the list of heiresses hit the betting book of White's, he'd been invited to her house for dinner to discuss a property deal with Hatton and some others. She hadn't been present for the dinner, but on his way out, Will had heard her laugher, and like a sailor to a siren's call, he followed it all the way to the library. The moment was still vivid in his memory.

"Shall I embark on a journey of spinsterhood? Is that my fate? It must be hard being a dream . . ."

"Are you all right?" Will asked.

"Who are you?"

"I am William."

She scrunched her brows. "I do not know a William. What are you doing here?"

"I had business with your father." His gaze shifted to the glass pinched between her fingers. "I believe the more important question is what are you doing, my lady?"

"I'm having a deep conversation which you have interrupted."

"A conversation?" He glanced around the room. "With books?"

"Why not?" she challenged. "They are great listeners. They don't judge or criticize."

"I think you have had too much to drink, my lady."

"So they've been telling me. Well, since you are here, you might as well have some use." Blue eyes—almost the color of the clear, blue ocean—stared at him with renewed calculation. "Carry me back to my room."

Will blinked. "What?"

"You heard me, William, Knight of Hillstow. Carry me back to my room."

"Lady Harriet. You are drunk."

"I shall not deny it."

Will cocked his head has he regarded her. This was the first time they'd met after he had glimpsed her reading beneath the tree. And it was nothing like he expected.

"Very well. This Knight of Hillstow shall carry you up to you room. Please tell me the way."

"Much obliged."

Drunk.

And not just slightly drunk—the woman had been completely cup-shot.

Just like now.

After she had directed him to her chamber, she'd fallen asleep the moment her head hit the pillow. Luckily, no one had witnessed the encounter, but it had left a lasting impression on Will. He even believed he'd be able to approach her with confidence after that night, having accomplished a real conversation with her.

He'd been sorely mistaken.

Had she been drinking gin back then, too? Whatever she had consumed, it had completely washed the memory of him from her mind.

Why had she been drinking that evening? He'd often wondered. Ladies weren't meant to imbibe. At least not like that. But then again, he had no experience to draw from. Maybe they did more often than he thought. And no matter the reason back then, tonight she had turned to drink because of him.

"I have no qualms about earning the right to a real marriage."

"Are you sure? It might not be an easy feat."

"Nothing worthwhile ever comes easy, love. And you most certainly are worthwhile."

A fresh flush of pink infused her cheeks. "When did you get such a smooth-talking tongue?"

Hell if Will knew. But each time he talked to her, it became easier, less painful. He hadn't even broken out in a sweat once throughout their conversation tonight. "I'm just saying what is in my heart."

"There you go again, being all charming."

Will's lips twitched. "Perhaps I am a charming a man."

"Are you trying to hoodwink me?"

He chuckled. "That's not possible."

"It's good that you know."

He swirled the bottle between his fingers. "What if I told you we met once before we were engaged?"

"We met before?" Her brows scrunched. "I would have remembered if we had been introduced."

"We weren't introduced."

Her head tilted to the side. "Then how did we meet?"

Will leaned forward. "Do you always forget about things that happen when you drink?"

She pursed her lips. "I can't say. If I can't remember, then I cannot know what I've forgotten."

"Well, I must not have made a lasting impression. I'm hurt."

She pursed her lips in thought. "I cannot recall such an incident."

"I'm not surprised, though still a touch disappointed."

She smiled. "I'm sure you will get over it."

Will's gaze dropped to her mouth. All pink and tempting. He wanted nothing more than to kiss her. But he wasn't such of a beast that he would steal a kiss from a woman in her condition, even if she was his wife.

She touched her lips. "What are you looking at?"

His eyes lifted to meet hers.

"Your lips."

She blinked at him, then scoffed. "Hah! From charming to rogue in a second."

He didn't deny it. "They are a beautiful sight."

She dropped her gaze to his lips. "Yours aren't bad either."

Will nearly groaned. That was his wife. She managed to always match him blow for blow.

"Let's not explore that topic too closely just now."

"Why not?" A smile sealed her lips. "It's rather intriguing."

"Because I want to kiss you." Badly. A raging fire burned within him. And all it took was one look, one word from her to set him ablaze. He could imagine her leaning into him, her palms sliding up the front of his shirt, and then her fingers curling into the softness of his hair, kissing him back as though her world burned for him as well. Will nearly groaned, the sensation in his imagination almost as real as their first kiss.

"I suppose kisses aren't that bad."

Will started. "I beg your pardon?"

"If I say you can kiss me, will you?"

Christ, she was determined to drive him to the brink of insanity. What the hell was wrong with him? He'd nearly come undone by an imagined kiss. "I won't."

"You won't?" She sounded shocked at his refusal.

"You are foxed."

She laughed. "Where did the rogue go?"

The rogue as trying very hard to keep a grip on his wits. If he lost them now . . .

"The rogue will return when you are sober, because when I kiss you again, love, it will be a kiss that you will never want to forget."

Chapter Ten

HARRIET FELL BACK onto the sofa in the library and draped her arm over her eyes. She'd woken with a terrible ache in her temples and would have stayed in bed all day had her belly not forced her to hunt for food. She peeked down at the dress she still wore from yesterday.

Ah, a hot bath would do the trick right about now.

Why on earth had she thought it a good idea to drink gin last night?

A footman appeared at the door. "My lady, you have a caller."

A caller? For *her?*

No one except that wily Calstone and Leonora knew of her nuptials or that she lived here now. Well, and her family, she supposed. But given the circumstances, her father would wait until Leeds announced their wedding to the world before he spoke a word of it. Leonora had a tea party to attend, and Harriet doubted the duke would be calling on her.

She rubbed her temples. A dull ache clung there. She was in no mood to entertain. And she could hardly meet anyone in this state of disarray.

"Have Leeds meet them."

"His lordship is not at home, my lady, and the gentleman asked specifically for you."

Gentleman?

That caught her attention, and she peeked at the footman from beneath her arm. She recalled running into Rochester yesterday. Did he suspect anything? Or did this mean that Leeds had made the announcement of their marriage? Other than her father, maybe Calstone, and less possibly Rochester, Harriet couldn't think what another gentleman might call on her here.

Drat.

She shouldn't have emptied an entire bottle of gin. She must have been mad. She was surprised that she could even consume so much. Alas, the proof never lies. An empty bottle had stared at her the moment she opened her eyes.

"Well, let's have it. Who has darkened my doorway today? Did he give a name? Tell them I'm indisposed." She lifted her legs to wiggle her toes—she hadn't even worn slippers.

"He claims to be a Mr. Grave—"

Harriet leaped from the sofa before the footman finished. "Rohan is here? A big, hulking, red-haired man?"

"Er, yes my lady, that seems to fit the gentleman's description."

"Well, why didn't you say so?" Harriet dashed to the drawing room without waiting for a reply. Rohan was one of her closest friends. As dear as a male friend could get. And the very friend she had planned to meet in Charleston had her plan not gone awry.

Had her father directed him here? He had never approved of their friendship, even though they'd grown up on neighboring estates in Kent. The Graves family came from trade and they had made their riches on the sea, which had never sat well with him. He approved even less these days.

But why was Rohan back in London?

Normally he sent word weeks in advance of his travels. Otherwise, she wouldn't have had the confidence to board a ship to the Americas in the first place.

What a twist of fate!

Harriet burst into the drawing room, her eyes lighting on the mop of red hair. Their eyes met, and two mouths split into grins.

"Rohan!"

Harriet dashed across the room and launched herself straight into her friend's arms. He lifted her in a hug, the low rumble of his laughter ringing in her ears.

A sound she had always loved.

The sound of her laugh weaved through his as he twirled her in circles. His strength always left her in awe.

"Have you grown even bigger since I last saw you?"

He chuckled. "I've put on a few pounds," his eyes narrowed, "But nothing more. And all muscle."

"You are never going to forgive me for calling you fat, are you?"

"Never."

"It was only once!"

"Once was more than my heart could take."

She grinned as he set her back on her feet but still held onto her shoulders. "Let me have a look at you." His gaze traveled from the top of her messy head to the tips of her pale toes, twin lines forming between his brows. "What happened? Did you escape Bedlam?"

"Don't start trouble. I drank too much last night."

One eyebrow lifted. "Don't tell me . . . the batch from my last trip?"

"The very same."

He leaned in to sniff her. "Now that you mention it, you do reek like a tavern wench."

She curled a fist and punched his arm. "You dare point that out?"

He laughed. "You dare drink so much gin?"

She covered his mouth with her hand. "Hush! What if some-one—"

A throat cleared.

Hears you . . .

Harriet ignored the tightening in her belly and glanced over her shoulder to her husband who stood in the doorway with a fierce scowl on his face.

Tiny prickles raced across her skin.

She had yet to grow accustomed to using that title. Husband. Ah, but even with such a ferocious look, he was still heart-stoppingly handsome.

Do not get distracted, now, Harriet.

"Who are you?" Leeds directed at Rohan, his eyes not once touching her. The wolf had focused on his prey, and this time his prey was her best friend.

"Rohan Graves," Rohan answered before Harriet could introduce the men.

"I know who you are," Leeds said in a low voice. "I meant who are you to my wife?"

"A friend."

"A friend who embraces a lady like that?"

Oh, Lord. He'd seen that? How long has he been standing there?

"*Good* friends."

"A good friend who calls my wife darling?"

"*Childhood* friends."

"A childhood friend who provides her illegal drink?"

"*Best* friends."

"I see."

Harriet gave an awkward laugh. She, for one, couldn't see anything. The men were sizing each other up, that much she gathered, but there seemed to be an unspoken conversation nestled in those few lines they'd tossed at each other.

Whatever *that* dialogue revealed, however, clearly made Leeds unhappy, which in turn, and for some unfathomable reason, made *her* happy. Her mood suddenly improved exponentially. Indeed, Leeds's reaction to Rohan might reveal more of his character, a subject that Harriet was becoming ever more passionate about.

A memory hovered on the edge of her mind, a vague flash of

a man sitting in the doorway staring at her with gentle eyes, but before Harriet thought to grab hold of it, it vanished.

Had Leeds come into her room last night?

Surely not.

She blinked away the haziness and smiled at Rohan. "Shall I ring for tea? We haven't seen each other in ages."

"Another time perhaps."

"Why? You are here now, aren't you? The least you can do is join me for tea."

Rohan didn't mince words. "When I heard about your marriage, I came to see with my own eyes how you are faring."

"My wife is well."

Rohan arched a brow. "That remains to be seen." He patted Harriet on the shoulder. "I've retired from the sea and decided to settle down in London for the unforeseeable future. We have ample time to catch up."

"That is amazing news!" With the knowledge that Rohan would be in London, some of the weight on her shoulders lifted. This man would always be her champion. No matter what.

"Also, I've found a home for Chester. A reserve where he will be free to roam. My people will collect him later today. I thank you for taking care of him for me."

Harriet was overjoyed by the news. Even though she would like nothing more than to keep Chester, wild animals, no matter how docile, did not belong indoors. "Oh, it was nothing. I enjoyed caring for him." She gave a small pause. He must have gone first to the Hillstow townhouse. "Did you see my father?"

He shook his head. "Only Lady Hatton."

Oh. "That is good then. You were spared his grunts and grumbles."

He chuckled. "I rather enjoy them. In any case, I shall take my leave."

Harriet nodded, beaming at her friend. "I shall see you out."

"No need." He motioned to Leeds, who was shooting daggers at the two of them. "You have other business to attend to. We'll talk again soon."

"Very well. Don't wait too long. I want to hear all about your work and travels."

Rohan inclined his head and took his leave. Was it Harriet's imagination, or did the tension in the room intensify after Rohan left? She glanced at Leeds, who was as stiff as an oak tree. He hadn't moved an inch.

Brooding eyes dropped to her bare feet. "Why aren't you wearing any shoes?"

Harriet wriggled her toes. "I like walking barefoot in my home."

His gaze lifted to hers, and some of the tension there ebbed away. "You are still wearing yesterday's clothes."

"I enjoy repeating outfits."

He stared at her, searching, *probing*.

Harriet arched a brow.

"Do you remember anything from last night?" he asked.

She stilled. "*Should* I remember anything from last night?"

"What about Graves?" His head cocked to the side. "He is the one who gave you the gin, is he not?"

He knew about the gin?

"You came to my room last night," she observed more to herself than him. He didn't deny it either. That was the only trouble with gin. She could never recall the events clearly after she'd had a few glasses.

"It's him, isn't it? Graves. He's the reason you boarded the ship."

"Well, yes. It might have seemed reckless to you, but I did have a plan." A partial plan anyway.

"On the ship, you asked me if I would break the betrothal agreement if you loved another."

Oh. That. She'd completely forgotten her taunt from back then. Leonora's suggestion fleetingly came to mind. *Temptation. Seduction. Jealousy.* She could say yes. She could see how Leeds would react.

No.

I can't do that to him. Or to Rohan for that matter.

"I . . . do love him," she admitted. "But only as a friend."

"I see."

"What, exactly, do you see?" Harriet asked.

"A broader picture."

"Well, Graves is a friend. You have nothing to worry about on that score."

A look flashed in his eyes, and while Harriet couldn't quite decipher the feeling she'd provoked in him this time, her heart stuttered in her breast at the glimpse of it. Before she could gather her wits, he closed the distance between them in three long strides, his head lowering so that they were eye to eye.

"And what if I told you I'm discovering myself to be a jealous man, love?"

Jealous?

Her lips parted in surprise at his admission. "Surely you jest. What do you have to be jealous about?"

"I do not jest about such things." His gaze imprisoned her. "I found it quite tormenting to watch my wife leap into another man's arms and not mine."

"I thought you were out."

"I returned just in time to see you dart into the drawing room with joy."

She bit back a smile at his sour tone. "Well, you scared him off, didn't you?"

"He'll be back." Leeds brushed the back of his hand over her cheek. "And another thing, love, if you wish to drink, I won't stop you. Though I prefer it not be contraband. You never know what's added to that stuff."

She blinked up at him.

Another flash of memory skittered across the planes of her mind, this one more vivid. Two eyes locked on each other. Teasing . . . "Last night . . ."

"Did you finally remember?" His lips curved into an amused

smile.

And Harriet knew she was in trouble.

Just what exactly happened last night?

AH, HELL.

Will had never felt so clouted in all his life. Beholding his wife in the arms of another man, hearing them laugh together as if they shared a treasure trove of secrets—though it had lasted but a minute, it must have counted as one of the tortuous minutes of his entire life. And there had been a lot of minutes over the years.

Jealousy, on the other hand—he never thought himself to be a man who would succumb to such base emotions. But when he remembered Harriet mentioning a man she might love when they were on the ship, his world tilted. Back then, he hadn't taken her words to heart. He'd believed she'd say anything to get him to bow out of the betrothal agreement. After all, he hadn't glimpsed her interacting with any gentleman at any ball. He certainly would never have thought in a thousand years that she might have meant Rohan Graves.

In that minute earlier when he had seen them together, he thought those words might have been true. But just for that minute.

If Harriet truly loved Graves, he was sure she would have clung to that ship with all her might. Also, upon observing Grave's reaction to their marriage . . . well, there wasn't much of one beyond a brotherly sort of interest. Their friendship must run deep.

He didn't mind that she had friends. He even didn't mind that one of them was Rohan Graves. He just wanted his wife to leap into *his* arms with joy.

"Did you break into my room last night?"

Will came back to his senses.

"As I said yesterday, love—*my* room. Unless you wish to

share a room, then it becomes *our* room. And no. You forgot to lock the adjoining chamber's door. Even so, I still didn't enter, as it seemed you were quite determined to keep me out."

"Well . . . you have a history of entering my chamber uninvited, you know."

"So you said last night."

Her eyes narrowed. "What exactly happened last night?"

"Nothing much. We shared a few drinks over a conversation."

"A conversation about what?"

"This and that. You asked me to kiss you."

"I did not!"

"Are you sure? I thought you couldn't remember," he teased.

"That . . . that . . ." Her mouth opened and closed, and Will couldn't help feeling a surge of satisfaction. "You refused me!"

"So you *do* remember."

"I *just* remembered."

"Then you must also have remembered that you divulged your plan to me, though perhaps accidentally. Annulment, love?"

"What plan? I just wanted to ruffle your well-composed feathers."

That surprised Will. "You think me composed?"

"Aren't you? You are always so calm and measured."

He leaned close until their noses almost touched. "Trust me, love, I am neither of those things when it comes to you."

Her cheeks flushed.

"Also, it's rather careless tossing out words such as annulment. Aren't you afraid I might drag you off to the country and lock you in another one of my chambers?"

"I would like to see you try." Her eyes lit with fire. "In fact, you might want to be cautious yourself. I don't mind doing the same."

Will scrunched his brows. "Drag me off to the country and lock me in your chamber?"

"Exactly."

"Then how about I take you up on that threat?"

"You . . . honestly! What kind of rogue are you?"

"A charming one?"

"Well, at least you do not deny the basic foundation of your character."

She must not have recalled that particular part of their conversation. "You know, you still have misunderstandings about me, but I will clear them all up in time. In the meantime, I shall wait for you to lock me up."

"My God, just when I think you've reached the highest level of madness, you surprise me with another level."

"If knowing that no other man would care for you the way I would is madness, then I welcome it."

"Oh? And in what way will you care for me?"

"With utter devotion," Will said, every word announced firm and clear. "After all, I have to *earn* my position as a real husband."

"Ah, right. I do recall saying something to that effect. Well," she gave a small cough behind her hand. "You should do as you see fit."

"Then are you prepared for me to woo you?" Will asked. She looked so unsettled by the prospect that he couldn't help but want to tease her.

She snorted. "What do I have to be prepared for? You are the one doing the wooing."

"Prepared for"—he brushed a tendril of hair between his fingers—"me. And all your impressions of me to be overturned."

"Well," she danced away from his touch, her cheeks infusing with more pink. "I do admire your confidence."

"Would you like to attend the Stewart ball?"

Her eyes rounded. "With you?"

"Once you bathe, yes."

Her mouth opened and closed, before she directed a glare his way. "What a rude thing to say!"

Will stopped teasing her. It was only fun if they both enjoyed it. "Who else if not me?"

"I just mean, no one knows about our marriage."

"It's still some days away, but it's a good place to make our first appearance. Unless there is another ball you wish to attend?"

"No, no, the Stewarts' event is fine." She yawned. "You also had gin last night. Why do you look so good when I look all rumpled?"

"I'll have the servants prepare a bath for you." His gaze lowered to her pale, almost blue, feet. "You should warm up before you catch a chill."

She nodded. "I shall appreciate it."

"And you look lovely, Harriet, rumpled and all."

She blinked at him, her eyes all but accusing: *Are you blind?* "I shall leave you to your business," she said retreating from the room with a wave of her hand, all but dashing off the moment she reached the door.

Will shook his head, chuckling.

He had never known an urge this acute—the urge to dash after her and hug her into his arms.

Before he had met Harriet, he always watched from a distance with what he understood to be a sense of yearning. Since he had firmly, unashamedly stepped into her world the day he signed the betrothal agreement, everything in his life had changed. He had come face to face with a fiery woman who did not back down, followed her own mind, and gave him a piece of it without preamble.

Will loved it.

No all he had to do was show her how much.

Chapter Eleven

Harriet nibbled on a slice of lemon cake as she stared at Lady Leonora and Lady Selena chatting across from her. Once Leeds had left that morning, she quickly followed suit. She'd been cooped up in that house for days and needed to get out for a while. Every room in their house was enveloped in the scent of that man.

Not that his scent was a *problem* problem.

But Harriet found that she quite *liked* the way he smelled, and *that* was a problem. She shouldn't be liking anything about her husband. Not his scent. Not his handsome face. Not those heated eyes that seem to look straight into her soul. Not this soon.

Woo her, he had said.

So her husband wanted to woo her. She didn't know what to make of that, only that it would serve as a distraction to her own goal. Just like his scent. And the flowers that he sent her every day along with a different note in each.

You looked lovely this morning, *love*. Your smile is like sunshine, *love*. When are you going to lock me away, *love*?

Love! Love! Love!

Her cheeks warmed at the recollection of all those adorable little notes. So unlike the man himself.

One thing she had come to learn of her Leeds—he was a dangerous man. Dangerously handsome. Dangerously charming.

When he wanted to be. And dangerously tempting.

Gah! She shouldn't have been so tempted, but she was. Even after she'd had an unwelcome and embarrassing surge of drunken memories.

Asking him to kiss her? Could the earth swallow her whole?

"How is married life so far?" Leonora suddenly asked, sipping from her teacup.

Harriet shrugged. "So-so." Liar. But how could she describe the whirlwind of emotions brought on by her husband?

Selena placed her cup and saucer on the table. "Leonora said that your father arranged a union between you and Leeds?"

Harriet nodded.

"A marriage of convenience, isn't that how you put it?" Leonora teased. "How did your husband take the news that he was merely convenient?"

Selena tilted her head to the side. "Yes, do tell."

"He took it . . ." How to put it? "Like a breeze."

Leonora laughed. "So well? See, I told you he was *dreamlike.*"

"If he is so dreamlike, why didn't you marry him?"

"Because he didn't ask for *my* hand."

Harriet rolled her eyes heavenward.

"Leonora said there were wagers involved," Selena said.

"I'm not sure," Harriet replied. "Leeds mentioned wagers when we first met. Have you heard any rumors circling the gossipmongers?"

"Why don't you just ask him?" Leonora reached for a cake. "I'm sure he would tell you if you do."

"I'm not that curious about them. If they even exist."

"You suspect he lied?" Selena asked, curious.

"At first I was suspicious. But I don't think he would lie to me." Since the start, he had been direct in his approach. Quite honestly, she hadn't thought to ask him again about the wagers. After his declaration to woo her, every time he looked at her his gaze was full of flames, she'd recall her drunken conversation, and she either fled or became too flustered to think about anything else.

"No, I haven't heard anything, but I shall keep my ears open. I could ask my brother if you would like?"

Harriet shook her head. "No need." She still didn't care about the wagers. What could there be to get excited about? Where there were fortunes to be made, there would surely be wagers to follow.

"Wait," Leonora said. "You haven't told us *how* you informed your husband that he entered a marriage of convenience."

Harriet shrugged. "I locked him out of my chamber." Well, she'd not wholly succeeded, but that was not the point. The message had been conveyed. And Leeds had respected her decision. *Ah, drat.* She can't think about that night without recalling everything else. It seemed like a dream almost. Not only that, but the memory seemed to overlap with a more distant one, one she couldn't quite grasp yet.

Leonora's mouth dropped open and her teacup tilted. "So you didn't actually inform him?"

"I believe she informed him with her actions." Selena grinned. "Well done."

"I'm surprised," Leonora murmured, dabbing at her dress where droplets of tea had spilled in her surprise. "Given that man's commitment to securing you, I hardly believed he'd leave you such a way out."

"Leeds, he . . . he can be as unmovable as a mountain, but he has his moments." More than she anticipated.

"Have you been peeling some of those layers back?" Leonora asked.

Selena arched an intrigued brow.

"Naturally. My plans haven't changed." Though, why did it feel like her husband was the one doing the peeling?

Leonora narrowed her eyes. "Then why do I get the impression that you are preoccupied? Do not tell me Leeds has swayed you before you could discover any of his true motives." Her smile turned bemused. "I stand by my words. *Dreamlike.*"

"Of course not!" Was it so easy to see? *Not the sway part.* She had not been swayed. But the preoccupied part? That much was true. "I've been chipping away at his exterior."

Selena smiled behind her teacup.

"And stop calling my husband *dreamlike.*"

Leonora burst out in laughter. "Very well, I shall stop if it bothers you so much."

"I am *not* bothered."

Leonora nodded with a knowing smile, and Harriet leveled a glare at her.

Selena set down her cup. "Ladies, ladies. How about we do away with the tea and enjoy a glass of sherry?"

"We'll need more than one glass," Leonora said with a wink.

Harriet balked at the thought of drinking. She glanced at the clock. "It's noon."

Leonora motioned for a footman to retrieve sherry. "When has that ever stopped us?"

"Leeds has already accused me of being a drunk."

Leonora sputtered tea all over the table. "He did *what?*"

"Well, not in so many words, but I'm sure he alluded to it." She couldn't remember his exact words. But he also didn't care that she enjoyed a glass here or there, so he must not care all that much. But then why would he? He would probably love the chance to tease her again!

"What did you do for him to make such a remark?" Selena asked.

Harriet shrugged, deciding to admit this much. "I got drunk on our wedding night after I barred him from his own chamber. Normal wife stuff."

Selena burst out laughing. "Remind me to come get some helpful hints from you if my brother ever arranges a marriage for me."

Leonora chuckled. "Me too."

"Your situations will be different from mine, I'm sure."

"You're right," Selena said. "My brother would never arrange a marriage for me. He treasures his life too much."

"I wish I could have a brother such as that," Harriet murmured with a smile. Her half-brother was still a boy, and they weren't close at all.

"Trust me, he is the worst." The footman came with the sherry and three glasses. Selena filled each one to the brim.

"Are you attending the Stewart ball later this week?" Leonora accepted her glass.

As did Harriet. She took a small sip. Not that bad. "Yes, Leeds and I shall be attending."

"Splendid!" Leonora exclaimed. "It shall be the first time you attend a ball as a married woman. The *ton* was quite shocked when the news was announced in the papers this morning. I daresay all eyes will be on you."

"Perhaps I should claim a headache then." There was a reason she'd been a wallflower.

"No! You must go! You must show all the people you are still Harriet Hillstow, a force to be reckoned with."

Harriet cast a doubtful glance at her friend. All she could hear was: *Everyone is going to look at you like they might look at a bug under glass.*

She loathed that the most.

However, she was not the sort to hide away, headache suggestion notwithstanding. Plus, the event would get her out of the house again. Declining to attend would mean another night alone with him. While the house was big, there seemed to be no hiding from him.

Leeds was everywhere.

Which was to be expected. Except something felt *different* than before. She could barely catch a breath, her awareness of him had become so strong, which caused her wits to scatter everywhere. This man was playing havoc with her mind. She needed to find a way to turn the tables.

"And you know," Leonora continued after a pause, "balls are the perfect opportunity to dazzle your husband with your beauty and uncover all his secrets in his dazed state."

Dear Lord.

Harriet didn't know about dazzle, but she could find a way to use the Stewart ball to turn the tables a bit, could she not?

Would Leeds ask her to dance? To take a stroll in the garden beneath the stars?

Stop it, Harriet. That's not the focus here!

The spot between Harriet's shoulder blades flared with a hundred tingles that raced up to the nape of her neck. Her brows furrowed. She only ever felt the sensation when *that* man's eyes were on her.

Her husband.

Harriet's frown deepened.

The next moment, a footman appeared at the door. "The Marquess of Leeds is here, my lady."

Harriet's eyes widened.

Leeds was here?

Her shocked gaze sprung to Leonora, whose eyes also seemed to say, *your husband is here?*

Leeds suddenly loomed behind the footman, giving everyone a start. His eyes settled on Harriet, and she saw his features visibly relax. Had he been worried she had run away?

"Lady Leonora, Lady Selena," he greeted. "My apologies for interrupting your tea."

Leonora waved his apology aside. "Would you care to join us, my lord?"

He gave a stiff nod and strode over to take a seat next to Harriet, who glanced at him with a small frown. The moment he settled in beside her, the familiar scent of tobacco and leather assailed her senses.

Lawd, why did the man have to smell so good? Could he not have smelled like goats and farm animals? And why did he search her out? She was about to ask when his low voice filled the room.

"I wanted to take you for a drive through Hyde Park in the phaeton," he glanced toward the window, and the darkening clouds gathering there, "but the weather is turning quicker than I hoped."

He wanted to take her for a drive?

Why did that sound so familiar? Ah yes. The day he came calling with a special license. Was this another excuse or was he in earnest? Harriet stared at him. How to make sense of him? He looked stiff, uncomfortable, and a shade of red coated his jawline that disappeared beneath his cravat. Yet here he was, apparently in earnest about staying at her side.

Harriet felt her heart thawing.

Good or bad?

Harriet couldn't tell.

WHAT THE HELL is wrong with to me?

Will couldn't remember the last time he'd been so frantic in his life. He sighed and tossed a brandy down this throat. He had arrived home and had been promptly informed his wife had gone out to call on friends.

To be fair, this was no *unordinary* thing. Women gallivanted about town all the time. And of course, Harriet could visit friends and go shopping as much as she pleased. However, the moment the butler informed him that she had left, ice cold shards pierced his chest. He'd been roughly tossed back to the moment he'd stepped into her house and discovered she'd taken flight.

His calm had evaporated a breath of air, and he exploded into action. He would not feel at ease until he found his wife—which he did. Using an extremely thin pretext, though one he had planned to fulfill if the weather hadn't turned.

And much to his astonishment, she had neither scolded him nor questioned him. She had accepted his arrival with ease.

Will took another swallow of his drink.

What did that even mean?

"Looking to drink away your woes?" Calstone dropped into a

chair across from him.

"Something to that effect."

"Your wife serving up trouble for dinner? Is that why you're in a club and not at home?"

Will shook his head. "I made an ass of myself today."

"Oh, and that's a problem? I thought you would have become used to the feeling by now."

"To the devil with you. The problem is, I'll do it all again."

"I take it the lovely Lady Harriet is involved?"

Will nodded. "Is it wrong of me to want to keep her to myself?"

"Ah, newly wedded bliss. I'll admit, it's rather unfashionable to want to occupy all of your wife's time. Unless it's a love match, which is even *more* unfashionable, and you know me, I'm nothing if not fashionable."

"You are full of shite, that's what you are."

"To answer your question, I don't think it's wrong. Fashionable or not, it's natural to want to be close to the person you fancy." Calstone glanced at a few men laughing loudly several tables away. "Especially if there's mischief afoot." He turned back to Will. "Did you hear the betting book has been stolen?"

Will gave a nod. "Who hasn't?"

"You're not worried?"

"Should I be?" He had already plucked Harriet from the marriage mart. Also, he had told her about the wagers, though she hadn't reacted to it the way he thought she might have. If she didn't care, then Will wouldn't care either. "I've more pressing matters to address anyway."

"Such as?"

"My wife."

Calstone chuckled. "Ah, yes, your obsession does seem to run deep. Do tell."

Will explained the proceedings of the day, his reactions and fears, finally freeing his chest of its pressure.

"And that opinionated little thing said *nothing*?"

"Don't call my wife a little thing."

"Very well, very well," Calstone said lifting his hands in surrender. "Are you perhaps suffering from a case of separation distress? I've heard it often happens with mothers and their babies."

"Balderdash."

He did not suffer from separation distress or whatever Calstone called it. And he certainly wasn't going to lay his soul down on a table in White's for his friend to dissect.

"Come now, I'm merely trying to cheer you up."

"How about leaving?"

"But then I can't tell you about Mortimer."

"The duke? What about him?"

"I heard he is on the hunt for the betting book, along with some other sots, but he's been officially tasked by White's."

"What does that have to do with me?"

"You really haven't been paying attention to what is happening here."

"Like I said, I have more pressing matters."

"Yes, yes, your wife. Why don't you just confess your love to the woman already? It's not as though she will chase you away with a pitchfork."

Don't be so sure about that. "She's not ready."

Calstone crossed one leg over the other and tapped the table. "She's not ready or you are not ready?"

"Both, I suppose."

His friend leaned forward in his chair. "Let me ask you, when *will* you be ready?"

Will considered the question. "When she no longer suspects my every step to be somehow a move against her." Though, in truth, he may have made some progress on that front today, in spite of himself.

"Has the dowry been transferred?"

Will nodded. "Into an account under her name."

"Have you informed *her* of that?"

"No."

"Why ever not?"

Will arched a brow. "By law, even though her name is on the account, it's still mine."

"Dear Christ, man. Have you truly lost your intelligence since you met that girl? It's still a gesture of intention."

Will paused. Then shook his head. "It's a miniscule one."

"So what if it is? She needs to understand your intentions, doesn't she? Why don't you help her out a bit? I'm sure a part of her believes you married for her dowry—it's a large one, after all. So convince her you have no need of it and no intention of touching it."

"She would just suspect it a scheme of some sort."

"Perhaps at first. But she won't think that forever. What else have you been doing?"

"Sending her flowers."

"Ah,'" his friend said impressed. "Good for you. What else?"

"Notes with the flowers."

Calstone pressed a hand over his heart. "Even a note? You have come far, old chap. What do you say in the notes? Are they snippets of poetry? You wouldn't write your own, so from which poet did you borrow?"

"No poetry."

Calstone's face fell. "No poetry? Please don't tell me you just wrote 'Sincerely Yours, Leeds.'"

"Is there something wrong with that?"

Calstone gave him a weary look.

"I wrote more than that, all right. She looks lovely, and that sort of thing." The first note had been the hardest. He hadn't known what to write. So he just decided to write what came to mind. Little messages from his heart.

"Well, I suppose that's already more than one can usually ask from you. I'm sure you are melting your wife's heart as we speak."

"I can't tell if you are being sarcastic or not."

"Upon my honor," Calstone's hand returned to his chest, "I am not."

Will scoffed. "Either way, it's too soon to tell." But she had been blushing a bit more often recently.

"Have you seduced your lovely wife yet?"

Will shot his friend a hot look. "I'm not answering that."

"No need, I can guess the answer. Perhaps it's time to show her what she might be missing, heh?"

"Wipe that smile from your face."

Calstone laughed. "It wouldn't hurt, would it? Courtship is a seduction of sorts, too, you know."

"I shall take your advice into consideration."

"Please do." Calstone suddenly cursed. "Don't look now, but a rat is on his way.

Will spotted Cromby and clenched his jaw.

"Leeds, old fellow! There you are!" Cromby exclaimed as he neared them. "I heard you married one of the heiresses! Good for you, good for you! Too bad you never set a wager in the book or else your coffers would be overflowing now."

"What an arse," Calstone muttered beneath his breath.

Will scowled, deeply, sharing his friend's sentiments. The only thing he could see when he looked at Cromby's face was a man who had once taken advantage of his wife and had tried to lay his filthy hands on her.

Will gripped his glass tightly before he tossed back the remaining liquor and rose to his feet. "Don't speak of my wife."

Cromby started, then gave an awkward laugh. "Can I not congratulate a friend?"

"We are not friends."

Cromby frowned. "What do you mean? We've always been friends, old fellow."

"We have never been friends."

Calstone leaped to his feet as well. "Leeds here is having an off day. Let's give the man some space."

Will sent a glare his friend's way, which Calstone returned

with a warning look of his own, motioning to people flicking glances their way.

"Of course," Cromby said. "We all have such days."

Will reigned in his temper. Calstone was right—it did no good to cause a scene in White's. He needed to be smart about the entire affair.

"I suppose even a mouse can give a man trouble. Of course, with her dowry—"

"Cromby," Will bit out. "I told you not to speak of my wife."

The man gave another awkward laugh. "I didn't mean anything by it. No need to get into a tiff because of a woman, is there?"

Will saw red.

He lifted his fist to remove the man's jaw, but was promptly stopped by Calstone, who kept a pleasant smile plastered on his face while he quickly moved to stand in what would have been the arc of Will's punch.

"Now is not the time," Calstone said in a lowered voice over his shoulder. "We'll handle this another way. A more permanent way."

Will clenched his jaw tighter but allowed the tension to roll off his shoulders. Damn it. Calstone was right. Again. No need to sully his fists on dirt when there were other ways to sweep it out the door. Cromby was a notable ass, but he had a large following of reprobates. Better to deal with him with a bit of caution. The last thing Will wanted was for any repercussion or reprisal to reach Harriet.

"Let's go," Will growled and strode away. There were better things do anyway. Like uncovering more ways to make his wife flush bright pink.

Chapter Twelve

HARRIET HAD A secret.
A big secret.

A big, big, big secret.

The biggest secret she'd ever had. She was practically burning up with the secret. This morning, two days after her tea with Leonora and Selena, she had received an invitation to attend tea with Lady Ophelia Thornton. And she hadn't been the only lady invited. What had followed her arrival there was rather shocking.

Leeds hadn't lied.

There really was a list of heiresses with her name on it. And there were tons and tons of wagers about those heiresses—who would marry them, how quickly they'd be married, how much money they had. However, that wasn't even the most shocking part.

Lady Ophelia had sneaked into White's and stolen the betting book! It had been on full display at the ladies' tea.

Quite frankly, Harriet was in awe of Lady Ophelia. What woman dared to sneak into a gentleman's club and steal their property with no one the wiser?

Remarkable.

The ladies had all been in uproar, of course. And while Harriet hadn't been happy, either, she couldn't fully commit her mind to the subject.

And whose fault was that?

As if announced, the connecting door to her chamber opened and the very culprit strode in wearing nothing but a dressing gown.

What on earth was he up to now?

At first, it started with flowers and notes. Those hadn't stopped. They arrived every day like clockwork. It was only in the recent days, however—after she invited him for a nightcap, which turned into a sort of routine now—that her husband had been driving her hot, chaotic heating spells by flaunting his *body*. A few buttons undone here, sleeves rolled up there. But this was a first.

To make matters even warmer, he constantly occupied her thoughts. Night and day he commandeered them. Not even her dreams were spared!

And the sight of him tonight was no different. Harriet's heart pounded in her chest so hard she could hear the beat, but she still managed to narrow her eyes on the man and demanded, "Is this how you show up to have a drink?"

He glanced down at his attire. "Is there something wrong with my attire? You're in your dressing gown as well."

"I'm still wearing a night rail."

"Shall I go change?"

"No need," she handed him a glass of gin, compliments of a new bottle Rohan had given her last week. "The contraband is almost gone."

He nodded and took his spot on a leather armchair while she curled up on another one—two recent additions after their nightcaps started. Her gaze trailed over him. How many times would she need to stare at him before he became less attractive?

"How is the duke doing? I heard his chatter in the halls earlier today."

"Annoying as ever."

Harriet smiled. "He is like a brother to you. Of course he is annoying."

"What of your brother? Do you get along?"

Harriet shook her head. "He is too young and busy with his studies."

Leeds nodded but didn't probe any further. "You can have Calstone."

Harriet laughed. "Lord no, you keep him." She took a sip of gin. "You know, you can drink something else. I know you don't like this stuff."

He shrugged. "Helping you finish it is better than you finishing it alone."

"Sound reasoning."

"You truly like the taste?"

Harriet rolled a sip on her tongue. "It's better to say I've gotten used to the taste."

"Cognac tastes better."

"I shall be sure to try it after this bottle is done." They settled into a comfortable silence, sipping their drinks.

"My mother used to enjoy nightcaps such as these when she was still alive."

"With your father?"

Harriet shook her head. "No, alone. Sometimes I'd sneak in her room to keep her company before she chased me away." Much like she did with Leeds every night.

"As long as I'm here, love, you will always have someone to accompany you for a nightcap."

Another companionable silence lengthened.

She should ask him.

Why did you marry me? Why the rush? Why the fiery determination? Because of those wagers? Leeds, being a member of White's, would have heard about the betting book, right? Could she risk asking, risk inadvertently betraying the other women's confidence? But still, those wagers had apparently been enough reason for her father to marry her off, but surely they could not account for Leeds going so far as to jump into the Thames after her. Could they?

In the end, she didn't ask. She didn't want to disturb the harmony of these moments, which were becoming ones she looked forward to. What if she didn't like the answer?

No, there would be other opportunities. For now there were still other, less delicate layers she could peel away.

"You should return to your room if you are finished."

"But I like yours better." He smiled. "You are in it."

Lawd. There he went again, melting her bones.

Harriet observed him from beneath her lashes, her cheeks, neck, and ears burning. He wouldn't push. He'd leave if she kicked him out. But . . . she didn't really want to. "Save these words for your little notes, will you?"

He chuckled, and then fell into a moment of silence before he said, "Your dowry was transferred to an account in your name."

Startled, she asked, "What?"

"From a legal standpoint, I know the gesture doesn't mean much. But it's yours." A pause. "I've no intention of ever touching it."

Harriet didn't know how to respond to that. In the end, she could only ask, "When did you do this?"

"The day after we wed. I'll have my solicitor send you the details."

"Why didn't you tell me this from the start?" He probably hadn't thought it important enough to mention.

"I didn't think it would matter."

Just as she thought. "Well, it matters," Harriet said. Even though, by right, it all still belonged to him, it mattered. "What made you tell me?"

He dragged a hand through his hair, drawing her attention to the lines of his face. Hard lines. But handsome. "I was reminded that the things I might take for granted are not necessarily the things others take for granted."

Others—meaning her.

"Let me guess, a certain duke has something to do with this revelation?"

The lips curved upward, and Harriet couldn't help but notice the tempting arch. Those lips that had kissed her once, and many more times in her dreams, in each instance stealing a bit more of her breath than the last. She blinked away the memories and dreams that surfaced in her head. This was not the time to notice her husband's lips! Lord, his lips alone might just be the biggest catastrophe of her lifetime.

But he hadn't married her for her dowry.

"How did you guess?" he asked.

Her impression of the duke raised just a bit. "He is oddly wise for a full-grown infant."

The soft sound of a chuckle teased her ears. "A fitting description."

"In any case," Harriet said, "thank you."

He inclined his head.

While they were on the topic, she might as well question him about one rumor that she'd read about him once. "Do you gamble?"

A brow shot up. "Gamble?"

Harriet almost laughed. The man sounded as if he'd just heard the most foreign word! "You know . . ." The urge to tease him claimed her. "That thing men do that costs them their entire fortunes."

"I don't gamble."

"Then, do you know about the rumors of you being a renowned gambler?"

He scowled. "I don't read the gossip rags."

"Well, according to them, you spend most of your days in gambling dens."

"And you believe that drivel?"

"Smoke usually accompanies a fire." What else could she say?

"Have I been in a gambling den? Yes. Calstone dragged me to one once. He gambled, not me." Those burning eyes bore into hers. "I don't gamble, love. I shall put that in a note for you tomorrow."

She laughed at his disgruntled expression. "No need, I believe you." Yet another rumor that seemed to be untrue. Also, if Leeds truly were a notorious gambler, chances were he would not be giving her dowry back to her.

"I'll still put it in a note. Then it will be on paper in my handwriting."

"You are quite a mystifying man," Harriet murmured.

"I am an open book, love." He paused for a bit, seemingly searching for the right words. "At least I am to you. When you are ready, all you need to do is read through the pages."

Harriet smiled. "That might be the silliest"—*but most endearing*—"thing anyone has ever said to me.

"Even Graves?"

"Rohan? Mostly what comes out of his mouth is vexing." She tugged at her dressing gown. "We are just friends, you know. Like Calstone is to you."

"And still I find myself rather envious."

Harriet searched his gaze. "Why?"

"Graves got to meet you while you were a young girl. He gets a part of you that no one else can hope to receive."

"There are more parts," Harriet said softly. "One's heart isn't just made of one compartment."

"Then there is hope."

Leeds couldn't want her heart, could he? No. Surely not. The mere thought seemed almost preposterous.

But the flowers . . . and the notes . . .

Harriet didn't quite know what to make of his words, but they did leave a trail of stuttered beats in her pulse.

Will set his glass down on the table and rose. "I shall take my leave then."

Had their drink finished so soon?

"Wait." She rose as well, placing her empty glass next to his.

"Is there something else?"

Yes. No.

Yes.

"You've come all this way dressed like that just to leave?"

He stared at her blankly.

"Well?"

"What are you saying, love?" he asked gruffly. "I don't want to misunderstand."

"I'm saying you can sleep next to me, beneath your own bedding, of course."

His glance turned skeptical. "Are you foxed?"

"From a spot of gin? No. Do I look foxed?" Foxed, no. Crazy . . . possibly.

"No, you look lovely as always."

She smiled at him.

"Then . . . I shall go get my bedding." He disappeared in a flash.

Lord Almighty. *What did I just do?* Her gaze turned to the bed. Big. Enough space for both of them.

No problem . . .

WILL OPENED HIS eyes to the vision of his wife's sweet face. His gaze flickered over her long lashes. They were like feathery fans resting against her cheeks, casting delicate shadows on her pale skin. The lines of defiance that often filled her features were smoothed away in sleep, leaving behind an expression of innocence.

A rush of warmth and contentment washed over him as he took in her serene expression—one he hadn't seen since they'd become betrothed.

Will traced the curve of her jawline with his fingertips, marveling at the softness beneath his touch.

Lord, he wanted to kiss her.

Her lips, slightly parted in slumber, held the promise of sweet whispered words and tempting kisses. The rosy hue of her cheeks hinted at the dreams that played in her mind, perhaps filled, if he was arrogant enough to believe it, with him.

Perhaps I can become a poet after all.

As always, the beauty that radiated from her entranced him, especially in the simplicity of waking up beside her.

A sense of awe settled within him.

This woman, his wife, held his heart in the palm of her hand. She was not even aware of her power. Though Will was sure she, with her sharp wit, would soon realize he was wrapped around her every word.

Her presence in his house, his life, had brought light that had been missing for years. Even if she never gave up her heart, there was simply nothing better than spending a day by her side. This woman completed him in ways he had never thought possible.

Will brushed a strand of hair behind her ear, reveling in the soft touch against his fingertips. He drank in the sight of her, committing it to memory. Given her unpredictability, he was not guaranteed a spot beside her again tonight. He found it rather remarkable that she had allowed him to stay at all. This could be considered a giant leap in the right direction.

One's heart isn't made of one compartment.

Ah, Christ.

Sweeter words could not have been said to him in that moment.

When it came to Harriet, Will was a selfish man. He wanted to occupy every chamber of her heart. But he would settle for claiming the territory of at least ninety percent. When he said he didn't gamble, he hadn't lied. He didn't gamble with money. He respected his blunt too much to lose it on a bad hand or the roll of a dice. But he did gamble in a way. And the stakes were much higher than any monetary fortune.

He had taken a gamble when approaching her father and asking for her hand. And now he was gambling that he could win her heart.

Will slipped from the sheets, careful not to disturb his wife, and padded over to the connecting doors. His gaze flicked over her baubles as he passed her dressing table, landing on a plain silver hand mirror. Before he knew what he was doing, Will stopped and reached out to clasp the looking glass and settled onto the small stool.

He lifted the mirror to his face.

Will stared at his reflection, his eyes flicking over his somber countenance weathered with lines of age and years of practiced restraint. There was nothing handsome about his face, at least not to his eye.

His reflection stared back at him, unmoving and aloof.

Will summoned a smile.

Dear God.

Was that how he looked when he smiled? Had he always looked so damn uncomfortable?

He curved his lips a bit more, but the attempt felt forced, lacking the warmth that should accompany a smile. He tried again, focusing on the delicate muscles around his mouth, the subtle movements that would transform his visage from something cold to something warm.

This look was even worse than before.

What a disaster.

He lifted his chin and mouthed, *you look lovely, Lady Harriet.* How many times had he practiced that particular line in the mirror? Too many to count. Come to think of it, he'd not been struggling in his conversations as much lately as he had in the beginning. They flowed more easily now.

Also, the line had changed, had it not?

You look lovely, love.

Will placed the mirror down with a grunt. He glared at the thing, before picking it up again.

He didn't need to practice lines anymore. But his smile . . .

The corners of his mouth twitched, but the smile remained distant, failing to reach his eyes. It was as if a veil of coldness clouded the true nature of his emotions, preventing them from realizing their full potential.

He flashed a row of white teeth.

Bloody hell.

This was even worse. *The* worst. He should never, ever, show his teeth when he smiled. Such an unnatural expression . . .

What the hell am I doing?

Calstone, that blackguard. This was all his fault. Did he really look like he smelled something foul when he smiled? Did that even make a whit of sense?

He would probably never be able to rid this face of its solemnity and embrace a more carefree existence. But he wanted to try.

For her.

Will scrutinized his reflection, searching for the missing spark, the ease that Calstone enjoyed but seemed to elude him. He had never thought about how his face seemed to others—not until Calstone had pointed it out—even though he had always known he was seen as cold and indifferent at times.

Perhaps there was an art to smiling. Like boxing. And if one practiced enough hours a week, one could master the intricacies. Like he had done with his stammer. He thought of Harriet, the ease with which she laughed. Her smile always came naturally and was truly a thing of beauty.

Will wanted to smile like that.

Surely he could conquer a smile?

If you can conquer your stutter, you can conquer your smile.

With a renewed determination, his wife's beautiful face in his mind, Will straightened his posture and looked into the depths of his own eyes. He thought of every one of her smiles he'd caught, even the ones that were rife with challenge. The way she tilted her head back, the way she swayed as she walked, the way her eyes flashed with anger when he crossed a line. . .

Slowly, his lips curved upward, a smile emerging from the depths of his being. He studied every angle of his reflection, the solemn lines fading, replaced by a flicker of affection. Was this what was called smiling from the eyes?

Better.

His face, however, still looked as though he was about to join a circus act. Stiff. Unnatural. Almost foolish.

But at least there were no teeth.

"What are you doing?" An amused voice came from behind him. "Why are you smiling into my mirror like that?"

Will slapped the mirror back onto the table. "Like what?"

"Like smiling is some foreign form of facial movement."

Ah, Christ. There truly was no hope for him.

Will smiled. Probably. "It's not."

She suddenly laughed, and Will thought that he would smile every day for her, regardless of how odd it might look, if it meant he'd be met by that beautiful sound.

"Very well, I am convinced," she said, sitting up. "You are most entertaining in the morning."

"Then you should allow me to stay here tonight as well. I can entertain you every morning."

"I've never heard a more obvious hint."

"Should I entertain you some more?"

She adjusted her position to sit cross legged as she stared at him. "You can answer a question for me."

"Of course."

"Why *did* you marry me?"

Will turned to fully face her. "I already told you."

"Yes, yes, I'm beautiful, intelligent, and unattached. I believe that was the exact order."

Will paused. "You remember even that."

"How can I forget?" She gave him a dry look. "No one has ever called me beautiful *and* intelligent in the same sentence. However, there are many women who are beautiful and intelligent. But you picked me."

"I shall tell you the truth then," Will said, almost coming up short when her eyes widened, and a glimmer of anticipation entered their depth. He nearly chuckled.

"You will?"

He nodded. "But not today."

Her face fell. "Why not?"

"I need a bit more time."

Two lines appeared between her brows. "For what?"

The corner of his lips twitched. "To woo you."

She fell back onto the bed. "How anticlimactic. Have you not been wooing me? I'm already your wife." She snuck a look at him. "I even let you into my bed."

Will rose to his feet. "But you still don't trust me—not as I would want you to. I'm not sure you'd believe what I would have to tell you."

She peeked at him from the corner of her eyes. "So you first wish to gain my trust? By *wooing*?"

Will nodded. "Is there a better way?"

"I wonder. Well then woo me faster, or I might lose my patience."

"And what happens then?"

"Who knows? I may start to sow misery and mayhem."

"You might as well."

She sat up. "Why?"

Will strode to the door. "When you are sowing misery and mayhem you'll be thinking about me." He shot her a heated look. "So scheme away, love."

"You insufferable oaf!"

Will escaped the chamber just as a pillow hit the door. He laughed. Today was going to be a great day.

Chapter Thirteen

"D O YOU WANT out of the marriage?" Rohan asked Harriet as they strolled through Bond Street.

"The fact that you are asking me that means you have a way, I assume?"

"I always have a way."

Harriet chuckled. She didn't doubt that, but she also believed her husband might be just as brutal in his methods as Rohan, if not more so.

"Don't stay such things out loud—you never know who might be listening." And she didn't want to see these two men— each powerful in their own right—go for each other's throats because of her. "I don't want out."

"Are you happy then?"

"Well, I'm not unhappy. Besides, Leeds lived up to the prom- ise I made my mother. He fought to be with me, and he's not a bad man."

Rohan grunted. "I'll reserve judgment, then."

"As long as you try."

"I still can't believe you nearly set off for Charleston. You could have met with a dangerous situation, darling."

"I've already been scolded, thank you very much," Harriet said. "I just wish I could unwrap all of his layers already." She'd been rather miffed this morning at his arch exit from her chamber, until she received a bouquet of flowers with a note that read: *I don't gamble, love.*

How many bones did she have left to melt?

"Just like a woman. Always wanting to dig up a man's soul."

"Oh, pish. That is such a male thing to say." She cast him a sidelong glance. "I've always wanted true partnership in a marriage. It suddenly feels as though it might be possible. Is that greedy of me?"

"Most greedy, indeed, darling," he drawled with a smile, and Harriet found herself smiling back.

"He is wooing me, you know."

"Ah, and is it working?"

Yes. Each flower, each little note, pulled at the strings of her heart. And this morning—Harriet suddenly laughed. Lord, oh, Lord, this morning had been . . . she couldn't even put into words what *that* had been.

"What are you laughing about?" Rohan asked, and Harriet realized with a start that she had completely lost the thread of their conversation.

"I caught Leeds practicing his smile in the mirror this morning," she admitted.

Rohan blinked at her. "I truly don't know how to respond to that."

Harriet's lips quirked. "No need."

"Well, that answers my question then. His wooing is obviously working, even if it is a bit unorthodox. Who practices smiling in the mirror?"

Her gaze trailed over all the people roaming about the street. "People who don't often smile." She glanced back at Rohan. "Has Chester settled in?"

"He has," Rohan said. "I also saw your father yesterday. He resembled a thundercloud. Are you still not speaking?"

She shook her head.

"You accepted Leeds but did not forgive your father?"

"Leeds at least asked for my hand. And assumed reasonably

that my father would have told me to expect it. What my father did . . ."

"I don't know much about fathers—God knows mine was never present—but I suspect your father did what he thought best, no matter how skewed. He didn't make that poor of a choice for you, did he?"

Harriet peered into a passing shop. "Let's change the subject." She wasn't ready to delve further into the topic of her father.

"Very well. Your husband seems to care for you, if that is any consolation against strained relationships. If it's not, there is always his wealth. And he has no gambling debt or any skeletons that I could dig up."

Harriet shot her friend a surprised look. "You investigated him?"

"Of course." He patted her head, and Harriet swatted his hand away. He laughed. "While I won't interfere with your decisions, I at least want to make sure you are cared for."

"Well, thank you, but I already asked him about the gambling rumors. Those gossip rags are the worst."

"When have you ever paid attention to the gossip rags?" Rohan asked. "They say you are a mouse."

That again.

"You have a point," Harriet murmured. "In fact, he allocated my dowry into an account for me to use as I wish."

"An admirable gesture."

"So I thought as well."

Rohan nodded. "Your husband has no obvious vices. His closest friend is the Duke of Calstone, and his favorite pastime is boxing."

Boxing? No wonder his arms felt so strong. "So not a speck of dirt."

"If there are any specks, I have yet to find them."

"Well, that's that then." Harriet sighed. "No need to keep digging. All I need now is the reason why he married me."

"You still believe he has one he hasn't told you?"

"Oh, I know he hasn't told me all, since I asked him plainly and he said I'd have to wait for his answer."

Rohan laughed. "Leeds seems to be quite the interesting man."

Harriet thought of Leeds's cramped smile this morning and almost wanted to laugh again. Ah, yes. That must have been the funniest sight she had ever witnessed. The image was one that she could draw upon whenever her mood turned sour.

As her husband slowly revealed more of himself to her, she questioned more and more the origin of his motive. Could it really be as nefarious as she had at first believed, or could she have been wrong? Could it be something else entirely?

Perhaps Leonora had a point. Perhaps she should use the Stewart ball to dazzle Leeds and draw out the answer she wanted. Curiosity was a loathsome thing. As was waiting to discover all of his secrets.

She sighed.

It wasn't like she wanted to harp on the subject, but the man had turned her world upside down. She wouldn't be content until she was sure she knew the full reason why.

"It has to be said," Rohan murmured, "he's done you quite the favor in one way. If not for him, these days you would be spending all your time fending off the tricks and traps of fortune hunters."

Harriet sent him a hot look. "Are you saying he was in the market for a wife, and I was easy pickings because of those wagers?"

"That is not what I said . . ."

"Implying something is the same as saying it."

Rohan lifted his hands in surrender. "I'm merely saying he did you a favor, and whatever answer you might be looking for, be prepared. You might not like it."

"Whether I like it or not, I still want to know!"

And if Leeds had married her because of the wagers . . . because she had been easy to pluck because of them . . .

Harriet's heart clenched.

He had said from the start that he and her father were only trying to protect her. But why would he *want* to protect her? Perhaps that was the better question to ask. Not why did he marry her, but why did he get involved at all? Why protect her? Why not seek a formal introduction before the wagers?

Lord, the man's mind was like the most complicated of riddles!

And on top of all these troubles and riddles, she still had *the secret* weighing on her. A secret that would finally be spilled at the Stewart ball. She had promised not to breathe a word of it, so she wouldn't, even though she was dying to confide in Rohan. And yes, even though she wanted to tell Leeds, too.

Gah! That way madness lies. Best to keep such tangled thoughts at bay.

Rohan pointed at a shop window. "Those are pretty ribbons. Do you want one?"

Harriet scoffed. "Who is skirting around the subject now?"

"My instinct for self-preservation is well-honed."

Harriet rolled her eyes but followed Rohan into the shop. She needed a pretty ribbon for the upcoming ball anyway, and this was a good distraction. "On the topic of marriage and easy pickings, when are you planning to take a wife?"

Rohan laughed. "Do you want me to share in the misery of being leg shackled?"

"Does it look like I'm miserable?" Harriet asked. "I'm coming to find marriage has its perks." Ah, see. She just had to think about that face this morning and her mood brightened.

"Oh? Like what?"

"Marry and discover for yourself."

"If I do find a woman who is willing to put up with me, you shall be the first to know."

"Please do," Harriet said, browsing a row of bright ribbons. "Oh, and the gin you gave me is almost finished."

"You want more?"

Harriet gave a thoughtful pause. "No need. I think I shall try Cognac next."

"Leeds swayed you over?"

"He promised it tasted better." She lifted a pretty pink ribbon. "What about this one?"

"What color dress are you wearing to the ball?"

"Blue."

"Light blue? Navy blue? Royal blue?

"The same color as a clear blue sky?" Harriet murmured, thinking of the dress she had prepared.

Rohan searched through the ribbons and pulled out a blue ribbon. "Like this?"

She looked over. "Yes! That one will do."

Rohan nodded, then said, "There is another reason why Leeds might have married you."

"Oh? Pray tell."

"He fancies you."

"Fancies me?" Harriet laughed, but she couldn't stop the butterflies from fluttering their wings in her belly. "I don't think so."

"Why don't you think so?"

"Men who get married in a rush don't fancy the women they marry. There is always another reason." A scenario suddenly occurred to Harriet, spurred forward by a remembered phrase. "Since he did not marry me for my dowry, perhaps he married me because he had no choice."

"Lord, do I even want to know what's going through that head of yours?"

"Inheritance!"

Rohan arched a brow.

"What if his father left a stipulation in his will that Leeds must marry before a certain age or else he will lose all of his unentailed inheritance?"

Rohan stared at her blankly. "You read too many romance novels."

"It does fit the situation though, does it not? It would also explain why he took the wagers as an opportunity to propose marriage."

"He still chose you over all the other heiresses."

"That's right." Harriet pursed her lips. "Perhaps in that regard I was the more convenient choice. All the other heiresses are pretty, strong, and outspoken."

"Instead of letting your imagination run wild, why can't you fathom that perhaps the man fancies you?"

"Because Leeds has no lack of prospects. He could have any woman he wants, yet he chose me. A wallflower."

"There is nothing wrong with you, Harriet."

She agreed. But . . . "I'm no diamond."

"There are more beautiful jewels on this planet than diamonds, darling. Perhaps Leeds saw what you fail to see."

"When did the two of you become such close friends for you to take his side?"

"Believe it or not, I'm on your side." His gaze turned thoughtful. "It's true that many women would have wed your marquess at the snap of his finger. But sometimes the most obvious answer is the true answer. Perhaps you are clinging to resistance because you are still clinging to old dreams and are scared to get hurt."

"Is that so wrong?"

"How the hell would I know?" Rohan asked. "Dreams, however, are not unyielding objects—they can reshape and are never lost. Just think about that."

Harriet snatched the ribbon from his fingers. "What books have *you* been reading lately to become so sentimental?"

Rohan chuckled. "Perhaps I have taken a liking to romances."

Harriet snorted. "Well stop. If I start believing your nonsense and thinking that my husband fancies me and you turn out to be wrong, I shall make you parade the streets of London in a gown as punishment."

"Threat received." He selected a few other ribbons. "Shall I purchase these for that day?"

"So you admit you are merely stabbing in the dark with your assumption?"

"Nothing is ever certain."

"Well, the theory of his inheritance is still plausible."

It certainly made more sense than the idea that Leeds might actually fancy her. Harriet scoffed. It was the most absurdly impossible notion that ever existed.

※》》》※《《《※

"JUST BECAUSE YOU are glaring at the door, doesn't mean your wife is going to walk through it sooner."

Will directed that same glare to Calstone. "We should have detoured to Bond Street."

"And hunt your wife down in public? Trust me, what we are doing is for your own good. You need to show her that you trust her. Even if you don't."

Will cursed. "I trust her."

"Yes, yes, it's Graves you don't trust. I understand."

"You don't sound all that convinced."

"I'm merely leaving you space for reflection."

Will grunted. How to explain? All his nerves were on edge. He did trust his wife. Strangely, he even trusted their friendship. What made him nervous was not this, but what was being said between them. What if Graves didn't approve of him? Just how much sway did he hold over his wife's opinion?

Get a grip on yourself, man.

Harriet was a woman with her own mind.

The only course of action was ignoring the pit in his stomach that threatened to become a cauldron of uneasiness and returning home at the urging of Calstone instead of peeking into all the shop windows on Bond Street.

Why?

Because, however uncomfortable he felt now in not knowing

just where she was, Will trusted their progress.

"You are courting your wife, remember?" Calstone said. "Since this has never been a conventional courtship, adjustments are to be expected."

"Such as?"

"Embracing your wife's friends."

"Is this not me embracing their friendship?"

"I'm giving myself and my skills of persuasion credit for this one and hoping you take it as a lesson from me for the future."

"Christ, the stuff you say sometimes."

"Am I *wrong*? Other than that, compliment your wife daily, and spend as much time with her as possible to build your connection."

"Spoken like a true married man."

Calstone shrugged. "It's much the same as keeping a mistress happy."

"You have a mistress now?"

"Lord, no. Demanding creatures, those. Learned all I needed from my father."

Will scoffed.

"In any event, I did some digging on Graves."

Now *that* intrigued him. "What did you uncover?"

"Nothing much. The man is a phantom."

"I suspect he is smuggling gin."

Calstone shrugged. "If he is, he is doing a damn good job. I've not heard a whisper of such dealings."

Will waved a hand. Harriet hadn't denied that her bottle was contraband, but it was pointless to debate matters they had no hope of dissecting. "What else?"

"He bought a house in Mayfair."

So the man was hadn't lied on that front.

"His family has been acquainted with the Hillstows for years, though they cannot be considered friends. Other than that, the family increases their fortune in the transport of goods and they own a veritable fleet of ships. He has two younger brothers managing those."

"Transport of goods . . ."

"If they are smuggling, they are very good at what they do."

"Connections?"

"Strong."

"Probably because he supplies them all with gin," Will muttered drily. The liquor wasn't bad, either.

"He's a powerful man to have on your side."

Will was gathering as much. Not that he kept company with people on the basis of what they could do for him. "Then you should befriend him."

"Me? What about you?" Calstone asked, looking mildly surprised.

"I already have you. That is more than enough for me."

"I'd reconsider if I were you."

"And why is that?"

"Can a woman and a man be *just* friends?"

Blackguard. "Why the hell would you toss out a question like that?"

"Though this be madness, yet there is method in it."

"Just say you want me to befriend the man for my wife's sake. Christ."

Calstone laughed. "But this is much more fun."

"I'll be sure to remember this fun when you find a woman you adore beyond reason."

Calstone reclined in his chair and set his boots on Will's desk. "If that happens, I will have deserved it."

"It's good that you know. Now get your muddy boots off my desk."

Calstone retracted his legs. "Fine, fine. I see the real problem here."

Will shut his eyes. Listening to Calstone made his temples throb.

"You still haven't seduced your wife into your bed."

His eyes snapped open. "What the hell does that have to do

with anything?" And he had slept next to her. That could be considered a great advancement from sitting in the doorway.

"That is why you are uneasy with Graves."

"It's not, trust me. Harriet compared Graves to you."

Calstone's head snapped up. "Me? I'm a damn duke."

Will shrugged, purposely declining to add further context.

"Now I *must* meet this man."

You do that. Will shut his eyes again.

He had fallen for a woman with spark. That spark was what he loved most about her. A spark he would never dim. If there were any shortcomings in their relationship, they were his. But no matter his shortcomings, there was one thing Will didn't lack—determination. And that determination was directed to one objective—win his wife's heart.

Even if that meant embracing Graves as a brother.

He might not like it, but he would do it.

"I suppose your wife hasn't seen you naked yet." Calstone suddenly piped up again. He should never have confided a single thing to his friend. The man would tease him all his life for the blunders of the past week.

Will inhaled a long-suffering breath. "Just go ahead, spit it out. Where are you going with this?"

"Well, as your aim is to court your wife, and seducing your wife with your body is another method of courtship, perhaps it's time to elevate your *wooing*?" His temples throbbed more painfully.

"You have such exceptional arguments. Why don't you write a play?"

"Brilliant idea," Calstone said. "But only if you agree to take the role as male lead."

Will snorted his answer.

"Back to seducing your wife. All you need to do is plant a seed of seduction in her mind. Tempt her."

Will furrowed his brows. "We've kissed."

"I'd have questioned your ability as a man if you hadn't." Will rolled his eyes, and a wicked glint entered Calstone's gaze. "Don't you think it's time to show a bit more skin? Show your wife what she is missing."

Will eyed his friend, who smiled like a fox "A bit of skin."

Calstone shrugged. "A chest. Something *else*."

"Just bloody stop."

"Here me out, old chap," Calstone pressed on. "If you're going to probe your wife about her outing today, why not do it naked?"

Naked?

Will twirled the thought in his head. This wasn't the worst idea. In fact, it could be one of Calstone's better ones today. Not that that was saying very much. "I retract my earlier rebuff."

Calstone waved his comment aside. "You know how I am. Your rebuffs flow over me like a rain droplet on a leaf. I barely hear them anymore."

Will cast his eyes to the ceiling. "Good for you." He crossed one leg over the other. "You are suddenly full of ideas."

"Good ones, heh."

The corners of Will's lips twitched. Ah, his friend meant well. Parading about the house nude might not be the best course of action, but Calstone had still given him an interesting idea. If he had to wait for his wife's return, why not wait in her chamber? *Bathing.* She would never expect such brazen behavior from him, but neither could he be censured too strongly for simply trying to stay clean. He wasn't sure if it would work, since it could not be considered a usual method of courting, but who was to say what was normal or not? They were already married. The playing field had changed. And if he happened to imprint the memory of his naked body on Harriet's mind . . .

Will shot to his feet.

"Finally see the light?"

A grunt.

He would wait for his wife in her chamber. If he was going to bathe, he must consider how long it took to prepare hot water.

He might not have much time.

His mind sparked with all the other ways he could tempt his wife in the future. Later, he could read a book in the nude on the bed? No. Shirtless would be better. Best to leave a bit for the imagination in such cases. He wanted to tempt her, not scare her with an intimacy she wasn't ready for.

He slanted a look at Calstone. "You can see yourself out."

Chapter Fourteen

HARRIET STRODE DOWN the hall to her bedchamber still preoccupied with the conversation between her and Rohan. The man had done it on purpose, planting seeds of doubt sprinkled with a flavor of anticipation. She understood why he had done so. She knew Rohan well enough to know that her hasty wedding and runaway attempt beforehand had disturbed him, even though he didn't say so. The less he said about the matter, the more Harriet understood how uneasy what happened to her had made him. He must be regretting not being here for her, which was why he had launched an investigation on his own and attempted to redirect her mind onto something else. Something more hopeful.

And it had worked.

Drat him for knowing her so well.

Harriet didn't plan to speculate much on the theory that Leeds fancied her. It was just too bold to claim. However, the idea did serve as food for her romantic soul. And the taste was sweet.

She pushed open the door to her chamber and stepped inside. A subtle fragrance of lavender assaulted her as well as a waft of . . . steam?

Harriet furrowed her brow, her gaze meeting the most provocative sight she had ever come across in her entire life. Not that she'd come across many, but this . . .

Ought to be outlawed.

In the center of the chamber stood a bath. In that bath lazed a very striking, and presumably very naked, man with a broad chest on display. Damp tendrils of hair curled on his temple, making him appear more god than man.

Her package dropped to the floor.

Lord. Save. Me.

This was her husband.

And he resembled a hero straight from one of her novels. Which was startling enough, but what made it jaw-dropping was that this was *Leeds*. Stone-faced, shockingly persistent, and breathlessly unyielding Leeds. Bathing. In her chamber. As though he had not a care in the world! As though this was the most normal thing to do.

"Ah, you are back, love."

"What are you doing?" Harriet managed to croak out.

He arched a brow that seemed to indicate that it ought to be obvious what he was doing. "I'm taking a bath."

"I can see that," Harriet snapped. "Why are you doing so in *my* chamber?"

He shrugged, and simply said, "Our chamber."

She pointed to the adjoining door. "Your chamber is over there."

He scooped a handful of water to splash over his arm and shoulder. "The servants must have accidently brought the tub here. "What could I do?"

Harriet rubbed her temples. Clearly, Leeds was up to something, and that something was meant to drive her insane. "You are trying to provoke me, aren't you?"

The corner of his lips lifted. "Not at all."

"You cannot sell this innocent act to me, *love*." Harriet's gaze pulled to his chest before flicking up again. Heat spread all over her. "Even if the servants made a mistake, you have not taken a bath at this time of day before."

"You've noticed my bathing habits?" He sounded intrigued.

"More like the lack thereof."

"My wife is calling me dirty. How mortifying."

Harriet harrumphed. Her husband had gone from a charming rogue, to a tempting rogue, to a downright shameless rogue! She pointed to the door. "Get out."

He arched a brow. "Now?"

"Yes, *now*."

"Are you certain that is what you want?"

"Yes!"

"As you wish." He rose from the tub, water dripping from his sculpted body. *Almighty heavenly Lord.*

"Sit down!"

"Honestly, love, now I'm not sure what to do."

Harriet covered her eyes with the palms of her hands. "Lawd, will you get back into the tub already!"

He chuckled, and Harriet peeked between her fingers, watching him lower back into the tub. But it was too late. The vision of his body, and all his manly bits, had been seared into her skull. Burned into every last nerve. So this was the body of a boxer?

She resisted the urge to fan her face. It appeared she was the one who must leave. Why hadn't she thought about that sooner? It seemed that Leeds had finally succeeded in scrambling her brain.

Harriet turned on her heel and marched toward the door. "Since you cannot leave, I shall be the one do so."

"You don't want to join me?"

Her steps halted, and she whirled in astonishment. "I beg your pardon?"

His eyes danced with amusement. "The water is still quite warm."

Her mouth nearly fell open. "Join you for a bath?" Had he lost his senses? What had happened between breakfast and now to prompt this shocking behavior?

"I've already slept in your bed, and we've established I'm not going to do anything you don't wish me to do. Why not join me for a bath?"

"Sleeping next to each other is different than bathing together." There was the nakedness for one. Also, skin sliding alongside skin.

He reclined back, placing his arms on either side of the tub, the picture of a relaxed male poised for seduction. "We shared the same mattress and the same linen. Is water really that different?"

"Breaking it down to the elements won't make your request any less absurd." She fanned her face, freezing at his smirk. Curse it! She yanked her hands behind her back, clasping her fingers together to keep them from acting as they pleased.

"You can join me in your chemise if you feel uncomfortable naked."

Was there even any difference? The garment would melt into her skin and provide little to no shield. "I'll pass on that offer, thank you very much."

"Have it your way."

Harriet stared as her husband shut his eyes indifferently, as though he had not expected any other outcome. He didn't think she would do it, did he? In fact, by the look of the man, he had been convinced the entire time that she would not dare. He thought he knew her, did he?

I dare, Leeds. Oh, I dare.

She narrowed her eyes on him, her gaze drifting over the droplets covering his chest to the water his torso disappeared under. She sauntered over to the tub, her lips curving into a smile as he opened his eyes again at her approach. A thrill of satisfaction trickled down her spine when she glimpsed the fleeting twitch of his brow. *Not that indifferent after all.*

She trailed a finger over the edge of the tub before dipping it into the water. "Warm."

His chest rose and fell. "I told you so."

"Extremely tempting. Are you sure you can handle me in your tub?"

Two burning eyes locked on her. "I can."

What had Leonora said again about temptation and seduction? This must be Leeds's effort at tempting *her*. She thought back to his unbuttoned shirts, rolled up sleeves, and yesterday's dressing gown. This must be the next step.

"You have grown quite bold," Harriet commented. "I suppose this is part of your attempt to woo me?" She paused. "All with the servants' help, of course."

He didn't breathe a word.

Harriet bit back a smug smile. She undid the buttons of her redingote and shrugged out of the garment, tossing it onto the bed with a smile.

His face lost all expression. "What are you doing?"

Her smile turned coy. "Didn't you want me to join?"

His brows drew together, only slightly, but enough for her to understand that he still wasn't sure she would actually do it, but he also wasn't sure she wouldn't.

"I want." His voice came out raspy.

"Then you shall have to help me with the buttons of my gown." She gave him her back. "I can't reach them."

A moment of silence.

Then, water sloshed before the light touch of fingers unbuttoned each one with slow deliberation. With each button he unhooked, her pulse seemed to throb harder.

One button.

Two buttons.

Three buttons.

Harriet swallowed, her nerves suddenly battling against her courage.

Dear Lord. What was she doing?

Am I really going through with this?

Too late now, Harriet.

"Why aren't you saying anything?" His whispered breath brushed against her ear, causing a tell-tale shiver to skitter across her skin. He'd done that on purpose, hadn't he?

"So lovely." You rogue.

Her mind went blank at the deliberate brush of his fingers, with nothing remaining but the towering presence of him at her back.

Naked.

Harriet shut the erotic memory of her husband standing up from the bathwater out of her mind. Only for it to pop right back in. Lean, rippling muscles. His thighs. And that thing.

Her face flamed.

Lord, oh Lord, oh Lord.

WILL SWALLOWED AS he undid each button of his wife's dress, the shock of her request still lingering in his limbs. Frankly, he couldn't tell what had possessed him to invite her. That hadn't been the plan. He'd merely wished to stir a blush into her cheeks. He loved the pink hue that unfurled across her skin because of him. Yet the invitation had rolled off his tongue as though it had always meant to be said.

And once again, she exceeded his every expectation.

His fingers had never trembled as much as they did in that moment. He let out a long breath as he retracted his hand after the last button.

"Done," he said, clearing his voice when it came out too gruff.

In a blink of an eye, the dress pooled on the ground.

She slanted a look over her shoulder. "The stays. Unlace them."

Had he entered another realm? He couldn't quite believe what was happening, but that still didn't stop him from undoing her stays, eyes never leaving her as he made short work of her corset. The entire chamber seemed to hold its breath, the only sounds being the gentle rustle of her shift and chemise joining the rest of her clothes and the slight movement of water against the sides of the tub.

His gaze trailed over the pale expanse of her back.

She turned her head and rested her chin on her shoulder. "No words?"

He had words. Two.

Almighty Heaven.

He'd succeeded in stirring the coveted rosy hue, but that was nothing compared to all her delicate curves and the slope of her body as she turned to fully face him.

A playful grin hung on her lips. "It's just sharing water, isn't that right?"

Ah yes, just one more foolish word that had once again come to nip him in his arse. How many times had this happened now? Many.

Don't call him a gentleman—he didn't avert his gaze, and could already taste the softness of her breasts in his mouth. They were the right amount of handful that made him want to reach out and love them. Her slender body still had enough curves to set his heart on fire.

"Still nothing to say?"

"You are lovely." Will thought the words might have stuttered out, but they were smooth, even though his tone had been pure gravel.

"So I've gone from looking lovely to actually being lovely. That is a step up."

She chuckled and held out her hand, and Will clasped it in his own as he helped her step into the tub. The soft haze of steam danced upon her delicate features, pulling at the breath in his lungs.

Beautiful, love.

That would be his note tomorrow.

Will sank back into the tub, his breath stalling when she followed suit, her legs sliding up against his as she settled across from him.

He suddenly questioned the choices that led him to this moment. No matter how he looked at it, he'd been caught in his own little scheme of temptation. The tub was not big to begin with, so they had to sit close to each other, leg up against leg.

Dear God, it felt marvelous.

It also felt dangerous.

He usually possessed exemplary restraint, but he suddenly worried it that might be obliterated today.

No, keep it together, Will.

He splashed some water over his chest, rubbing the spot over his heart. "You surprise me at every turn, love."

"Do you like surprises?" The sparkle in her eyes was unmistakable.

"Normally, they're too stimulating for my taste, but with you, I don't mind." *Surprise me every day. Surprise me forever.*

He squinted when she flicked her finger in the water, sent drops of water to spray over his face. "I would say that for someone who doesn't like surprises, you are certainly adept in handing them out, but you're probably going to respond with: *only when it comes to you, love.*"

Will chuckled, wiping his face. "Touché, love. You've come to understand me quite well."

"I wish," she said. "There is still a great deal I wish to understand."

Ah, yes. She wanted to know the reason why he married her. "You shall understand everything soon."

"Only a rogue would make a lady wait."

"Patience is a virtue."

She jabbed a toe into his flesh. "You are no gentleman, *husband.*"

That one little phrase sent him from slightly heated to molten lava. A flush spread from his jawline to his neck. He didn't know whether it was the term itself or her tone or both, but Will suddenly had a big, hard problem below.

He needed to distract himself.

Now.

"How was your stroll with Graves?" Will asked, sure the topic of Graves would cool him right down again. And indeed, it had been his intention to ask anyway.

"You know about that?"

"Of course," Will said, holding her gaze while he stealthily covered his *problem* with his arm. "Are you that surprised?"

"I'm more amazed you didn't join us on our outing."

"Would you have welcomed me if I had?"

"I welcomed you at Leonora's."

"That was different." Will would never admit that if it hadn't been for Calstone, he would certainly have joined them today.

"How so? They are all my friends." One, thin brow rose. "Is it because Rohan is a man? Is that why it's different?"

Was it just because Rohan was a man? "I'm not sure, myself."

"I don't mind you joining me when I visit with friends. Just like I know you won't mind if I do the same."

That was correct—he wouldn't mind. He loved spending time with Harriet. Any moment with her trumped anything else.

"I suppose I ought to thank you for not forbidding my friendship with Rohan. Most husbands would have."

"There is no reason to thank me. I'm not most husbands."

"You certainly are not," she said with a small smile. "But I know you do not like him, yet you tolerate our friendship."

"It's not that I don't like Graves. But I don't know the man well enough to form a favorable opinion of him. Since he is a friend of yours, however, I suppose he can't be that bad."

"I'm sure he feels the same way about you."

I'm sure he does, he thought wryly.

Well, one thing was true—this topic had served to help him with his problem.

"Would you like to me to bathe you?"

Will stiffened. "What?"

Her eyes darted to the sponge placed on the footstool beside the tub. She collected the sponge and lathered it with soap, a glint of mischief entering his gaze.

"Do you want me to bathe you?"

Christ, yes.

Which was to say, hell, no.

The problem that subsided a moment ago sprang up again.

Will quickly snatched the sponge from her. "I'll do it."

"You wish to bathe me?" Her voice cracked on the last note.

"Why not? Didn't you want to bathe me a moment ago?"

"Yes, but . . . I shall do it," she attempted to snatch the sponge back, but Will was faster, lifting the sponge above his head, out of her reach. "You can bathe me after, if you like." Harriet bathing him? It was a temptation too great to let slip away. But he might not be able, for obvious reasons, to return the favor if she went first, and Will really, really wanted to bathe his wife now that the option had appeared.

"Let me bathe you first," she insisted. *"Please."*

Will lost the fight.

What man could a deny his woman in the face of that plea? He certainly didn't have the strength.

He handed over the sponge, his arm in place to cut his desire from her view, lest he lose this chance altogether. But it was painful. So damn painful.

You can do this, Will.

She took the sponge and, after dipping it into the water, with a touch as light as a feather, she brought the sponge to Will's chest, tracing its contours with the utmost of care.

Will almost groaned.

He should have turned around to give her his back. Why the hell hadn't he done that? But he wanted to look at her while she bathed him. He wanted to carve every moment of this into his memory.

Soap left a path of bubbles where she trailed, creating a soothing sensation on his skin. Did she know what she was doing to him? Her unhurried strokes were pure torture.

His body hardened to the point he thought he might explode.

She dragged the sponge to his lower abdomen, her eyes fixed

on him with such focus, Will couldn't take it anymore.

He'd attempted to ruffle her feathers, but she had ruffled his instead. He'd been bested by his wife. He was man enough to admit that much. Though perhaps not to her.

He placed a hand over hers, his fingers moving to encircle her wrist. Her eyes lifted to meet his.

"That's enough," Will said, voice gruff.

"Oh? I've only washed a bit."

"You can wash me more another day."

She searched his gaze, and what she found there brought a deep flush to her cheeks, as well as in impish smile. "What about me?" she asked. "Did you not want to wash me?"

Could he?

No.

No. No. No. Bathing her was one of his top priorities, yes. But as expected, just not today. He wouldn't survive it.

"Next time. Next time I'll bathe you, too."

Her teeth flashed. "Are you sure there will be a next time? Perhaps this is your only chance."

"I created this chance, did I not? I'll create another." He gave her wrist a slight squeeze. "You're welcome to call me over whenever you wish me to wash your back. Or we can move our nightcaps to the tub. You know I'll accompany you as long as you'll have me."

"So bold!"

"Two bold peas we are then in one bold pod. So let's not stop here."

And Will wouldn't stop. Not until he possessed the one thing he wanted most.

His wife's heart.

Chapter Fifteen

The Stewart Ball

HARRIET STEPPED TOWARD the edge of the ballroom a bit breathless after her third dance of the evening. All with Leeds. She spotted one of the other women who'd been at Lady Ophelia's tea also leaving the dance and felt another prick of guilt.

In truth, Harriet had not thought a prick of guilt could stab so deeply. It was rather like a needle continuously piercing through a silk fiber embroidery base. She'd never imagined she would one day keep such a secret from her husband, though when she had thought *that*, she'd always expected her husband to be someone she loved, or at least someone she had built a connection with *before* they married. She hadn't started her marriage to Leeds with any of those things. But who would have thought that with each conversation, each encounter, each step of each dance, affection and trust would sprout and grow into a flourishing seedling?

And at least on this subject, Leeds had been honest with her. He told her on the first day they met that there were wagers, a list. She had acted like it didn't matter, and it hadn't—then. But she hadn't really known what the wagers were then. And somehow she still found herself embroiled in secret activities now, even conceiving the idea that would be acted out tonight.

She wasn't to take part herself, however. Leeds was too *pre-*

sent for her to actively participate in the planning for tonight, and she was far too preoccupied with her husband and the dangling bit between his legs. Well, to be fair, those images were recent additions that haunted her every waking thought. Which was probably why that persistent tinge of remorse had only started the moment she stepped from the carriage and beheld the bright lights of the manor that would soon be filled with mayhem.

Would Leeds be angry because she'd kept a secret from him? She darted a glance his way.

No, that rogue. Was he not still keeping a secret from her?

Harriet shook her head. This was not the time to dwell on secrets and whatnot.

Focus.

Right—the wagers.

They would all be exposed tonight. The men of the *ton* were about to receive a mighty surprise. Luckily, her husband was not one of the men responsible for creating that list or the list finding its way to the betting book.

A big, huge, extraordinary consolation.

Her gaze caught on a row of seats with a handful of ladies observing the men and women bustling about. She had once claimed a spot there amongst the wallflowers. Tonight, she didn't feel like a wallflower, and with Leeds at her side, she would never occupy that row again. Unless . . . she snuck another glance at him.

Oh, yes. There was no doubt in her mind. Leeds would surely join her amongst the wallflowers if she were to plop down there again. Even if that were to happen, though, she still wouldn't *feel* like a wallflower.

Not with his attention on her.

Like when he'd unhooked her buttons. Like in the bath. Like all the time they'd spent together in each other's company. His attention was a force unto itself, a ball of fire that could never burn out.

It was addictive.

Pure temptation!

Calstone appeared beside them with a grin. His gaze swept over her. "What a delightful sight. Married life seems to have brought a blossom to your cheeks."

Harriet cast her gaze heavenward. "What are you even saying, Duke?"

"You look lovely tonight, Lady *Leeds*."

Her cheeks flushed, and she caught her husband's heated look before his gaze paused on the ribbon woven into her hair. He averted his eyes.

What was *that*?

Harriet cleared her throat and returned the duke's grin. "Thank you."

Calstone inclined his head, his eyes sweeping over the ballroom. "Quite the crush tonight. I daresay the perfect night to come out, wouldn't you agree, Lady Leeds? Dances beneath candlelit chandeliers. Fabulous wine. Stolen kisses in garden strolls."

What was this man on about? "Are you informing us of your plans for the night?"

Calstone's smile slipped.

Beside her, Leeds chuckled. "He is meddling—that's what he's doing, love."

"You don't find the mood of the night romantic? This is your first event as a married couple. You must try *everything* tonight."

On the contrary, she thought it felt rather more like the calm before the storm. Nothing romantic about that. "Well, a ball certainly looks better while dancing than it does from a post against the wall."

Leeds took a tendril of her hair between his fingers. "You can't even imagine how much better it looks to me, love."

Harriet's heartbeat sped up. She didn't need candlelit chandeliers, fabulous wine, or stolen kisses in garden strolls to set a romantic mood. All she needed was Leeds's charming mouth. It melted her like nothing else.

"Come on now," Calstone insisted. "This is where reality meets the imagination."

"You and I have different views on that, Duke." She shrugged. "Unfortunately, the first night of my debut shattered that illusion."

Both men stared at her.

"What?" Harriet asked. "Why are you looking at me like that?"

"What happened on the night you debuted?" Calstone asked.

"Calstone," Leeds warned.

Calstone's gaze flicked between the two of them, but he didn't press further. *That's right.* She'd told Leeds about Cromby. He must have deduced the reason was that odious man.

"Well, I shall make it my life's mission to restore the magic of the ballroom for you," Calstone announced.

"Find your own wife," Leeds retorted. "If my wife wants any magic restored anywhere, I'll be the one to do it."

Harriet bit back a smile. "Boys."

Both men turned to her. "I think you've both forgotten I was a wallflower once. Now I'm one no longer. That is enough magic for me, thank you very much."

"You never belonged amongst them."

"Well, you certainly plucked me from them, did you not?"

Calstone groaned. "Have a heart. Flirting before the bachelors. That is considered unconscionably rude."

Harriet chuckled. "How about I introduce you to my good friend, Lady Leonora? I believe she is looking for a spot of fun."

A look of horror fell across his face. "Please don't do that."

"I think that's a brilliant plan," Leeds agreed.

"It's a bad, bad plan."

"Why? Aren't you looking to dance beneath sparkling chandeliers and take garden strolls? A spot of fun?"

"A spot of fun for a lady means something else entirely than it does for a gentleman."

"You are sure?"

"Leeds, old chap. Call off your wife. My heart can't stand her teasing."

Leeds chuckled, and Harriet grinned up at him. She did like her husband's laugh. He should laugh more and keep on practicing his smiles. The world would be a better place if he smiled a bit more.

"Why are the two of you grinning like fools? What did I miss?" Calstone asked.

Harriet laughed, catching sight of Rohan as he sauntered up to them. "Leeds, Calstone. Lady Harriet, you are the picture of radiance. Blue suits you."

"Graves," Leeds greeted with a nod.

"Ah, *the* Graves," Calstone said. "You are the good, childhood, best friend of our lovely Harriet. The Duke of Calstone, at your service."

Oh? *It seemed someone had been gossiping.*

"A pleasure to make your acquaintance." Rohan inclined his head to Calstone.

"Oh, the pleasure is all mine," Calstone said. "What brings you to this side of town?"

Harriet shot Calstone a frown.

Rohan, on the other hand, took the duke's question on a breeze. "The hope of a dance." He smiled at Harriet. "Can I add my name to your card?"

"Certainly."

"Is there still a spot on your card?" Leeds asked. "I thought I'd claimed them all."

Harriet blinked, glancing at her dance card. Leeds's bold scrawl had claimed all the dances. Her head jerked up to look at Leeds. "I can't possibly dance every single dance on this card." Even a reformed wallflower needed breaths between dances!

"All right, I'll let you off on some of them. We can have lemonades as you revive."

Was Leeds jealous over her friend? Still? She'd figured he would have become more used to Rohan by now and not mind if she scratched his name off one entry to give to Rohan. Apparently he still minded. She shouldn't enjoy it, she really shouldn't, but a thrill of excitement raced across the tips of her fingers.

Leeds's eyes never wavered from Rohan. "As you can see, her dance card is full."

Harriet wanted to pinch the man. "Next time, Rohan," she said, trying hard, but failing just as hard, to keep the laughter from her voice.

"Of course. I shall just have to beat your husband to your next dance card."

Leeds nodded, and Harriet glimpsed the slight twitch of the corner of his lips. "I welcome the challenge."

"It's *my* dance card."

Leeds leaned in close. "I too am *yours*, love."

Harriet melted into a puddle. Any more, and she would just evaporate into a mist of steam.

Calstone groaned. "Why did the two of you even leave the house?"

Rohan chuckled. "I'm starting to share that sentiment."

Harriet's entire body heated to what she was sure to be bright vermillion. She peeked at her husband. Slight red blotches could be detected on his jaw line. Their gazes met.

Be still my heart.

Was Rohan right? Did Leeds fancy her?

And what about her? What did she feel?

She liked her husband, yes. Flirted with him also. She even admired him in many ways. He'd said he would woo her, and he'd set out to do just that. So just who was peeling back the layers of whom?

Did it even matter anymore?

Her only initial requirement for this marriage had been to fulfill the promise she had made to her mother, that she would marry a man that would fight for her. A man worthy of being called her husband. She hadn't believed Leeds to be such a man at first, but he had proven himself worthy of her vow. After that, she had simply wanted to get to the bottom of his motive for their rushed marriage.

She hadn't had all that many expectations, really.

Did that still hold true?

No.

Day by day, moment by moment, she expected a bit more. A bit more laughter. A bit more affection. A bit more hope. Rohan had said dreams were not unyielding objects, that they could reshape and were never lost. So perhaps all her dreams for her future weren't as lost or out of her reach as she'd thought.

But what if . . . just what if . . .

They had just begun?

Could he do it?

No, you can't do it.

But what if he did do it? He'd done it once before, carried her off over his shoulder. But there were too many people here. They'd cause a scandal. Not that he cared about any of that. But Harriet might.

He couldn't do it.

I really want to.

She blushed so prettily. He wanted to whisk her off home where they could be alone. Perhaps he could wash her back. Make her blush some more. Chatter over a nightcap.

Will's eyes shifted back to his wife where she conversed with Graves, flitted over the ribbon in her hair. It had come from the package she had brought back after her outing with Graves. It annoyed him. A little bit. But only because he hadn't bought her a ribbon yet. He'd only been sending flowers and notes. Should he purchase some ribbons?

No.

Not ribbons.

Friends bought ribbons.

Husbands bought . . . other things. He'd put a list of ideas together.

"Why are you smiling like that?" Calstone interjected into his thoughts.

Not this again. "How am I smiling?"

"I don't know. It looks part wolfish, part smug. A wolfish, smug smile."

"I don't know what you are talking about."

"Me neither," Harriet said. "What's this about smug, wolf smiles?" She winked at him, and Will's entire body went rigid, a certain morning springing to mind.

He inwardly groaned.

"I'd like to see this smile. Do it again—it sounds rather intriguing." She laughed and lowered her voice to a whisper. "Perhaps I shall be entertained in the morning again."

That's it. He was dragging her off.

"What are you two whispering about?" Calstone asked. "You should just return home."

Yes. They should.

"Your marriage has been announced," his friend went on. "You've shown your faces, spare us the rest if this is all you have to offer."

"I'm not ready to leave yet," Harriet said.

Will wanted to curse. Loudly.

"In that case, come on Graves," Calstone said. "Distract me from the two of them. How have you been finding London?"

Graves arched a brow. "Dreary. Wet. Full of busybodies."

"I couldn't have described the place better myself."

"Don't mind him," Will said. "Sarcasm rolls right off him."

"Good to know."

Will brushed his hand against his wife's. She smiled at him.

"I can't even argue against it. It's true." Calstone patted Graves on the shoulder. "Join us at our club for a drink sometime."

Graves inclined his head. "Speaking of which, I've heard

there's been an uproar about your betting book."

"Ah, yes, the book was stolen right from under the members' noses."

"Quite the wagers going on in that book," Graves pointed out.

Will frowned. "What are you getting at, Graves?"

"Did you wager on a certain list?" Graves countered.

"Of course not."

"But the list *did* provide an opportunity," Graves pressed.

"Rohan," Harriet hissed.

"It's fine," Will said. "He has a right to ask. The wagers didn't provide opportunities so much as they provided incentive for mischief. If you are referring to me asking for my wife's hand, rather than an opportunity, it served more as an awakening of sorts. Does that answer your question?"

Harriet squeezed his fingers. Her clear gaze sent a ripple of comfort down his spine. He loved her eyes on him. He wouldn't mind if they never left him in this lifetime.

Perhaps it's time to tell her. To confess your feelings.

The impulse stuck in his chest and wouldn't let go.

He would tell her. He would tell her soon. The notes were a good place to start. He could build up his confession from there. All he could do then was have faith and trust that she was ready to hear the truth, as ready as he was to impart it.

"I daresay," Calstone spoke up. "Any sane man would seize the chance to marry such a captivating creature. Unfortunately, Lady Harriet never cast her gaze upon me."

"You don't want my gaze on you anyway," Harriet said drily. "You'd be shaking in your boots."

"Quite right."

His wife looked ready to deliver another quip, but her expression suddenly contorted. Before he could ask what was wrong, a hand clamped his shoulder and a familiar, grating voice laughed in his ear. "Leeds, old fellow. Glad to see your mood has improved."

He stiffened, and he shrugged the hand off his shoulder. "Cromby." The ice Will infused in that one word gave everyone pause.

Everyone except Cromby who didn't seem to notice or care. His gaze fell on Harriet. "Ah, Lady Leeds. Always a vision."

A bitter taste filled Will's mouth, and he cut off Cromby's line of sight with a shift of his body. "What do you want, Cromby?"

The man's face turned red at the blunt question.

A soft hand clamped his elbow as his wife stepped up beside him and directed a haughty look Cromby's way. "Lord Cromby, I was not aware you were acquainted with my husband."

Will hid a smile.

Ah yes. His wife was no coward.

Cromby's face went from red to vermillion. "We–"

"Aren't friends," Will said firmly, turning his gaze toward his wife. He had backed off in White's because that would have ended in fisticuffs. Blood. What he'd done in White's had been mostly for himself, partly for his wife. What he did here, he did for Harriet alone. "However, London is small, and you cannot help but run into all sorts of people."

She nodded seriously. "I have found that to be the case, too. It cannot be helped. There is always a jackal or two amongst a flock of sheep."

Will turned his back on Cromby, uncaring whether he left or stood there like a fool. Let this serve as a warning to Cromby and anyone who supported him. Will did not suffer their ilk.

"I can't believe you did that." Harriet looked up at him with wide eyes. "I can't believe *I* did that."

Will traced a finger over her chin. "I told you, the second I learned about your aversion to him, he was dead in my world. And," he lowered his voice, "you can do whatever you like."

Her face split into a grin. It was the first time she had shown him an expression like that, and one of the many knots in his heart slowly unraveled.

"Well, then, don't blame me when I do whatever I want in

the future."

"I won't."

"There the two of you go again. Why did I even come to this ball?" Calstone lamented.

"I've been questioning that for myself," Graves murmured.

"We should go for drinks and leave these two alone in their little world," Calstone said. He turned to Will. "Let me tell you, old chap, if you don't hold onto me, I'll be stolen by someone else. I can see the headlines now: The tradesman and duke—a shocking tale of love and betrayal."

Harriet nudged Will with an elbow. "Now might be your only chance to hand him over to someone else."

Graves shook his head. "Is he always like this?"

"Unfortunately."

"You say that after I jumped into the Thames after you?"

Will snorted. "That was your choice."

At that moment, a rush of titters exploded around them, and Will's gaze was drawn to the upper staircase, where four men appeared beside each other.

No. Not men.

Women.

Will recognized them almost instantly as Lady Ophelia, Lady Louisa, Lady Selena, and Lady Theodosia. Four of the heiresses on the list. He shot a glance at his wife, whose expectant, yet nervous gaze was riveted to the scene. No surprise in her eyes.

Whatever was about to happen, she was informed.

He thought back to when he'd followed her to Lady Leonora's house. Lady Selena had also been present then.

He glanced back to the women. A hush had fallen over the ballroom. All eyes on the scene at the top of the stairwell. It was impossible not to stare. Each woman wore well-fitted men's clothing. From boots to cravat to even a top hat. Each lady also carried a cane in one hand and a set of papers in the other.

Whatever they were up to, it wasn't proper.

It would cause a scandal.

All of a sudden, the women tossed their sheaves, and sheets of paper swept down over the ballroom like the first shower of an upcoming storm. Hundreds of sheets. Silence, but for the rustling of paper, filled the air.

Beside him, Calstone bent to pick up a page that flitted to their shoes, brows furrowing. "This . . ."

He handed it to Will.

Will poured over the content.

Dear God.

A page from the betting book.

A copy, to be more precise. Still, this did not bode well for anyone. His gaze returned to his wife, just in time to see her sneak a peek at him before averting her gaze again.

Ah, yes, she knew.

Will frowned. That she'd been privy to what would transpire tonight was not as alarming as her keeping it a secret from him. He hadn't worried when the betting book went missing—it had nothing to do with them. But he'd never considered that the heiresses were the ones behind its theft.

Christ.

And the club members were hunting for the book.

Club members like Cromby. And the Duke of Mortimer.

Will sighed. Judging from the whispers and flushed faces of the crowd, the storm that had been brewing since the book had been stolen had finally arrived. Now, all he had to do was keep his wife out of the tempest, even though Will suspected she was already right in the middle.

Chapter Sixteen

*S*PECTACULAR.

Paper fluttering through the ballroom like spectacular leaves in the wind. Harriet had been so preoccupied with her husband's direct cut of Cromby that she had almost missed the arrival of her friends and their marvelous performance.

They did it.

They actually did it.

And it exceeded even her expectations.

"What a brilliant spectacle," Calstone exclaimed, snatching one of the last copies from the air as it glided down.

A palm settled on her lower back. "Are you ready to leave?"

Harriet didn't want to, not yet, but she caught the concern on his face. He clutched one of the copies tightly in a fist.

"*Now*, you're leaving?" Calstone asked. "The show has just begun."

"You enjoy it then," Leeds said. He took her hand in his. "We need to avoid the aftermath."

"What aftermath?" Harriet asked.

"The one where wives start bludgeoning their husbands with candelabras," Graves said.

Harriet cast a concerned glance over the onlookers. At the moment, everyone was busy reading the copies, trying to decipher the content, what it meant. Some of the men knew what they were looking at—their faces could be told apart from the rest by their glowers and, in a few cases, their expressions of downright panic.

"Shall we?" Leeds asked.

Harriet nodded and allowed her husband to lead her from the ballroom. They had to pass her friends, and she sent them a small wave of support.

"Leaving already?" Selena whispered.

"Yes, I'll speak to you soon. You were all fabulous, by the way."

Selena waved her off with a wink.

Leeds retrieved their cloaks from a footman, and he helped fasten the garment before they stepped into the cool night's embrace. "The carriage will come around in a few minutes."

Harriet nodded. "Aren't you going to ask me if I knew?"

"I know you did." He looked at her meaningfully. "It was written all over your pretty face."

"Are you angry?" Harriet asked softly. He didn't look angry. But then, Leeds had a way of schooling his features so no one, not even her, could tell what he was thinking.

"I'm not."

"Are you disappointed?"

"No."

"Then what are you?"

The carriage arrived and Leeds wasted no time ushering her in. She settled into the soft cushions, eyes following him as he entered after her. He rapped on the roof and the carriage shot forward.

"I'm not angry," he said after a moment. "And I'm not disappointed. If anything, I'm concerned."

"Concerned about what? Wives bludgeoning the husbands with candelabras?"

"God no. That has nothing to do with me. However, you, on the other hand, are an heiress on that list. Four of them stood on that stairwell today, declaring to every member of White's who stole their book."

"You're concerned we might be in trouble?"

Dark eyes settled on her. "I cannot predict what might happen. That is my concern."

"What will White's do?"

"It's what they've already done, love. Since the betting book's disappearance, which I gather you know all about, things in certain quarters have been strained. They tasked the Duke of Mortimer to find it, and I heard that Cromby—the oaf—has decided to see if he can find it first."

That man again.

"My friends won't give back the book."

"Let them do what they please. So long as you are not put in harm's way."

Warmth swept over her skin. She had learned that Leeds had a very protective nature—a layer pulled back. It could make him appear abrupt and cold, but that was just a mask he pulled on to cover his concern. He might seem calm and unruffled to the outside world, but inside he must be grappling with a tempest of emotions.

"Aren't you going to ask if there is anything else I'm keeping from you? About the book?"

"I rather imagine a woman to be repository of secrets, is she not?"

Leeds was no fool. Those sharp eyes saw more than the average man's. They saw *everything*. One look from him and it seemed as though he saw straight into her soul.

"However," he went on, "I also know that not all secrets are ours to tell. But those that are, can you tell me? About what happened? Who stole the book?"

"You must have already guessed it was one of the heiresses. I can tell you that it's true. One of the heiresses did nick the book."

"But you can't tell me which one?"

She shook her head. "Is that important?"

"It's important if it's you."

Her breath hitched. "Why?"

"Because I don't know what methods will be used to get the book back, love. I'd rather you not be in the crossfire."

So protective. "Well, it wasn't me."

"Very well," Leeds said. "So long as this doesn't bring trouble to you."

"Are you going to put that in a note tomorrow?"

He tilted his head. "Perhaps it will say 'Stay away from anything dangerous, love.'"

"Does that mean I should stay away from you?"

"I'm dangerous?" He sounded surprised.

Yes. To my heart, my body, and my soul. It was rather frightening to realize how much access he had to her heart while not knowing how much of his heart she could reach. Others might claim that Leeds fancied her, but she was too nervous, too unsure of herself in this regard, to presume the same. And anyway, fancying wasn't the same as . . . well, as other things.

"Well, I've come to learn you are rather frighteningly charming when you choose to be," she said finally.

They stared at each other though the dimly lit carriage while the wheels ambled along the cobblestone streets, the rhythmic clatter of horse hooves mingling with the faint sounds of their breathing.

Awareness prickled her scalp, his imposing body taking up much more of the space now than it had on their way to the ball.

The air pulsed with energy, an undercurrent of allure that Harriet could no longer resist. The world outside ceased to exist, and in a moment of pure insanity, or perhaps sparkling clarity, Harriet reached across the space between them and traced the sharp line of his jaw. Even though he was freshly shaven, the rough rasp of stubble scratched her finger. She had been dying to do that since they had bathed together.

Her heart pounded as he leaned into her touch, his eyes never leaving hers, as though he didn't want to miss any nuance of her expression or reaction.

"What are you doing?" he whispered.

"I don't know." She withdrew her hand. "Testing something, I suppose."

"Do tell," he said, voice hoarse.

"The texture. Your jawline seems rather sharp."

He leaned into her palm. "And how does it feel to the touch?"

"Prickly."

Leeds scratched his jaw. "That can't be helped, I'm afraid."

"But it's not as hard as I expected."

Harriet froze when he reached out and traced the shape of her face with a finger.

"Soft," he murmured, "Just as I expected."

Lord, oh Lord, oh Lord.

"Why didn't you join your friends tonight?" Leeds asked curiously.

"Do I have the ability to keep such a thing from you, as closely as you keep watch over me?" Harriet countered.

"You have kept the details of tonight from me thoroughly enough."

"Yes, but would I have been able to leave your sight long enough for me to join them?"

"Perhaps not. But that's only because I can't keep my eyes off my captivating wife," he said softly. Suggestively. "But you did meet up with the ladies. *That* I didn't know."

"Well, it's like you said. We woman have our secrets, which means we have our ways."

"So I see."

"But I will have you know, I did feel a tiny pinch of guilt. But only once we arrived at the Stewarts."

A subtle smile quirked his lips. "I suppose a small pinch is better than no pinch at all."

She turned thoughtful. "I'm surprised you are taking this all in stride."

"I can be a reasonable man, love." He gave her a thoughtful look. "Did you want to join your friends?"

"A part of me did," she admitted. "The biggest part didn't. Would you have been angry had I joined them?"

"I'm not sure." He leaned in closer. "But I would have done what I have wanted to do since we arrived. Toss you over my shoulder and kidnap you home. I'd go mad from knowing other men had seen you in such tight-fitting breeches."

"*That* would have been your objection?"

"What else would there be?"

Harriet's heart gave a little summersault. The man was just too lethal. If he had unleashed this charm when they first met, she might have a *real* marriage by now. But even though their journey hadn't had a very good start, she couldn't quite begrudge the trials they'd had to face to get to this moment.

"Oh, there is still one more thing I must tell you." She grinned at him. "Tonight was my idea."

A breath of silence filled the space between them before he reached over and pinched her chin gently to hold her face before his. His gaze struck the air from her lungs.

"Leeds?"

"Promise me in the future you will include me in your plans, schemes, or whatever mischief you wish to embark upon." His voice dropped to a raspy whisper. "I'd rather be part of any schemes than left in the dark."

She covered his mouth with her hand. "Don't say another word."

His brow asked the question his mouth couldn't.

"I don't think my heart can stand another word. That being said, I'd be quite happy to include you in future plans, schemes, or mischief. I think you need a bit more of them in your life."

Harriet slowly withdrew her hand from his lips, her gaze taking their place. This mouth of his that surprised her around every turn was indeed tempting to silence. Perhaps she was still caught up in the rush of the night, and all the moments that had been building up between them, but Harriet suddenly found herself curious as to how it would feel to be the one to kiss Leeds.

And if ever there was a time for bold action, tonight was the night.

Their first kiss had been his.

This one—this one would be hers.

Then, as if moved by fate, or perhaps it was her heart, she leaned into her husband and kissed him.

DEAR GOD, WHAT was happening?

His wife was kissing him.

Will was intoxicated by the taste of her lips on him, even sweeter because she'd been the one to kiss him first—something he had never dared dream of so soon.

He balled his hands into fists to keep himself from pulling her onto his lap and deepening the kiss until they were both panting for breath. This moment was for Harriet . . . about Harriet. He wanted her to understand that she could take control, be in control any time and in any way she wanted.

Her hands settled on his legs and a jolt shot right through that *part* of him.

Bloody hell. Not again.

Another problem arose.

But Christ, her lips were soft and heavenly, and while her kiss could be considered more of a peck, the impact was devastating on his body. He could almost taste their shared breath. Feel the rhythm of their hearts pounding as one.

A low heat burned in his chest, and sparks ignited the air of the carriage. He breathed in her scent, the soft, peachy fragrance of her perfume was dizzying. Tension thrummed in his gut.

Her lips lifted from his.

Will shut his eyes. He didn't want the moment to end. He wanted *more*, but any more and his restraint would surely have snapped.

"Are you speechless?" Her amused question came. He opened

his eyes to catch sight of the delightful flush of pink that spread across her cheeks.

The color captivated him.

"Can I try something else?"

The question terrified him. "I'm all yours."

Will jolted when she placed both hands on his shoulders, then settled onto his lap. He sat still—completely still—as though a little exotic, untamed creature had ventured close and any movement might frighten it away.

He couldn't help but repeat his earlier sentiment to himself. *Dear God, what was happening?*

"What are you doing?" Will asked gruffly.

"I'm not sure myself." She playfully twirled the strands of his hair. "I'm acting only on impulse?"

Acting on impulse? "You are seducing me."

"Oh? Is *that* what I'm doing? Then it doesn't take much to seduce you, does it? I'm not even doing anything."

Not doing anything? She was driving him crazy. "Everything you do seduces me."

"Is that so? Then I am to gather you have no regrets yet? Not even jumping into the Thames?"

"No, I don't regret that," Will said without hesitation. He would jump into the Thames a thousand times if it meant catching his wife. "But I do have one regret." He finally, slowly, circled his arms around her to lock her in, admitting, "My biggest regret is not formally courting you."

"Why didn't you?" she asked.

Will inhaled deeply, collecting his thoughts. He had known this day would come. He had practiced his lines time and time again for just such a moment. It didn't make it easier, but unexpectedly, it wasn't as hard to begin as he'd thought it would be. "Few are aware of this, but most of my early childhood I suffered from a terrible stutter."

The hand teasing his locks withdrew.

"All the children, but especially the girls, would laugh and make fun of the way I spoke. Eventually, I just stopped speaking to them until I could improve the flow of my speech."

"That must have been quite difficult to bear."

Will shrugged. "It's long in the past. But in moments of extreme nerves for me, my stutter returns. When that happens, I choose to not speak at all."

"That is why you never courted me?"

"It might not seem like a big thing, love, but you make me nervous." Even now, his heart pounded in his chest like the hard beat of military drums. "The thought of stuttering through a courtship to the point where I couldn't form a coherent word was a rather horrifying prospect to me."

"But you haven't stuttered since we've met."

"I almost did, several times. Calstone intervened on occasion. He knows the signs. I . . ." Will cleared his throat. "I also practice my lines and sentences in my head over and over. Sometimes, taking a moment to repeat what I want to say in my head also helps."

"That certainly explains some things," she said softly. "I'm sorry you had to go through that in your childhood, but I appreciate that you told me."

A weight lifted from his shoulders. He'd told her. She knew now. And she didn't have a look of revulsion on her face. Nor one of pity. She stared at him with clear, bright eyes filled with gentleness.

"I was teased as a child too. Nothing like you were, mind you. But I was too shy of a child, and my face would become red as a crab in any social setting. You said I didn't belong amongst the wallflowers, but truthfully, it was the only place I could breathe."

Will tightened his arms. "You belong with me."

"You know, for someone who struggles with speech when they get nervous, you sure have a silver tongue. Does that mean you're not nervous around me anymore?" Her flush returned. As did her teasing tone.

"It means you have set my heart at ease, love."

A hand covered his mouth again. "Are these all lines you practiced?"

Will shook his head. They all came from his heart. He kissed the palm covering his lips and chuckled when she yanked it away on a gasp. "Do you want me to stop saying such things? I don't know if I can, though, even if you say yes."

She harrumphed. "Let's change the subject."

"What do want to talk about?" Will asked. He would do anything, talk about anything, as long has he could keep her in his embrace like this.

"You made an effort with Rohan today."

"Talking about other man while sitting on my lap. Tsk."

"Shall I return to my own seat then?"

"No, no. That seat has become cold. It's best to stay here. For warmth." Will suddenly remembered something. He didn't want to ruin the delicate mood, but he could not delay this much longer. "For another change of subject, your father sent an invitation for us to join them for dinner tomorrow."

She averted her gaze. "You go if you want to. I won't."

Will wanted to protest but decided against it. He had hoped that her resentment toward her father would have thawed a bit by now.

He inwardly sighed.

As long as resentment lingered in her heart toward Hatton, could she truly, *fully* accept their marriage? She might be treating them differently now, but they had both signed the devil's contract, as she had referred to it that time. Was it just a matter of time before she remembered that?

"He is your father, love. And you saw those wagers. He only wanted to protect you."

"I know," she said. "That is not why I am angry."

So it was still about how no one had seen fit to inform her. "Have you ever considered that he might have been scared as well?"

Her brows crunched together. "That's ludicrous."

Will shrugged. "It's something to think about."

"Nevertheless, I shan't be attending the dinner."

Will nodded. He wouldn't press any further. But he was curious—and half petrified—about the answer to a question he didn't want to ask but knew he must. "Do you still believe I stole your dreams and snuffed out your happiness?"

She started. "You remember that?"

"I always remember what you say," Will said, holding his breath as she pursed her lips in thought.

He already knew one of her dreams had been to find a love match, which was at least partly why she'd been so resistant to theirs. He, too, had his dreams. His first dream had been to marry Harriet. Now his dream was to win her heart. As for happiness, he already had *his* definition—his wife. Every moment spent with Harriet was a moment of happiness.

"I believed it when I said it." She said finally, not shying away from his gaze. "But I spoke in anger without considering what it actually meant." Her brows furrowed. "Does this make sense?"

Will nodded. It did.

"What do you believe now?" Will asked.

"I'm not sure I can say yet." She suddenly grinned at him. "But whatever my dreams and whatever my happiness, they are too big for one man to snuff out."

"I am relieved."

All Will had to do now was make his wife see that everything she hoped and dreamed for—everything she would ever desire— she already had it all within her grasp.

Chapter Seventeen

HARRIET GREETED TWO ladies as she passed them on the street while on her morning stroll the next day, and the distant notes of someone practicing the piano drifted through the air accompanied by a woman's off-key singing. In the past, it had been her habit to wander through the neighborhood each day after breakfast, weather permitting. It was about time she got back into a familiar routine that she loved. Though this ritual paled into comparison with the new ones she'd developed with Leeds.

Nightcaps before bed.

Sleeping next to each other *in* bed.

Waking up to find Leeds doing one thing or another. Like that first morning when she caught him *practicing* his smile. That still brought a smile to her face. She'd also caught him playing with her hair, writing notes, and just this morning, she'd woken up to him practicing what she presumed to be boxing jabs in his dressing gown.

He might as well have jabbed her in the heart for how striking he looked! And just why did the embarrassment that seemed to follow her bold behavior always seem to surface the next morning? Not *while* she had sat on his lap, and not even after they'd arrived home. No, it was this morning. When she opened her eyes to find him punching air.

The man seemed to have taken her suggestion to entertain her in the mornings very much to heart.

You belong to me.

Harriet patted both her cheeks as heat rushed to her face.

Well, for better or worse, they were together. The little boy who stuttered and the shy little girl with the crab-red face.

Let's just belong to each other.

A familiar figure exited a house further down the street. Harriet whirled, heart pounding, giving the person her back.

Had he seen her?

Please don't see me, please don't see me.

She glanced over her shoulder in time to glimpse the man enter his carriage. The last time she'd seen her father was when she'd stormed out of his study after she discovered he had betrothed her to Leeds.

The carriage jolted forward, and Harriet whipped her head back around, looking everywhere but the carriage as it passed her. She half expected the horses to draw to a halt and her father to leap out and . . . and what? Scold her? Apologize? Heaven forbid, embrace her?

She needn't have worried.

The carriage didn't stop. Her father didn't jump out. And she would never know what might have happened if he had. She looked to the familiar bold green door of her old home. She hadn't even realized she'd retraced much of her old route and circled back here instead of her new home.

Should she forgive him?

Leeds seemed to think so, though he hadn't put it in so many words.

No. She wasn't ready yet, wasn't ready to pretend that what he had done didn't matter. Even though marriage to Leeds was not as horrible as she first thought it would be and she found her husband more intriguing with each passing minute, the fact remained that her choices, her desires, had been utterly disregarded.

Ultimately, she'd never really blamed Leeds, however annoyed with him she'd been. He had asked her father for her hand, which was his right, courtship or not.

But her father could at the very, very least have told her Leeds had asked to marry her *after* Leeds had done so. It would have taken two minutes of his time. Were his daughter's wants not worth those two minutes? He had clearly known that Leeds planned to wed her by special license. Wagers or not, fortune-hunters or not, he could have demanded a normal wedding of Leeds or shared his fears with her. He could have *asked* her. But he hadn't even done that much.

Did she mean that little to him?

No, Harriet still couldn't forgive him.

With one last look at the door, she continued her stroll back to her real home. She would be better off focusing on her blush-inducing husband than on anything—anyone—else. He'd revealed to her his difficulties as a child, but he hadn't confessed anything else. Certainly, Leeds had some affection toward her. That much was clear from his little notes and flustering admissions but that hardly constituted love.

Ah, but they feel a lot like love.

In truth, they felt like a dream she had almost given up on. A woman could lose herself in all the hope that sparked in each one.

If her mother were still here, they could gossip about Leeds over a pot of tea. Mama had always given the best advice.

"Well, well, well," a familiar, rather grating voice interrupted her walk. "What do we have here? A little lamb, it seems."

Harriet turned to the voice and was confronted with the detestable face of none other than Cromby. She inwardly cursed her luck.

"My lord," she greeted before turning away and continuing on her walk. She refused to entertain this man. Hadn't Leeds made it clear at the ball? The fact that he still had the nerve to stop her in the street in broad daylight vexed Harriet to no end.

He blocked her path in a few strides "Running off so soon?"

What was the lout's problem? "My husband is waiting for me," Harriet said calmly. "If you will excuse me."

He didn't move. "Quite the champion you have in Leeds."

"He is an honorable man."

"Is he really?"

Harriet stilled. "Whatever do you mean?"

"It's not my place to say. However, he did make quite a fortune from your union, did he not?"

Hah! And you thank I shall lend my ear to you poisonous mouth? "Well, of course. I had a significant dowry, my lord."

Cromby frowned. "It's not your dowry of which I speak."

"Surely you don't mean the wagers in your notorious betting book."

"Ghastly affair, that," Cromby said, and Harriet had to restrain herself from rolling her eyes. "Still, I have to hand it to Leeds—he is quite the accomplished man. The *first* to cash in on the heiresses."

Harriet gave him a fixed stare. Did he truly believe he could cast doubt in her mind? Leeds had already told her—and told Graves when he'd also asked—that he hadn't placed wagers. She had seen the betting book at Ophelia's, and she hadn't glimpsed anything that would prove otherwise. Granted, the bold penmanship on the pages was hard to read and sometimes cryptic, but she didn't need to dissect each one to know she wouldn't find Leeds's name there.

She believed her husband.

Trusted him.

Her lips pressed into a flat line. "You, on the other hand, my lord, are the vilest of cockroaches, taking advantage of innocent ladies. How many more women have you forced your attentions on?"

His face turned red. "How dare you insult me, you little—"

"Oh, I dare." She cut him off. "And I dare to further say if you ever approach me again, you shall regret it for the rest of your days!"

His face darkened. "You think you can threaten me without any consequence?"

"I think you are a man without consequence, and soon the whole world shall know about it."

He took a threatening step toward her.

"Cromby." A hard, authoritative voice warned.

Harriet spun around. A man stood behind her, one neither of them had heard approach. He was tall, taller than even Leeds, and bore a cold countenance that made even Harriet want to straighten her back more. A *true* marble statue.

This was the Duke of . . .

"Mortimer," Cromby greeted, a tense edge to his voice.

Mortimer arched a brow.

The marble moved.

"I hope you are not detaining a lady against her will."

"What the hell do you mean by that?" Cromby snapped in belligerence. "Lady Leeds and I just happened to run into each other."

The duke turned to Harriet. "Is he bothering you?"

Harriet was still so shocked at the utter disregard the duke had shown Cromby that she'd momentarily drawn a blank. He didn't even attempt to stand on ceremony.

Well, if he didn't stand on ceremony, neither would she. "He is a bit of a bother, yes."

Cromby puffed up in anger. "You little—"

"*Cromby.*"

The man clamped his mouth shut.

Harriet's gaze darted between the two men, the undercurrent so sharp that she swore if she stayed any longer it would pierce her skin and draw blood. "Well then, Your Grace, if you will excuse me."

The duke seemed to want to say more but thought better of it. He inclined his head, simply replying, "Of course."

Harriet nodded before hurrying past them. Goodness! Cromby was certainly finding himself in a pickle these days.

Served the man right.

She suddenly couldn't wait to see her husband, and any moment now, his daily flowers would arrive with a note scrawled in his hand. Anticipation filled her as she hurried home.

⇒⟫⟪⟨

IMAGES OF HIS wife's lips, breasts, and water dripping from her collarbone caused Will to throw three consecutive punches to the same spot without thinking. He shifted on his feet but was unable to fully evade Harrison's jab to his ribcage in response.

The hit brought him back to the present.

"You are distracted." A right fist swung to Will's face, but he nimbly dodged the blow this time.

Of course he was. He woke up hard as steel from a damn near lethal dream of his wife in a bathtub. Just the memory of it stirred a reaction below. The only way to relieve the tension was to punch something.

"He has woman troubles," Calstone said from where he stood leaning against the wall.

Harrison, his private boxing instructor, raised his brows. "So that's why. You're venting."

Will scowled at them. "This is my weekly practice match."

"That doesn't change the fact that you're not practicing." Harrison motioned for Will to come at him. "You're venting."

"Nothing to be ashamed of," Calstone piped up.

"Shut up," Will growled, swinging his arm with more force than he intended and barely hitting his mark.

Harrison grunted, retaliating with a left punch. Will ducked and stepped around him, dancing three steps to the side. And he did not have woman troubles—he had a woman. She had wiles, and *that* was troubling.

"What exactly are these troubles?" Harrison asked. "Didn't you marry the woman of your dreams?"

Calstone laughed. "Not before the lady nearly ran off to the

Americas. We caught her back. Now his little wife has him chasing his own tail." He let out an exaggerated sigh. "It's hard to woo a wife."

"Seems like a woman I'd like to meet."

"Calstone," Will growled. "Why don't you take Harrison's place?"

Calstone waved his hands in surrender. "I'm not dressed for fighting. These are my new boots. I've tried a new hand lotion as well. Can't ruin the effect with boxing."

Harrison laughed. "So frivolous."

Will snorted. Calstone *was* frivolous, but he wasn't wrong. It was hard to woo a wife. There was no damn rule book. Was he doing too much, too little? He wanted to do much, much more, but that had nothing to do with *wooing*. Which was why Will had shown up for his private training match needing to expel the pent-up energy in his body. He *was* distracted.

And his body was impatient.

No one could claim he was not a patient man normally. But where certain parts of him were concerned, the word had started to wear thin. And that member was making the fact known.

So it was either vent here or drag her off to a secluded corner and ravish her. And since his wooing had yet to turn into true seduction, this seemed to be his fate for the foreseeable future.

Will and Harrison went at it a few more rounds before his partner stepped back and raised his hand in a signal to halt.

"Let's stop here for today," Harrison suggested as he massaged his shoulder.

"It's only been twenty rounds." Usually, they would practice up until fifty.

"Your uppercut was excellent today, as was your footing. Your mind was sloppy. I can work with the first and the second, but not the last."

Will straightened from his stance, wiping the sweat from his temple with his shirt.

"Thank you for putting up with it."

"At least you got some of your frustration out," Calstone said with a grin. "Direct the rest to your wife."

Harrison glanced at Calstone. "Are you purposely riling him up?"

"It shouldn't come as a surprise. It's been my favorite pastime for years now. Besides, the more I rile him up, the more he is able to vent out in boxing. You could say I am helping him."

"Let's practice every day from now on," Will said.

"Fine, but get your mind in the match when we train."

Will inclined his head. "I will."

"Now that the venting is over, I want to hear all about what your wife said about London's biggest scandal of the decade."

Harrison leaned against the wall, observing the two men. "Scandal of the decade?"

"Haven't you heard?" Calstone asked. "The *ton* is buzzing with news that copies of the stolen betting book were distributed at a ball by the exact chits who were being wagered upon."

Harrison waved the news aside. "I don't care for the distractions of the *ton*."

"Leeds's wife is in the betting book."

Harrison arched a brow at that. "Ah."

Will frowned. "What do you mean *ah*?"

"Is this part of the woman troubles Calstone referred to?" Harrison asked. "Can I assume that your wife has had a hand in the affair?"

"Smart man," Calstone exclaimed.

"Whether my wife had a hand in it or not, this matter has nothing to do with us."

"So she said nothing?" Calstone lifted a skeptical brow.

"She said plenty, *old chap*. But that is between me and Harriet."

Calstone pouted. "You're no fun."

"I've never been any fun. Why are you complaining now?" Leeds retorted.

A knock on the door interrupted them, and Harrison excused

himself to answer it. The moment he was out of earshot, Calstone asked, "Feeling better? It may have been just twenty rounds, but you went at it like a beast."

Will stretched out his shoulders. "Some."

"Do not fret too much. I have faith in your ability to win over your wife. It's impossible for Lady Harriet to resist your charms."

Will raised a brow, amused. "You know this how?"

"A man would have to be blind to not see the blatant—and let me add highly unfashionable and thoroughly improper— flirting going on at the Stewart ball. Set off beautifully by the fireworks of paper exploding above you."

"You are exaggerating."

"Am I? You have to admit, you've come a long way from when we were on a boat in the vast blue sea and her all her looks screamed 'off with his head!'"

"Bloody hell," Will muttered, tilting his head to flex his neck from one shoulder to the other. "Don't you get tired of sprouting drivel every day?"

"Don't mock my methods. Everything I do is to cheer you up."

"You make my temples throb."

Calstone shrugged. "They'll stop throbbing once you turn 'off with his head' to 'off with his breeches'."

Will looked daggers at his friend. "Vulgar."

"But true."

"My wife is not the cause of my headache." An evil twinge of mischief sparked in Will. "And while we are on the topic of wives, shouldn't you start thinking about producing an heir?"

Calstone gasped, clutching at his heart. "How dare you?"

Will's mood suddenly cleared.

Harrison returned, his face as dark as stormy clouds. Behind him, a man Will recognized as Charles Baily, the footman he'd instructed to find and inform him at once if anyone from White's knocked on his door when he wasn't in residence. The man stood with a touch of apprehension in his expression as he bowed to

Will. "My lord. Your Grace."

Will's mood plummeted again. "What's happened?"

"It's her ladyship, my lord," the footman said hastily. "One of the servants stepped out to the markets and happened to spot her while her ladyship was out on a stroll. It seemed that on her way back she was stopped by Lord Cromby. The Duke of Mortimer also appeared on the scene."

Will cursed, already dashing from the room. Cromby approaching him and Harriet together was one thing, but cornering his wife alone was another altogether. Encountering both Cromby and Mortimer—he couldn't imagine how she must have felt. One was a jackal that tried to push himself on her and the reason for the betting book debacle, and the other was in charge of retrieving that book.

This did not bode well.

Not for Cromby. Not for Mortimer.

Will flexed the muscles in his back.

He would not stand for this sort of treatment of his wife. Not today. Not tomorrow.

Never.

Chapter Eighteen

HARRIET SLUMPED DOWN on the chaise in the library—a quiet and soothing room—her heart still pounding from her confrontation with Cromby and the Duke of Mortimer. It was hard to believe that the duke, of all men, had come to her aid. She'd never been introduced to the duke, which made her all the more grateful for his assistance. If she'd had to face Cromby alone any longer, who knew what might have happened. She might have punched him, kicked him, and caused another scandal.

Though the duke's appearance couldn't be that much of a coincidence could it? The way he'd spoken to Cromby . . . he must know about the man's character and deeds.

I should have stayed in bed longer.

She lifted a small note and traced her finger along the ink.

I belong with you, love.

She brought the note to her nose and inhaled deeply, finding the traces of his scent. She loved her Leeds's wooing. His messages were never long. Always short and succinct. Even this method—flowers and notes—was direct, and yet it was the consistency that proved his sincerity. He never missed a day.

But . . .

She wanted *more.* And not just more wooing.

Impatience sparked in her breast.

The rogue tempts her with his perfectly sculpted body at their nightcaps, yet they only talk. The rogue tempts her with his presence in her bed, yet he only sleeps. She'd even joined him in a bath, but the only wooing then was the way he'd wooed her buttons undone! The man wouldn't even touch her with a sponge!

You, sir, are by no means a gentleman!

And yet he was a gentleman by every means.

She suddenly laughed, finding the entire situation to be extraordinarily funny. She wondered if he felt the same as she did. Probably not. Her gaze flickered to the flowers she'd set down on the table. Even they were taunting her.

Ox-eye daisies.

Meaning *patience.*

All his other flowers had been pretty and with various meanings ranging between purity, virtue, and the like. Leeds probably hadn't delved very deeply into the meanings of the flowers he'd chosen. But today's bouquet was pure mockery.

A commotion drew her gaze to the door, and it was followed by the sound of a gruff voice. "Where is my wife?"

Leeds?

"In the library, my lord."

The next moment, Leeds strode through the door, his sharp gaze darting to all corners of the room before settling on her. He was at her side the next moment.

His gaze roamed over her from head to toe. "Are you all right? I heard Cromby stopped you in the street."

Harriet arched a brow. "How did you know? It happened not even an hour ago."

"A footman came to inform me. And no," he said before Harriet could respond. "I'm not spying on you, love. It was pure coincidence that a servant saw the interaction. But they know to inform me when a member of White's calls when I'm not home."

"You're worried they will come looking for the book here?"

"One can never be too cautious."

"The women aren't in danger from your club, are they?"

"Not from the club, no. But there are too many unknown variables for my liking." He brushed a tendril of hair behind her ear. "You are sure you're all right?"

Harriet nodded. "I'm fine."

His hand moved to caress her cheek. "What did he say?"

"Nothing much." Harriet didn't want to relive the moment and neither did she want to involve her husband and cause him to do something that would land him in trouble. It was better to just forget that odious man altogether. "He was just being annoying as usual. I put him in his place, and Mortimer interrupted his bluster."

"Did Mortimer say anything else?"

"Should he have?" Harriet asked. "Do you mean because he is in charge of reobtaining the betting book?"

Leeds nodded. "It seems too much of a coincidence that both approached you at the same time."

"I had the same thought. But Cromby was just spewing nonsense, and the duke didn't say anything about the book, nor did he offer to escort me home."

"I don't like it."

Harriet smiled. "Then next time take me with to your boxing match."

"Training, love. And you'd be too much of a distraction."

"Oh?"

"Don't sound so intrigued. I was scolded today for a sloppy mind. Just imagine how much more sloppy it would have been if you were there."

"I don't know," Harriet said with a teasing drawl. "If I'm with you, you might do even better for wanting to impress your wife."

He paused, considering. "You might have a point."

She grinned at him. "So take me with you next time. Or have your private trainer come here."

"As you wish." Leeds's gaze searched hers. "Are you sure you are all right?"

"I'm *fine*." Her gaze fell on the flowers. "Actually . . ."

His good humor instantly disappeared. "What?"

She pointed to the flowers. "Do you know what they mean?"

Leeds glanced at the flowers, then looked back at her and said slowly, "I do not." A pause. "Should I? What do they mean?"

She snorted. "Patience."

Leeds fell silent for a moment, and then a low chuckle filled the room. "The florist must have sensed my mood and decided to mock me."

Leeds was impatient? Over what?

She wanted to ask, but his attention was suddenly drawn to the rows of books that covered the walls of the library. He motioned to the shelves. "Have you taken a look at my collection?"

Harriet followed his gesture to look at the books. "I have not."

He straightened and held out his hand. "Come have a look."

Curious, she placed her hand in his and joined him at one particular section, her eyes widening. She lightly traced the spine of the books with a finger. "Are these all . . ."—her gaze swung back to him—"Charles Griffin's books?"

He nodded.

"You procured them for me?"

"Don't you like them? I gathered you enjoyed his books. I also found some similar ones you might want to try. I've cleared an entire section for your books, too—books you may wish to choose for the library yourself, that is."

He had noticed her book preferences from the first time they met? "I do . . . I do like these sort of books, thank you." Her heart beat fiercely in her chest, as though it knew before she did that she was about to do something truly bold. Bolder than everything she had already done up to now.

This was the moment.

In the solitude of the library, with the scent of old and new books filling the air and the hushed whispers of knowledge and stories that hung suspended around them, Harriet made a decision.

This is right.

Leeds, a tall and foreboding figure, a man she hadn't chosen at the start but chose in the end, stood before a row of ancient bookshelves filled with her favorite books, looking devilishly handsome and absolutely clueless.

The man had a way to disarm her with his words.

Let's see if she could disarm him with her touch.

She reached out, lightly brushing her fingers against his arm. He turned to face her, his gaze meeting hers. That one look was all it took. The world around her seemed to fade away, leaving only the two of them.

Yes, I belong with you.

And she was done resisting temptation any longer.

Without a word, Harriet took a step closer, almost touching his body, delighting in the way two slight lines formed between his brows. The sounds of their breaths mingled, creating an intimate current that—she had a feeling—could never be disrupted.

She clasped the lapels of his coat between her fingers, rose to her toes, yanked him down to her height, and pressed her lips to his.

He froze. Not kissing her back. Not embracing her in his arms. Just froze. Harriet bit down on his lip.

A low growl exploded from him, almost like a beast, and his hand gripped her waist as her back collided with the shelf.

Lawd, it felt good.

He claimed her mouth fully, their tongues seeking each other in an urgency that belied the very meaning of the flowers he'd purchased that day. Harriet's hands found their way to his broad shoulders, then she drew them downward, her fingers lightly tracing the solid arch of his back. His arms squeezed her to him.

A thrill shot down Harriet's spine.

Harriet pressed herself into him even more, conveying all her unspoken words and hidden emotions in that one single act.

"Christ, love," Leeds breathed against her mouth. "What are you doing to me?" He pulled away, then leaned back in to brush his lips against hers one more time. "I can't get enough."

"Neither can I." She wanted more.

So much more.

She wanted to taste all of his flaws. All of his strengths. All of him.

She wanted it all.

"Let's belong to each other."

WILL COULDN'T SPEAK. He couldn't *breathe*. He couldn't do anything after those five words left his wife's lips except stare at her. Emotion clogged in his throat, and all the words he wanted to say stuck on his tongue. Almost like the wings of a butterfly caught in its own cocoon, unable to unfurl.

This isn't happening.

Will had fantasized about this moment more times than he could tally in his mind. He had been imagining her lips swollen from his kisses, her body spent from his loving, since he first glimpsed her beneath that tree on that sunny day, laughing as the wind flipped the pages of her book.

He opened his mouth to respond.

Closed it again.

His wife leaned over to press a kiss against his throat, her fingers replacing her lips when she pulled back. He couldn't tear his gaze away.

She smiled at him. "It's all right. You don't need words to speak."

The cocoon split apart.

Will framed Harriet's face between his hands and claimed her lips in a passionate kiss. He needed to touch her. Needed *her*. Like air. He couldn't live without air. He couldn't live without her. Craved her presence, her sweet blushes every second of the day.

She held all the power, all of him.

"Christ, you smell good."

Her lips arched in a smile against his. "Not as good as you."

"I smell like sweat."

"I like it." She sniffed before inhaling deeply. "As astonishing as it sounds, your smell is quite alluring."

Will cursed. "You can't say things like that, love."

"Why not?" she whispered, stroking his jaw.

"Because . . . God, Harriet, love, you are the very bloody heart of me. You control every beat." A word from her and all of him would evaporate as though he never existed. That was her power. But sweet words? How could his heart handle the frenzy they provoked?

Her hands shoved in his hair. "Then don't stop kissing me."

Will didn't deny her. He leaned to capture her lips again, his tongue sweeping into her mouth. Soft. Sweet.

Addictive.

He *had* to occupy every corner of his wife's heart. He *had* to claim every inch of her skin. He *had* to wake up to her each morning. He would never get enough of her. So in every touch, he confessed the intentions of his heart, his soul.

Her hands passed down his back, stopping at his buttocks.

When had they left his hair?

Bloody hell.

"*Love.*" He reached down and bunched her skirts up, his hands trailing over the silky stockings on her legs until he reached her thighs. "Can I?"

She pulled back to look at him. "Aren't you?"

"I . . . I . . . am?" Will suddenly doubted his intellect. His entire brain froze up. Yes, he *was*, but he wanted to know what she . . . *was*? See? It didn't make any sense. "I want you."

"I can feel that," she murmured.

Will looked down. He didn't know why, but he looked *down*. As if to somehow see that she *could* feel. And when he did see, he wished he hadn't. Because he hardened. Un-bloody-comfortably hardened. He was so uncomfortable he wanted to undo his breeches right then and there.

"Do you want me to stop?" Will slowly retracted his hand, releasing her dress.

"Don't," she reached out to snatch his wrist, keeping his hand locked on her leg. "If you stop now I might just bash you over the head with a Charles Griffin." She thrust her hips against him, accepting, *owning,* his desire. Her desire. "I don't want you to stop."

Will's pulse leaped. "You know what this will lead to?"

"I know. And I want all of you."

Will almost choked on emotion, the words finally rolling off his tongue. "You belong with me. And I with you."

"Then what are you waiting for?" She looked up at him, revealing the pale arc of her neck. She smiled. "I'm in your arms, yet you still doubt what I want?"

"Then I shall be more frank," Will breathed, trailing his mouth along the column of her neck. "This will consummate the marriage. This will make our marriage *real.*"

She framed his face in her hands. "I want real, Leeds."

"Will. Call me Will."

She beamed at him. "I want real, Will. A real marriage. With you."

He rested his head on her shoulder. "Who am I to stand in the way of such resolve, love?" He breathed in deeply. "I am not that strong of a man."

"Oh?" she breathed. "Then please," she murmured in a voice barely audible. Breathless. "Let me see you at your weakest."

He stared transfixed into the soft crystals of her eyes. He didn't require any further encouragement. His control had been hanging by a thread, and she snapped it with that last request. He caught her lips again, and this time, he plundered instead of cajoled. He no longer held back.

He wanted to claim her.

Possess her.

Become truly hers.

His hand resumed its previous mission, tracking over the skin of her leg. "Christ, Harriet," he growled. "If I can't have you now, you might as well slit my wrists."

"So impatient."

Will cursed, and his hand paused. "But this is the library." Had he lost his damn mind? Yes. *Yes* he had. And he didn't want to reclaim it.

"Is that a problem? Oh, right," she murmured with a glance to the door. "What if someone walks in?"

"If they enter it means they didn't knock." He lowered his voice. "This is still madness."

"It *is* quite scandalous . . ." She sounded so delighted that Will felt his whole body thrum with lust.

"You started it, love."

"Yes, and I always finish what I start." She wet her lips, and Will followed the action hungrily.

Christ.

She was killing him. With every kiss. Every small touch. Every little word. *His tempest.* His salvation. His hope.

A blush stole over her cheeks. "Why are you just staring at me, Will?"

"You are beautiful."

"Why thank you, but shouldn't you be doing something *else*? Like kissing me. Touching me. Anything *but* staring at me, Will."

Will didn't need to be told twice. He crushed his mouth down against hers again, giving his wife what she wanted. He didn't know when or why she had decided that he had earned the right to become a real husband in every sense of the word. But now that he had, he wasn't going to let any moment to *be* real slip him by.

Will dropped his head into the hollow of her neck and inhaled deeply before he trailed his tongue down the smooth, delicate arch of her neck to her collarbone.

"It's your first time. We should do it in a bed."

"This is perfect," came her quiet reply. "Don't make me wait any longer."

Will groaned. She had no idea what those words did to him. He couldn't wait any longer either. His entire body ached with the need to be inside her.

"As my wife wishes."

His hand dragged from her leg to her center while the other hooked below her buttocks and lifted her, anchoring her to the shelf at her back. He guided her leg to wrap around his waist.

"*Oh*," she whispered as he cupped her core with his hand.

"So soft," Will whispered in her ear, his finger pressing deep into her. "So warm. How does this feel?"

"Strange." Her eyes met his, and he trailed his lips over her bright pink cheeks.

"Just strange?"

"Good too. Intriguing."

"Strange, intriguing, and good." He slowly pushed another finger inside of her, capturing her gasp on his lips. He then nuzzled her neck again. "How about now?"

"Full. Stimulating."

Another finger. "How about now?"

She half groaned, half complained. "You are teasing me, aren't you? It feels *full*."

Will nipped at her neck in response. "This is just the start, love."

Finally.

Chapter Nineteen

H ARRIET HAD A revelation.

The best relationships were not those that were created from dreams and wild fantasies but from the chemistry that sizzles between two people in a true moment—chemistry that held all the potential to transform into something more . . . something like love.

Harriet felt that sizzle now.

She had daydreamed about being held in her husband's arms, had been tempted by the charm of his attempts to woo her, and now she finally lived in the breathless anticipation of becoming truly one. And while they had in no way had the perfect start, this moment between them tasted perhaps a bit sweeter for it.

Her body felt alive with his touches.

His fingers.

Lawd, it was only his fingers. She remembered what the *other* part of him looked like. What would that feel like?

Her arms looped around his neck and she pulled herself closer to his chest. As close as she could get.

"Wrap your other leg around me," he said huskily as he fumbled with the front of his trousers and his fingers were replaced by *that* hard object.

She did as he instructed, the position thoroughly erotic and more scandalous than anything she could ever have imagined.

They were about to make their marriage real. As real as any marriage could get, and she didn't feel even a murmur of fear or hesitancy. Excitement coursed through her veins.

His eyes never left her as he pushed into her. He looked magnificent, with his flushed cheeks—*finally*—disheveled hair, and his gaze boring into her with so much emotion she couldn't begin to decipher all that lay within their depths. But what she did know was that she wanted to dive into them. Untangle each and every complicated fiber of his being.

A gasp was drawn from her lips as he filled her with all of him. "This feels different," she breathed, arching into the shelf.

"Different how?"

"Different *big*."

Harriet felt herself burn beneath his hot gaze. "Does it hurt? Tell me if it hurts."

"Just kiss me." The sting didn't matter. Only him. "Kiss me, Will. Don't hold back."

"Damn it."

Then his lips brushed over hers. Achingly tender. His tongue danced with hers as they explored each other's mouths. Slowly, he started to thrust inside her. Their kiss turned to something else. The rhythm more frantic—a bolder dance.

Wicked. Oh, so wicked.

She was reeling from desire that started off as a hungry spark but quickly transformed into a ravenous fire. She embraced every moment of it.

Her lashes fluttered as she lifted them to meet his gaze, pulling back to draw in the air he stole from her lungs. He had mercy, his head lowering so that his tongue could drag over her collarbone and up the arch of her neck.

One of his hands cupped her breast through her dress, and a half-strangled moan left her lips. Her head fell back, and the pounding of his hips pushed her harder up against the shelves of books at her back.

"So damn good," he growled in a low, strained whisper. His

teeth grazed the lobe of her ear, before retaking her mouth in an urgent kiss.

The warm scrape of his tongue enticed a moan from her, and she writhed against him, seeking more. *Will.* In answer to her unspoken plea, he thrust deeper. Harder. It was almost too much for her. Her entire body was on fire. Alive with need. A throbbing sensation stirred deep within her.

A whimper escaped her lips, a prayer of need, and she pushed her fingers desperately into his hair, gripping the tufts tightly as she held on. All her life she had searched for someone to share the perfect life, the perfect man with the perfect circumstances, never quite knowing what perfect really meant, what it was she was really longing for.

She longed for this. She longed for him, perfectly imperfect.

"Will . . ." She didn't know what to demand from him, so Harriet let her body do all the guiding, but for his name. It exploded from her like a declaration of something not yet spoken.

His chest heaved. "I love your name on my lips."

Laughter stirred in her chest, a note of daring. "I love your lips on me."

He pushed into her harder, stronger, faster. "They will never leave."

Lawd, what that man and his mouth did to her. She arched into him again, shifting her hips to take in more of him. If there was more to be had. She didn't want to miss out on anything. Not an inch.

"I love that expression on your face." His eyes caught hers, and Harriet couldn't look away from the raw, naked arousal there.

"What expression?" she breathed.

"Like you're almost coming undone."

I am coming undone.

Harriet wriggled her hips to urge him on. "More. Everything."

He didn't disappoint. This man never did. Taut muscles

strained against her body. Every shove was hard and deep. Her body would be sore tomorrow. Her back would ache, too. She didn't care.

"Is this what you want, love?"

"Yes," Harriet breathed. "Exactly this."

"Bloody hell, Harriet . . ." His face buried in her neck. "Tell me you are mine." He caught her gaze, his eyes bright. "Tell me I'm not dreaming.

Her hands left his hair to cup his face. "I am yours, Will. And you are mine."

A growl, or a curse rumbled deep from his chest. His head fell to her shoulders, his rhythm not once stopping.

She pulled him tighter against her. His pace became more urgent, setting a thrilling tempo. A rush of emotion assailed her. Harriet clung to him, tightening her legs and curving into him, meeting each thrust with the same urgency she felt in him.

Harriet had never imagined she would do anything so wicked, so erotic. And in a library no less. The books and their adventures within the only witness to the flames that erupted between them.

She inhaled the scent she had never been able to escape as her body hungrily accepted him, searching . . .

Her nails bit into his jacket.

His hand gripped the shelf behind her as he claimed her, all finesse gone. Books tumbled around them as a thousand sensations exploded inside her all at once. The sensations were so strong that Harriet started to tremble, a wave of pleasure exploding over each nerve of her body. His other hand's grip on her waist tightened as his strokes turned rough, more powerful.

A hoarse curse left his lips, followed by her name. Then he shuddered against her, his chest rising and falling with strong heaves. They stayed like that for a moment. Two moments. Three.

The hand that held on to the shelf joined the other around her waist. Then, without warning, the support of the shelf disappeared and he carried her to the sofa, laying her down on the pillowed surface and joining her there.

Soft. Much better than books.

He cupped her cheek, trailing kisses along her jawline. "Are you all right?"

"No." A rush of warmth overwhelmed her at the raspy note in his voice. She wanted to hear that tone from him every day. "I'm even better."

His face nuzzled hers. "So am I."

Now that her heart didn't drum in her ears any longer, a distant rustle and bustle of servants could be detected. "Do you think anyone heard us?"

"Even if they did, they wouldn't dare say anything."

Harriet shut her eyes. "Should I be embarrassed? I don't know how to feel now. I'm still in a daze."

"You don't need to feel embarrassed about anything, love. This is your home."

He sat up and gathered her into his arms. Harriet squirmed to find the most comfortable position, allowing his warmth to envelope her. Her gaze fell on the flowers, and she smirked. What patience?

"You had better not stop sending me flowers or notes now that we have entered a real marriage." Harriet peeked at Leeds.

The corner of his lips inched upward. "I didn't woo you just to get you into my bed."

"Oh? Then why did you woo me?"

His finger poked her cheek gently. "For these blushes."

Her cheeks grew hotter, and he chuckled. "Rogue," she muttered.

"Shouldn't we retire to our chamber to freshen up?"

"Give me a moment." He placed a soft kiss on her shoulder. "I'm not ready to let you go."

She wasn't ready to let him go either. She could feel his heart still pounding against her back. The rhythm was most comforting. "I can feel the beat of your heart."

"Would you mock me if I said it's beating for you?"

"I wouldn't mock you." She glanced at him. "Or would you prefer that I tease you until the day you breathe your last breath?"

"God, yes. Words to give a man eternal hope." He tucked a strand of hair behind her ear. "How are you feeling?"

"Are you asking about the state of my body or the state of my mind?"

"Both."

"My body feels all tingly," *awakened*, "and my mind still feels like it's gone," *numb*, "into slumber. Yours?"

He smiled. "About the same."

She leaned back into him. "I could stay like this forever. Let's never move."

He chuckled and hugged her tightly. "I can think of a more comfortable place to settle."

"The bed?" Harriet tossed out a guess.

"It's comfortable," he drawled with his lips pressed against her ear, causing an onslaught of shivers to spiral down her spine.

"I have a better place still," she countered. "The tub. I can lather your entire body with soap."

"That sounds nothing like comfort but very like torture."

"Rogue."

But a charming one.

"Are you sure you don't want to join me?

Will stared at his wife who was teasing and taunting him from the bathtub. He was tempted, so very tempted, but he would not be able to hold himself back if he joined her. Christ, just thinking of their lovemaking a mere hour ago in the library, against a damn bookshelf of all places, made him rock hard. Again. Well, honestly, his hardness hadn't fully gone away to begin with, and his wife was not making it easy to resist her.

But, damn it. He'd thought it would be torture to be in the bath with her. He hadn't expected that it would be more tormenting watching her from outside the tub.

Honestly, he was still in a state of shock. He almost wondered if he had been knocked senseless by Harrison and would soon be awakened by a rough shake. Or knowing Harrison, another punch.

"I'll wash up after you."

"Suit yourself, but I'm warning you, there might not be any warm water left."

"Consider me warned." *A cold bath might be better anyway.*

She grinned at him—a mischievous grin that he knew could only herald pain. And he was right. Her leg unfolded from the water and into his view, the heel of her foot resting on the edge of the tub. "As you wish."

Will groaned. Provocative minx.

He could not deny that the rogue within clamored to be let loose again. Now that he had savored the sweet taste of his wife, he couldn't get enough.

He needed to remain rational.

Patience.

Restraint.

It would be too easy to escape into his wife's touch, and he wanted so much more than that. And no matter how many times she told him she was fine, it had still been her first time.

"Aren't you cold?"

Will caught her gaze dropping to his exposed chest. He grinned. "Hot."

"You are doing it on purpose, aren't you?"

He scratched his chest. "What exactly do you believe I'm doing on purpose?"

"Reclining on the bed, showing off your muscles. It's as though you are attempting to seduce your wife."

"The very wife who is bathing naked in front of me?"

She grinned cheekily at him. "The very one."

"Just who is attempting to seduce who here? At least I have my trousers on."

"It's still not enough." She slanted a glance at him. "At least cover yourself with a bedsheet. You might be wearing trousers but are they are not hiding your arousal."

Will glanced down.

Yes, that part of him stood rather proud. And wanting. And not at all pleased that he was not joining his wife in the tub.

Should he just toss caution to the wind?

No.

Absolutely not.

He was not a beast, however much he wanted to be. Oh, God, how he wanted to be. But gazing upon the soft glow of her skin, the elfin smile on her lips, and the look of contentment in her gaze, only one question came to his mind. "Are you happy, love?"

Her eyes drifted shut. "So happy."

He could very well see that. "I don't mean in this moment."

She lifted an eyelid, peeking at him. "Then what do you mean?"

"In general," Will clarified. "Are you happy?" *Have I won your heart?* Taking the next step in their relationship didn't mean he had succeeded. So long as he was on the right course.

"I am not unhappy," she said slowly. "Though I could be happier."

"Tell me." Will wasn't against dropping to his knees and begging for her to tell him all the ways he could make her happy. He'd been serious earlier. He would never stop wooing his wife, even if she were the happiest woman on earth. He would pluck out the stars from the sky to keep it that way if that's what it took. "What can I do for you to be happier?"

"You could join me in the tub."

"Anything but that."

She burst into laughter.

"What else?" Will said gruffly.

"A spot of gin would be nice."

Truly remarkable. "Is that all it takes to make you happy? Gin and a naked man?"

She flicked droplets of water his way. "You forget about flowers and notes."

"Of all the things you could demand, you choose the simplest things."

"I have come to understand that happiness is not something to be pursued, but something to claim." She splashed water over her neck and shoulders before lifting her gaze to him. "And you can claim it in the simplest things."

"Like gin and naked men."

"And flowers and notes." She cast him a curious look. "What about you?"

Him? "I'm a simple man."

"Let me guess the things you require." She gave a thoughtful tap on her chin before teasing, "Well it can't be bathing with a naked woman because there is one before you. So perhaps boxing and nightcaps with your wife?"

"And kisses, and touches, and wooing said wife."

"But still not bathing with a naked woman?"

"Like I said, I'm a simple man. Bathing with the naked woman before me is a complication she will regret in the morning, which means *more* complications for me."

"I have to tell you that is in direct contrast to the wants and needs of the woman in the tub. She wants you in the tub, she needs your chest pressed up against her back."

Will groaned.

Was this how his wife felt every time he said something that made her blush?

"I am not an unreasonable man." He aimed a hot look her way. "There are other things I can do to satisfy you."

"But would I want them?" She tapped at the water with a finger.

He shouldn't ask. Her answer would probably kill him. But

he couldn't help himself. "What do you want, love?"

"Tell me three of your life's dreams."

Dreams? Three? Will studied her from the bed, pondering. "What will you give me in return if I do?"

"What do *you* want?"

Your heart. "A kiss."

One brow flew upward. "Only that?"

He shrugged. "If you really want to know about my dreams, a kiss is the price."

"Very well, I accept your condition."

Will rose from the bed and strode over to the tub, a flash of satisfaction pulsing through his veins when her gaze trailed over his chest down to *that* part that refused to settle down. He hadn't expected all this, that his racing back home from boxing practice would lead to her accepting him in the most intimate way. He had kept his heart hidden from her as he had tried poorly to woo her, but he would no longer hold back.

He leaned over to look his wife in the eyes. "My first dream is not so different from yours."

"Oh?"

"It has always been to wed the woman of my dreams."

Her eyes went wide.

"My second dream," he trailed a finger over her cheek, "is to make love to her every day."

Her lips parted.

Will smiled. "And my third, most sincere dream is to capture her heart."

"Will . . ."

"And just in case I have not been clear, love," Will said, brushing his lips against hers. "That is why I had no choice in marrying you. That is why I couldn't give you up no matter what. You, Harriet Hillstow, are the woman of my dreams. You always have been."

Chapter Twenty

HARRIET HILLSTOW WAS a dream-woman.

A woman in a dream state, rather. *A dreaming woman.*

In the days that followed her husband's startling confession, to say her relationship with him had changed would be the understatement of the season. They could hardly keep their hands off each other.

He'd left her quite in a daze that day. But he hadn't pressed her or even expected a response to his admission. He'd just kissed her madly, sealed his three dreams—his declarations—with a scorching kiss that had robbed her of her breath.

William Fitzgerald Hamilton, the third Marquess of Leeds, had not started out as the man of her dreams. But he had become hers. That much could no longer be in doubt.

He was the man of her dreams. And she, apparently, was the woman of his.

This was what she had wanted all her life. This was what she had dreamed about.

Love.

Which was why, since she hadn't yet declared anything of her own, she wanted to purchase him a gift, something he could always cherish, and it had taken the better part of a week to decide on the perfect one.

A pocket watch.

One with a bit of sentimental meaning.

Only time will tell.

On that, Calstone had been right. Time had revealed quite a remarkable tale. And with a watch as a gift, she hoped it would stand as a reminder that time would continue to reveal a truly precious life for them together.

Harriet browsed at the selection of watches displayed before her.

"Which one do you like?" Selena asked. Harriet had dragged both Selena and Leonora along with her to help her choose.

"I'm not sure." She pointed at a gold watch with the intricate design of a wolf on the case. "That one seems most fitting."

Leonora laughed. "Are you saying your husband is a wolf?"

"Wolves are majestic, loyal, and charming beasts," she countered with a smile. And devoted to their family. And Harriet was now part of his.

"Well, I *am* surprised your wolf hasn't picked up on your scent and made his presence known." Leonora shot a suspicious glace around the shop as if to make sure he hadn't suddenly materialized nearby.

Harriet laughed. "I quite enjoy his unexpected visits. But he has business today, so there will be none today."

"So, we can relax and speak freely," Selena said with a wink.

Harriet nodded.

"And Leeds knowing that you know all about the book and the wagers hasn't affected your home life?" Selena asked.

"Not really."

"They made quite a splash in ballrooms, though." Leonora said. "Wives are revolting against their husbands. Daughters are kicking up fusses. It's quite entertaining to watch. I heard there is even a women's club that formed and has started their own betting book."

"What?" Selena exclaimed. "Where can I sign up for that club?"

"I'm surprised you haven't received an invitation," Leonora

said, "since you are part of the reason for all the chaos."

Harriet chuckled. "Well, I, for one, don't think I'd have time for such a thing." Her husband occupied most of her days. And nights.

Selena snorted. "Must be the early bliss of married life."

"The wagers never bothered you at all, Harriet?" Leonora asked.

"I'd like to know about that, too," Selena muttered. "They've been hell for me."

Harriet thought for a moment. "Well for one thing, I never really had the chance to give them much thought to begin with. I had other more pressing things happening in my life."

"Like getting married—*because* of those wagers."

"Then I suppose I ought to be thankful. If not for that list, who knows how long it would have taken my husband to approach me. He can be shy at times." Though shy might not be the right word. But they might have missed their chance altogether.

Her friends looked at her as though she sprouted horns, and Harriet laughed. "I said at times."

Selena tapped her chin. "So, you are saying I should get married if I want to escape the miseries of these wagers?"

"I said *no* such thing!"

"It would be the most effective way," Leonora pointed out. "Harriet is a prime example of how ineffective they are once you marry."

"Please leave me out of this," Harriet said. "I'm different from the rest of you in this regard. My part in the whole affair was done almost before it began."

"Did you ever peek to see if Leeds made a wager?" Leonora asked.

"I never saw his name on the pages I glanced over at Lady Ophelia's, and he told me he didn't," Harriet murmured. "Nothing more is necessary."

"You are right, you *are* different from the rest of us," Selena said. "Still, you have the betting book in your possession. How can you not be simply poring over the wagers?"

Harriet shrugged.

Two days ago, she'd visited Lady Phaedra Sharp, one of the distributors of pages at the Stewart ball, who had stealthily sneaked the book to her in the form of a gift. Her husband had arrived on the scene soon after, so she could hardly refuse the offered gift without raising suspicions. However, the book had been burning a hole in her traveling case stuffed under the bed ever since she'd accepted it. She didn't know what to do with the thing.

And, as she was not scheming any mischief with it, she hadn't told Leeds. She would keep the book, and the secret, just for a little while.

"What exactly is happening with you that's made your life hellish?" Harriet asked. She pointed at the watch with the wolf and told the clerk, "I'll take that one."

"Shall I wrap it for you, my lady?" the clerk asked.

"Please do."

Selena leaned against the display case and, casting a quick glance around, whispered, "Do you truly want to know? Then I shall tell you. That irksome fellow has been following us this entire time."

"What irksome fellow?" Harriet's eyes widened. "Oh. *That* irksome fellow."

Leonora leaned in as well. "Who are we talking about?"

Selena cast a glare at the shop windows. "The Earl of Warrick."

Leonora glanced around. "The Earl of Warrick is following us? Why? Oh, wait. This is an *heiress* thing, am I correct?"

"Quite right," Harriet said.

"Don't look around!" Selena admonished. "I don't want him to know that *I* know he has been clinging to my shadow. I want to teach that wastrel a lesson first."

"Have you spotted him today?" Leonora asked.

"He is lurking somewhere behind a carriage off yonder." Selena shook her head. "He thinks he is so smart. That man must have a pea for a brain."

"Well, at least his motives seem to be protective. You can rest at ease," Leonora said.

"Speaking of protective men, you should take the book off my hands as well. Leeds is already uneasy with White's"—*and Cromby*—"searching for the book. Do you know how uneasy I am? Every time he enters the bedchamber I stare at the bed, and he misinterprets my gaze. He thinks I have an obsession with it." *No need to say more.*

"Me?" Selena shook her head. "With my brother hounding me and that brick of a man following me around, I can't. Besides, my brother knows all my hiding places."

"So, find one he would never expect," Harriet pressed. She wanted to get rid of that blasted book. "Think about it. You could taunt your brick-shadow man with those wagers. Your brother as well. A bit of reading and you'll see what they've been wagering."

"I never thought about it that way." Selena's eyes suddenly brightened. "I've seen the wagers about us, but I never combed the book for other entries. It would be interesting to see what silly things those two have been betting on. Perhaps I might get some blackmail material to put that dog on a leash."

Harriet laughed. "Then it's settled. After we are done here, we'll go and fetch the book."

"Still not comfortable keeping secrets from your husband?" Leonora asked.

"Would you be?" The clerk handed over her parcel, and Harriet dropped the coins in his hand. She nodded as she turned to leave. "Besides, have you looked into Leeds's eyes? It's as if they stare straight into your soul. I can't even be certain he *doesn't* know."

Selena chuckled.

Leonora bit her lip. "Can I have a peek at the book?"

Selena nodded with a sly grin. "Of course. Do you have

someone specific you want to search for? A certain rake, perhaps?"

Leonora scoffed.

They exited the shop and spotted Lady Ophelia and Lord Rochester.

"I didn't think I'd run into you today," Ophelia exclaimed in surprise and smiled at Harriet. "Are you taking your mind off those nasty gossip rags with shopping? You shouldn't believe everything they print."

Harriet blinked. "I beg your pardon?" What nasty rags and what were they saying?

"Ophelia," Rochester said, shaking his head.

Ophelia paused. "Oh."

Harriet's heart skipped a beat. "What have the gossip rags said now?"

Ophelia tugged at her skirts. "Perhaps you should—"

"Tell me," Harriet urged. She hated suspense! "Please."

Ophelia sighed. "I'm not sure how much of it is true, but the papers claim your husband was spotted with his mistress the day before last, escorting her into a gaming hell."

Mistress? Gaming hell?

Harriet burst out laughing.

"Harriet?"

Leeds had a mistress?

Lawd, where did the papers ferret out their stories? Leeds couldn't possibly have a mistress. The man might as well have been attached to her side. And the times he wasn't, well, even in those times, no gossip rag could convince her that Leeds had a *mistress.* In fact, she didn't know what was more improbable. The mistress or the gambling hell. Both were equally absurd.

Someone must bear Leeds a grudge.

"What utter nonsense!" Selena exclaimed.

Leonora nodded solemnly. "He wouldn't keep a mistress."

"I agree," Rochester said. "Leeds is a private man. And he is not messy. By the looks of it, Lady Leeds agrees as well."

She waved a hand, still trying to contain her chuckles, retreating a few steps to gain her composure, lest she bowl completely over from laughter. Oh Lord, that was so unexpected. And the look of worry on their faces was just as amusing. Might she use this to tease Leeds tonight?

"Harriet!"

Her gaze lifted to the horrified faces of her friends. What on earth . . .?

The moment the realized she'd strayed a few steps farther than intended, a black cloth covered her head.

Harriet dropped her parcel in fright, and she knew only darkness.

WILL STUDIED THE ring he'd just picked up at the jeweler's with a sense of pride. He'd had the bauble commissioned the day after they married. He would never admit it, but up until the moment the priest declared them man and wife, Will had been holding his breath.

A part of him had lived in a suspended state from the moment he signed the betrothal agreement. As though his dreams were finally within his reach, yet still impossible to grasp. Even after she had accepted the betrothal agreement, and his rather awkward proposal, he'd kept holding his breath until the vow left her lips on their wedding day. At times it still seemed like a dream to him.

If it was, then let him never wake up.

Unfortunately, he had a friend named Calstone and that friend chose that moment to barge into his study, waving a newspaper in the air.

"Have you read the papers?"

Will snapped the ring box shut. "No. Why? Have you caused another scandal?"

Calstone scowled. "When have I ever caused a scandal?"

"The gossip papers are riddled with them."

The duke scoffed. "They don't know *I* am behind them, so it doesn't count."

"If you say so." Will eyed his friend. He appeared genuinely out of sorts. As if he had rushed here in a great hurry. Calstone never rushed. He might saunter, skip, or even hop, but he never rushed.

"Damn it, that is not the point." He slapped the newspaper on the desk. "This time it's about you."

"Me?" Will frowned. "I didn't cause a scandal." He paused, then nodded. "The special license debacle. Though I would hardly consider it a scandal."

"Much worse than that, old chap."

"What can be worse than that?" Will racked his brain. His cut of Cromby? People might gossip but surely that was not newsworthy?

"How about you being spotted with your mistress in broad daylight entering a gambling house!"

Will scowled. "I don't have a mistress."

Calstone tapped the paper. "You do according to this. Now I am well aware of your nature and the sort of man you are, but is your wife? I suggest you explain to her before she catches wind of it from someone else."

Will leaped to his feet. "She wouldn't believe such trash."

"Are you certain? Would you stake your life on that assumption? Your pretty wife has been skeptical about your character from the start. Or have you forgotten how she boarded a ship to the Americas to get away from you? Where is she, by the by?"

"She is out shopping with her friends." He'd wanted to accompany her but had been pulled away by his man of affairs.

"You are doomed, then," Calstone said. "Most women read the gossip rags before they leave for outings. Your wife is bound to hear of this before she returns home."

Will slapped a hand on the desk. "Damn it! Who could be

behind this?"

"Do you still have to ask?" Calstone raised a brow. "You've offended only one person recently that I can think of who would deliver you such a low blow."

"Cromby," Will growled. "That bloody weasel."

"Seems like just the sort of cowardly thing he or one of his cronies would do. Not only did you cut him at the ball, but you and Deerhurst also had him blacklisted from all the clubs in London."

Will balled his fists. "He deserved it."

Their gazes flew to the corridor as the sound of a slammed door reached them.

Calstone chuckled. "Seems your wife has learned of your rumored affair. I shall have your tombstone commissioned."

"Shut it," Will bit out, striding from the study, ready to explain to his wife what utter nonsense the absurd rumor was. What met his sight, however, was not a furious wife, but two very frantic friends of hers.

"What's wrong?" Will demanded. "Where is Harriet?"

"Let me guess," Calstone drawled from behind him. "At the docks?"

Will glared at him. His wife wouldn't dash off without confronting him. She wouldn't flee at all. Peel his skin from his body maybe, but not run away. In fact, he hadn't truly thought she would believe the rumors until the arrival of her friends.

"What docks?" Lady Selena burst out, heaving for breath as though she'd been running at full speed. "Kidnapped!"

Will froze. "Say that again?"

"Yes, please," Calstone said. "Our lovely Lady Harriet has been *what*?"

"Harriet has been kidnapped!" Lady Leonora reiterated. "She—she's gone."

Will shut out everything else and simply asked, "When? Where?"

"Just now," Lady Leonora said. "We were at the shop purchasing a gift for you." Will's gaze flicked to the package she lifted up. "When we finished, we ran into Ophelia and Rochester and learned . . . well, we learned . . ."

"About Leeds's mistress," Calstone finished for her.

Damn it. "Don't say it like that. People might misunderstand. I don't have a mistress."

"That's a relief," Lady Selena said, patting her chest. "We have enough rogues in London as it is. However, Harriet was, well, I don't quite know what she was, she started to laugh rather hysterically when she heard, and in that moment of inattention, three men set upon her and dragged her into a carriage. They even covered her head with a sack! Ophelia and Rochester set out after them. We came here." She inhaled deeply.

Will's heart sank.

Laughed hysterically? Three men? A sack over her head? Fury, unlike what he had ever experienced exploded in his chest. Who dared do this to his wife? To him? There would be hell to pay today.

Focus, Will. One thing at a time. He returned to that thought which had helped him maintain his sanity in the past. He could not falter now.

"Who would do this to Harriet?" Leonora asked, her brows drawing together in concern. "What do they want? This can't be because of the wagers, can it?"

"Cromby's doing?" Calstone asked.

Lady Leonora's eyes widened. "Cromby? That lecher? Why would *he* do something like this?"

"That snake!" Lady Selena exclaimed.

"Leeds here cut off some of his routes," Calstone said, kneading his knuckles. "Now it seems Cromby is wishing for death."

"I can speak for myself, Calstone."

Calstone nodded. "Yes, but I know how you hate it."

"By Jove, do the two of you always bicker like a man and wife?" Selena muttered. "We should get down to business."

Leonora nodded.

Will's jaw clenched. "If it's Cromby, his motive is revenge."

"Would he hurt Harriet?" Leonora asked.

"No." He would be a dead man if he did. If even one hair on her head were harmed . . . "Cromby wouldn't take the chance. But I need you to tell me everything about the men who took her in as much detail as possible. Do not skip over anything, no matter how insignificant you think it might be."

Selena nodded. "I've an excellent memory."

Will turned to the footman and spoke with a calm he was not experiencing while his mind whirred. "Have the kitchen prepare tea." The man nodded and disappeared. "Lady Selena, you said Lady Ophelia and Rochester set after Harriet and the men who took her?"

"Yes," Lady Selena said. "They will send word as soon as they can."

Will wanted to dash off immediately, but the only way he could help his wife now was to remain composed and gather as much information as possible without losing his damn mind.

And then he would find the bastard, Cromby, or otherwise.

And he would kill him.

Chapter Twenty-One

HARRIET HAD NEVER been so frightened in her life. Not that time when a spider crawled onto her bed. Not a few weeks ago when she found herself on a small boat in the ocean. Not even the time Cromby had forcibly slobbered over her cheek.

She had been kidnapped.

The moment the thought struck, a measure of calm settled in, enough to be able to remind herself that it had been done in the presence of her friends, and they would never allow her to just be whisked off by some unknown foes. She had no doubt they would be dying of worry, but by now, her friends would have sprung into action—divided to conquer. They would have rushed to inform Leeds, perhaps even Bow Street, and maybe even set out after her.

She estimated the carriage ride had been about twenty minutes or so. The kidnappers had then left her alone in the carriage for approximately twenty seconds before a man opened the door and gathered her up into his arms. They had entered a house, or what she at least thought to be a house.

Presently, she was being tied to a chair by the man who'd removed her from the carriage. He wasn't one of the kidnappers from the street. He smelled different. More freshly clean. An expensive cologne prickled her nose. Harriet thought it vaguely familiar.

Where have I smelled that scent before?

"Who are you?" Harriet demanded. "What do you want?"

Silence.

"I am talking to you, mister! The least you can do is answer me! Why have you taken me?"

The man chuckled.

Harriet lost her temper and started struggling against the rope. The bindings weren't tight enough to hurt her, but not lose enough for her to struggle free. "When my husband finds you, you will not be spared! If you let me go now, he might be merciful! *Might.* A big, fat might!"

"Your husband is the reason you are here, darling."

Harriet froze.

That voice.

The bag that covered her vision was ripped off her head, and a big, red-haired man with a cocky grin stared down at her.

"Hello, darling."

"Rohan Ingrid Graves! What is the meaning of this?"

"Tsk." He crossed his arms over his chest with a deep scowl. "There you go again using my middle name. You know how I hate it."

"I use it exactly because I know how much you loathe that sweet, feminine middle name! What is the meaning of this? Do you know you almost scared me half to death? I thought Cromby kidnapped me!"

"That little coward? He is too afraid to incur the wrath of your husband."

"And you are not?" Harriet glared. "He will not forgive you for this."

"He will warm up to me in no time. After all, I only have your best interests at heart."

Hah! Don't count on it. Leeds was one of the most protective, devoted men she knew. He would not let Rohan off lightly. Confound it! Why did her friend have to do something so ludicrous?

"My interests *are* his interests!"

"That's true. I know you probably won't believe me, but it was necessary to do this."

Harriet blinked up at her friend wide-eyed. "You are right, I don't believe you. How was this necessary? You have finally lost your mind. Untie me! Right. Now."

He shrugged. "It's all part of the plan. Granted, I only had a few hours to pull it together, so it might be a bit rough around the edges."

"What *plan?*" Harriet shouted. "If you don't release me now, I shall have Leeds skin your hide." She paused. "*And* I shall tell the whole of London your middle name!"

"Tut-tut. Before you do all that . . ." He pulled a folded newspaper from his inner coat pocket. "Have you read the news lately? Your husband has been quite busy according to the rags."

Harriet blinked.

Dear Lord.

Was this about Leeds and his so-called mistress at the fictional gaming hell? And like that, the bulk of her temper lost its fervor. Has the whole of London lost the plot? Her husband was not that sort of man.

"Is that why you are doing this? You kidnapped me because my husband has a rumored *mistress?*" Harriet scowled at her friend. "I thought you put no stock in gossip rags. And if you say anything about smoke and fires I shall scream your ears off."

"You are the one who usually speaks of smoke and fires. I'm merely trying to help you."

"How is this helping me? If you want to kidnap someone, go kidnap the author of the article."

"That would have served no purpose."

Harriet glared. "Rohan, I am only going to say this once. I am happily married."

"Yes, yes, I saw as much at the Stewart ball."

Her eyes went wide. "You saw as much, but you are still doing this? You crazy man, you are interfering in my marriage.

Do you find me so weak that I cannot confront my husband if I have a grievance with him?"

"This isn't *just* about your husband."

Harriet stared at her childhood friend at a loss for words. The man had gone mad. But she knew him well enough to understand no matter how much she screamed and scolded, he would not budge an inch. She also knew he had a good heart, despite whatever *this* was. In his mind, his intentions were good. In hers, she wanted to box his ears! So be it then. Let Leeds deal with him. *See if I save your hide.*

So infuriating! "I still don't understand one thing."

He arched a brow. "What is that?"

"Why the hell am I tied up?"

He laughed. "So I can be certain you don't run away."

Urgh. "Why are all the men in my life so impossible? And why would I run away? Wait, what did you mean this isn't *just* about Leeds?" She was missing something.

"Just sit tight and relax."

"Relax my arse! I'm tied up like a pig for slaughter." She wanted to rub her temples from annoyance, but she couldn't, which only annoyed her *more*. "How exactly do you see this playing out? If the authorities get involved you might be arrested."

"You would send me to jail?"

"I might not, but Leeds would have no qualms, I'm sure. You haven't told me this brilliant plan of yours? Just what do you hope to accomplish today?"

He tossed the paper aside, dragged a chair opposite hers, and sat, elbows resting on his knees. "Trust me this once, will you? When have I ever let you down? As for how I see this playing out . . . your husband and your father will barge into the house, frantically calling your name. I might receive a punch or two, of course, but it shall be worth the family reunion, I think."

Harriet's breath stalled. "My father?"

Rohan nodded. "I sent some people to inform your father

that you've been snatched up and where he should go to find you. He will collect Leeds, and they will both come rushing to your aid."

Was he serious? "This is your plan? You are doing this because of my *father*?" Her eyes widened even more. "Is this why I would run away?"

"Smart."

Harriet fumed. "You are so sure your little scheme will unfold as you believe?"

"Granted, there are variables I cannot account for since it was a last-minute plan."

"Spurred on by the gossip column?" she guessed.

"I saw an opportunity to help a friend," Rohan said calmly.

"Untie me, Rohan."

He sat back and crossed one leg over the other. "You remember the months that followed your father wedding his current wife?"

She scowled. "What about them?"

"You didn't speak to your father for half a year."

Her heart pinched. "What does that have to do with anything?"

"You were miserable in those months. Your father was miserable. You might have Leeds now, but I know how much this trouble with your father bothers you."

Harriet recalled that time well. She and her father had only returned to speaking terms after . . . after this rascal before her tricked them both into the same carriage, switched out the driver, and set them to the countryside!

Lawd, she didn't know how to feel about this. Back then, she hadn't appreciated his methods either. But in the end she'd also been grateful to him. Mostly. This time, however, it wasn't just her and her father involved.

There was also Leeds.

"Also," he went on. "As a bonus, you can see how your husband fights for you once more."

"Rohan Ingrid Graves," Harriet hissed. "You shall rue this day."

Teeth flashed. "I know."

He knew but he didn't care. *One day, you will know what it feels like to fall flat on your face in love. See if I don't meddle in your life then! In fact, why don't I just play matchmaker and find you a lady that will keep you on your toes?*

For now, Harriet just hoped her husband would arrive soon so she could get out of these bindings.

Her father, on the other hand . . .

This entire situation was ridiculous. Utterly absurd. Beyond ludicrous.

Rohan Graves, just you wait!

THE MOMENT CROMBY appeared in Will's line of sight, he threw a punch. No hesitation.

Cromby hit the floor instantly. Breathing, but otherwise lifeless.

"What now?" Hatton asked, raising his brow. "Didn't we want to question him?"

Will shook out his hand. He had wanted to do that ever since that night at White's. "He will wake up soon." He turned to Calstone. "Search the house."

Calstone nodded and motioned to the servants who had followed them in. "We'll leave no stone unturned."

He'd been holding in his anger, the chaos brewing inside since he'd learned of his wife's disappearance. Cracks now began to form in his calm, spilling out tendrils of panic. The details the ladies had provided hadn't helped narrow down Harriet's kidnappers or where they might have taken her. He'd nearly worn the carpet thin while waiting for Rochester to send news.

But when Hatton had burst into his home, waiving a newspaper in hand, all his good intentions had turned to smoke. After calming the furious man down, assuring him he had not hurt his daughter and that he didn't have a damn mistress, he couldn't hide the fact that Harriet had been taken.

There was really only one way to put it.

Hatton had exploded in a fit of rage.

Will nudged the unconscious Cromby with a boot. Something felt off. No matter how he looked at it, Cromby was a coward. Harriet probably wasn't in this house. If Cromby *was* behind Harriet's kidnapping, then most likely he had one of his henchmen do the work.

Hatton stepped up beside Will. "I regret it, you know."

Will turned to his-father-law, not needing to be an expert in fatherhood to know what the man meant. "I know."

"Does she hate me?"

"She is hurt," Will admitted. "But she is your daughter. She doesn't hate you."

Hatton sighed. "I knew she would object to the marriage, which was why I never told her. I believed I was doing the right thing. She's always had a romantic heart, but I feared for her future."

"That is no excuse," Will said, then sighed. "You should have informed her, and I should have courted her. We are both in the wrong."

"She was like this when I married Delia, too."

Will arched a brow. "You didn't inform her of that wedding, either."

Hatton pursed his lips. "It was because I married right after my mourning period ended."

Ah.

Will could not imagine how Harriet must have felt. She had felt pushed out by Hatton and his new family, but it wasn't Will's place to tell his father-in-law that. He doubted Harriet had, and she wouldn't appreciate it if he did so in her absence.

"It's no use dwelling on past mistakes," Will said. "We can only go forward from here."

Hatton nodded. "My invitation for dinner still stands."

"I hope you understand that I won't force her to reconcile with you. I support my wife no matter her decision."

"I see that I at least didn't make a mistake in permitting you to marry her."

Will chuckled. "Do you really think it was your decision? Up until the moment we married, I fully expected her to find a way to jilt me. And even standing before the priest . . ." He shook his head. "She could have said no. She owed neither of us anything. To presume otherwise. . ." He didn't need to finish that sentence. They both understood.

Cromby groaned.

Will crunched his knuckles. "Seems like this cockroach is about to wake up."

"Good," Hatton said, a steely edge entering his voice once more.

Cromby opened his eyes, clutching his jaw. "What the devil?" His eyes fell on Will, and he roared, "What is the meaning of this, you blackguard?"

"I will only ask you this once, Cromby," Will bit out. "Where is my wife?"

The man's face contorted. "What are you talking about? How the hell would I know where your wife is?"

"She has been kidnapped, and answer the question," Hatton growled.

"For Christ's sake," Cromby snapped. "I don't know anything about your wife. I didn't even know she was missing, damn it."

Leeds hunched down beside the man, jabbing a finger at his chest. "You are the one who spread the rot of me having a mistress and entering a gaming hell." A statement. A fact.

"Is that the same as kidnapping?" Cromby growled, levering himself into a sitting position. "You humiliated me and blocked me from all the respectable clubs in London! You expect me to take that lying down?"

"You don't deserve to belong to any respectable club after all you've done."

"Agreed," Hatton said, stepping on Cromby's shin. "Leeds asked you once, now I shall ask you once. Where is my daughter, you filth?"

Cromby cried out in pain.

"Damn it, I don't know!"

Will rose and punched his fists together. "Do you believe him, Hatton?"

"Every word from his mouth smells like shit."

Cromby spluttered. "This is common assault! You cannot just accuse people left and right of kidnapping and batter them in their own homes!"

"*Don't*," Will shot the man a menacing glare, "speak to me of assault if you know what is good for you. "You accosted my wife once. Who is to say you didn't take her now?"

"I never touched your wife!"

Will's brow shot upward. "Didn't you force a kiss on her?"

"That . . . that . . . lies!"

"You are denying it?" Will asked. Just when he thought Cromby couldn't become more loathsome a character, the man proved otherwise.

"He did what?" Hatton said in a low—very low—voice, his chest rising and falling with each deep breath.

Panic crossed Cromby's face, and he tried to scramble to his feet.

Hatton lifted his leg and stomped down. His boot landed squarely on Cromby's chest, pushing him back to the floor.

"Damn it! I'm sorry! Nothing happened, did it? She still married you!"

Will sneered in disgust. Once a coward, always a coward. He suddenly didn't want to breathe the same air as this bloody bastard.

Calstone appeared with the servants and shook his head, and Will let out a breath of relief even as the tension in the muscles of his shoulders pulled taut. Because if she wasn't here, just where the hell was his wife? There was something they were missing.

"Are you sure he doesn't know anything?" Calstone asked, grim.

Will shook his head. "I believe he is telling the truth."

Will pinched the bridge of his nose, thinking.

"Leeds," Calstone suddenly patted his shoulder and motioned to the door. Rochester leaned on the doorframe, a wry expression on his face.

"It seems I missed all the fun."

"Harriet?" Will asked quickly.

"We have her whereabouts." He motioned with his finger and a boy, no older than sixteen, appeared at the door. "I also found this lad skulking about. Seems he is searching for Hatton."

The boy stepped forward and bowed. "Begging your pardon sirs, but I was told to tell you a lady has been kidnapped and give you the address."

"Who told you?" Will demanded.

He boy clutched his hands together. "I don't know, sir."

"The address?" Will asked.

"Same as the one I followed your wife to," Rochester said. "This kidnapper also relayed that the lady shan't be harmed."

The boy nodded enthusiastically.

Will clamped a hand on Hatton's shoulder. "Let's go." He wanted to find his wife and put an end to whoever kidnapped her, then take her home and nestle into her arms.

"Wait a moment." Hatton rolled up his sleeves. A thunderous look contorted Hatton's complexion. "Let me deal with him first. He dared touch my daughter."

Will didn't argue. He walked out, leaving Cromby to Hatton. "I'll wait for you outside."

Chapter Twenty-Two

"Isn't it courteous to offer your victims tea? I'm parched."

"My servants are off for the day." Rohan glanced at the cabinet. "I can offer you some sherry."

"No, thank you," Harriet says cheerily. I'd like to be clear-headed when my husband beats you to a pulp."

"So ruthless, darling."

Harriet snorted. "You remember he practices boxing, don't you?"

"I've been in enough tavern fights to hold my own."

She gave him an incredulous glance. "Are they the same?"

"Is there much of a difference? It's the weight of the punch that matters."

The weight of the punch . . . Harriet tilted her head. Rohan was about the same height as her husband, but bulkier. His punches would probably be heavy and well-placed, but somehow she knew, just knew, Leeds would win a fight between them.

"I don't know much about boxers, but I imagine them to be highly disciplined. Extremely agile."

Leeds was certainly agile. She could attest to that.

"Your husband takes boxing *lessons*, darling. No matter how you look it, it's not a fair fight."

"We shall see."

How much time had passed? Her body was starting to ache in

protest at sitting still for so long. And her chin, her ear, and her nose were itching all at the same time.

"Just who did you send to my father? A snail?"

Rohan glanced at his pocket watch. "Something must not have—"

The steady sound of the front doorknocker echoed through the house.

Harriet's ears perked up. "Leeds?" Her father?

Rohan's brows drew together. "Would he knock so calmly?"

He would if he's learned I'm here with you.

But Harriet decided not to enlighten her friend. Whatever came his way, it would serve the ruffian right, including her new matchmaking plan for making him fall in love against his will.

Though truthfully, she was almost certain she would do a disservice to any woman she might match with this beast. Whoever the woman, *she* would have to be the one to tie Rohan down, or she might be trudged all over!

Rohan rose to his feet. "I shall go see who it is. Not a sound from you."

Harriet rolled her eyes. "Are you mistaking me for a *real* kidnapping victim?"

He smirked. "You *are* a real kidnapping victim."

Red-mop ruffian.

She glared at his back as he strode from the room, straining her ears for any indication of who had arrived. A moment later, male voices filtered through the corridor to the drawing room. Faint, but discernible.

Had Leeds found her?

She shot her own smirk at the door Rohan had left through. Leeds was here. She knew it. Her scalp prickled with awareness. A curious thing, but a thing nonetheless.

This little scheme of Rohan's—she was ready to put an end to this madness. She wanted to return home. Bathe with her husband. Cuddle in their bed.

The voices faded, followed by an unmistakable thud, then

footsteps, and then a familiar voice called her name. So breathtakingly familiar.

"Harriet?" That gruff, gloriously male voice called.

"I'm here!" Harriet called out, her entire body brimming with excitement.

The door slammed open and Leeds filled the doorway. Large, striking, and all hers.

Lawd, she loved him.

"Damn it! I should have walloped that bastard harder!" He was at her side in three strides, kneeling before her. "Are you all right? Are you uncomfortable?"

"My nose is itching."

His gaze lowered and he reached out to scratch the tip with a finger. "Here."

"Up," Harriet said, amused. "A bit to the left. Now my left eyebrow."

"Why don't I just untie you, love?" He started to work at the knot in one of the ropes.

She glanced beyond her husband. "Where is Rohan?"

"In the hall. He's . . . resting."

Harriet couldn't stop the grin spreading across her face. "I told him not to go up against a boxer. They are agile."

His gaze met hers. "Agile, hm?"

She nodded, her gaze once again moving to the door. "Is my father here?" Harriet asked, not certain why she whispered.

He paused in uncoiling her bindings. "He is." A slight hesitation. "If you don't want to see him, I can—"

She shook her head.

It was time to face her father.

She wriggled her arms. "Hurry."

Leeds made quick work of the bindings. "As a seaman, I'd thought he'd be at least more adept at tying knots."

"I don't think he was trying too hard," Harriet said as she rose to her feet, stretching out her limbs.

"Harriet?" a soft voice came, and her head lifted to meet the rueful gaze of her father. Her pulse leaped.

They stared at each other, neither speaking. A moment passed. Two. Three. Until Harriet couldn't take it any longer.

"Rohan decided to meddle and—"

"I'm sorry—"

They both fell silent again.

Her father was the first to speak again, clearing his throat. "Are you well?"

Harriet stood straight. "I am well."

He scratched his head. "I know it doesn't mean much now, and I don't expect you to forgive me right away, but Harriet, I am truly regretful, and hopelessly sorry for the way I dealt with this situation, with your betrothal. I should have informed you. You are my only daughter, after all."

Emotion clogged in Harriet's throat. She didn't quite know how to respond. She'd imagined all sorts of scenes that might happen when she faced her father, but none of them prepared her for the remorse that wove through his apology.

That was all she really ever wanted: an apology. To know she mattered. That she hadn't been cast aside.

Harriet hesitated. She wasn't ready to join her father for dinner. Or pretend that he hadn't done what he'd done. She . . .

A hand settled on the small of her back. Firm. Reassuring.

Leeds.

Her husband, the man of her dreams.

She nodded to herself. She couldn't pretend nothing happened, but she could do one thing. Was *ready* to do one thing. "I accept your apology, Papa."

This I can do.

His shoulders sagged in relief, his gaze taking in the rope on the floor for the first time. "That bastard tied you up? Should I drag him back here and beat his—"

"No need, no need," Harriet interrupted, trailing off when two pairs of eyes settled on her. How to explain? Rohan had gone mad?

"Rohan is meddlesome when it comes to family, and he considers me family, so he once more meddled. I don't know if Papa recalls the time when our driver drove us to the countryside . . ."

Her father cleared his throat. "So that was him?"

Harriet nodded.

"I see." He cleared this throat again. "This one was a bit extreme."

"Yes," Harriet said. "I agree." And yet, like the previous time, she couldn't bring herself even now to stay angry at the man.

She glanced at her husband. He looked calm. Almost too calm. Like the first time she had met him. "Will? Are you all right?"

Those dark eyes locked with her. "No." He suddenly kneeled before her, clasping her hands in his. The scene was so familiar her eyes went wide. "What are you doing?" she hissed in a low voice.

"The newspaper," Leeds said. "What they said about me."

She cupped his cheek. "I know it's not true. It's quite preposterous. It's not even a very good attempt at smearing your name."

"I knew you wouldn't believe that drivel," he muttered. "Then the hysterical laughter . . ."

Hysterical? Is that what her friends had told him? She grinned. "I found it rather funny. Hysterically, so, yes."

He brought her hand to his lips to kiss it. "I love you, Harriet. I love you so damn much I can scarcely breathe from it at times." Clear eyes held hers. "But don't feel pressured, love. I'm still very determined to win your heart."

She placed two fingers over his lips. "You already have it."

He blinked up at her. "I already have it?" He repeated against her lips. A bit dumbly, and Harriet laughed.

He lowered to his haunches, bringing them face to face. "I love you, Will. Madly."

He averted his gaze, drew a deep breath into his lungs before slowly exhaling. He met her gaze again. "Christ, Harriet. In the next life, let's reverse roles."

Harriet blinked. "Reverse roles?"

He nodded. "You chase me."

"Absolutely not!" She narrowed her eyes on him. "I'm warning you now William Fitzgerald Hamilton, you'd best fight for me in all our lives."

He chuckled. "Yes, Lady Leeds. I shall fight for you in all our lives. But before we get to that, do me a favor. Say it again—my full name."

Harriet paused. The look in his eyes, so filled with love. Hope, tenderness, love, all blazed in his eyes. It was almost too much for her to bear.

"So demanding." She pretended to roll her eyes before cupping his face between both her hands. "William Fitzgerald Hamilton." She leaned in to press her lips against his ear. "You are mine. I am yours."

"Thank God," Hatton suddenly grumbled. She'd almost forgotten he was there.

"Agreed." Leeds smiled at her. He rose to his feet, pulling her up with him.

Clapping came from the doorway. Harriet looked over to find that ruffian Rohan leaning against the wall. "It seems that my work here is done."

"Crazy fool," Leeds muttered.

The room suddenly filled with her friends Selena and Leonora, as well as Rochester, Ophelia, and Calstone.

Warmth flooded her.

"Too many damn people," Leeds muttered, clasping her hand in his.

She nudged him with her shoulder. "Let's escape."

He glanced at her. "Do you have a plan?"

"*The Royal Oak.* Just carry me off again."

Her husband, never one to disappoint, did exactly that.

WILL COULDN'T KEEP his hands off his wife.

"I want you again," he murmured against her breast, biting down on the soft flesh. He chuckled when she pushed him away. "I'm already a wolf in your eyes. Wolves ravish beauties."

"Do you like the watch?"

He kissed the finger which held the ring he had bought for her. "Yes. And is this to your liking?"

She smiled and held up her hand, tracing a finger over the blue sapphire stone. "I love it." She slanted a look at him. "What made you choose this stone?"

He kissed one eye. Then another.

She laughed. "Very well, I understand. My eyes."

"Also the blue dress you wore at the Stewart ball."

"And here I thought men didn't notice such things."

"I notice everything about you, love." He shifted to pull her firmly into his embrace, sliding a leg over her thigh to keep her in place. "Especially all the moans you make when I love you."

She pushed at him, her face brightening to a delightful pink. "Stop it, I have some things I need to confess."

He pulled back to stare at her. "You have my full attention."

She bit down on her lips.

Will drew his brows together. "I am not going to like these confessions?"

"What? No, I mean, I don't know. One maybe, but the other . . . I'm not sure."

He pressed a chaste kiss on her lips. "Just tell me, love."

She nestled deeper into him. "I made a promise to my mother on her deathbed."

Will froze, but said nothing, allowing her to collect her thoughts and say what was on her heart. He intertwined his fingers with her, observing her.

"I promised her I would marry a man who would fight for

me. A man who proved himself worthy."

Will went still, his muscles tensing. "Then . . ."

"I dashed off that day as a test to see what you would do. Not just that, but everything I did up to the moment I agreed to marry you was to see if you were a man who would fight for me. If you were worthy. Obviously, I found the my answer—I married you."

Will's heart squeezed. Hard. He rested his temple on her bosom, collecting his thoughts. Emotion burned in his eyes.

"Bloody hell," was all he could manage.

A small hand patted his back. Soothing. Will started trailing kisses over her the swell of her breasts, up to her collarbone, her neck, until he finally reached her lips. He pulled away. "I have a confession too." He nipped at her chin. "Or more truly an accusation."

"An accusation?"

"Yes, your memory is atrocious. Especially when you drink."

"That's your accusation?" She suddenly blinked. "Did I do something when I was tipsy?"

"Tipsy?" His hand roamed the length of her leg. "Woman, just call it what it was—foxed."

"Very well, *foxed*. Now tell me, what did I forget?"

"Me. You forgot me."

"What?" she asked, startled.

"The day we first met."

Her brows scrunched. "Yes, the day you flaunted a special license in my face."

"I did nothing of the sort, and that is not the first time we met."

"Impossible. I would have remembered if I had met you before that moment. Unless . . ." Her eyes narrowed. "You said I was foxed. But that would mean . . . it could only have been . . . but no, that was a dream. Wasn't it?"

Will chuckled at the levels of confusion that flashed over his wife's face. So he had been a dream in his wife's mind since that day? He bit back the grin that threatened to split his face.

She jabbed at his chest. "Did you carry me to my room?"

"No," Will denied firmly. "I'm a mere marquess. Only a knight is allowed to carry—" A hand covered his mouth, and two blue eyes blazed at him.

"It *was* you!"

Yes, love, it was me.

He traced a finger over her waist. "Shall the knight ravish the lady now?"

A sprinkle of mischief, a glint of challenge filled her face. "But I have one more confession, or have you forgotten?"

Will paused in his actions. Oh yes, one he probably wouldn't like and one he would. Did that mean this one was . . .?

She leaned in close, her whisper of soft, feather light touch. "The betting book of White's is under our bed."

The End

About the Author

Tanya Wilde is an Award-Winning author that developed a passion for reading when she had nothing better to do than lurk in the library during her lunch breaks. Her blazing love affair with pen and paper soon followed after she devoured all their historical romance books! In 2020, she won the Romance Writers Organization of South Africa (ROSA) Imbali Award for Excellence in Romance Writing for Not Quite a Rogue.

When she's not meddling in the lives of her characters or pondering names for her imaginary big, white greyhound, she's off on adventures with her partner in crime.

Wilde lives in a small town at the foot of the Outeniqua Mountains, South Africa.

Website – www.authortanyawilde.com
Instagram – instagram.com/tanyawilde
Facebook – facebook.com/groups/843373666456177
BookBub – bookbub.com/authors/tanya-wilde